THE LAST CROSSING

The Finger Lakes Mysteries Book 3

ELIZABETH MEYETTE

BORIS PUBLISHING

Published by Boris Publishing

Copyright © 2018 by Elizabeth Meyette

BORIS PUBLISHING

ISBN: 978-0-9960965-3-9

❦ Created with Vellum

Prologue

✣

Christmas Eve, December 24, 1968

"What do you mean, you can't be my maid of honor?" Jesse Graham's joy ebbed as if a soprano had hit a sour note in "O Holy Night." She frowned at her best friend over her amber longneck bottle of Genesee Cream Ale.

"Well, there's a chance I won't be given permission. I just think you should ask someone else, Jess." Maggie Keegan flipped off the cap on a second beer and set the church key on the coffee table.

"I'm not asking anyone else, Mags. You've been my best friend since ninth grade. I want you beside me when I take the plunge."

"I've requested a meeting with Sister Therese. I'll explain to her that you are *most* unhappy. I'm sure that will sway her." Maggie extended her arms, giving an exaggerated bow.

Jesse threw a Santa Claus pillow at her, but it bounced off the armrest and back toward her. "Shut it, Sister Angelina."

"Seriously, even if I could be your maid of honor, I'd have to wear my habit. Are you sure you want a black and white color scheme for your wedding?"

"It works. Joe will be in black and white. So will Marty. I can find a wedding dress with a black sash or black sleeves. It'll be perfect."

"I'll talk to Sister Therese." Maggie took a swig of beer.

Jesse studied the Christmas tree balanced in the corner of the room. *Why do I always pick a crooked one? Pity, I guess. Who else would choose that tree? Me and Charlie Brown.* They had spent an hour chipping at the base of the trunk to get it straight in the tree stand, but the upper trunk leaned precariously to the left. The colorful lights twinkled off the streams of tinsel that hung from the branches, each one carefully placed individually.

It was beautiful.

"I love Christmas." She sighed. "It's so romantic." Jesse held out her hand, gazing at the diamond ring Joe Riley had just given her.

Maggie smiled. "Oh, Jesse, I'm so happy for you and Joe. You two are perfect for each other. And who could have planned it better? Two redheads marching toward their future together. Fortunately, Joe doesn't have the usual red-headed temper." Her dark brown eyes danced with mischief.

"Are you saying I do?" Jesse grabbed the pillow from where it had landed on the floor and threw it at her again. Her aim was better this time, and it bounced off Maggie's short, dark, pixie haircut. "Hah! I gotcha, Sister Angelina!" She loved to tease Maggie using the name she'd chosen ten years ago when she took her vows with the Sisters of Saint Joseph. Jesse hugged another pillow. "Marriage with Joe will be heaven." She studied her best friend, who could be a stand-in for Audrey Hepburn. "Tell me, why would such a beautiful woman as you take a vow of celibacy? Chastity, for God's sake—oh, I guess that would be why."

Maggie threw the pillow back at her, and it sprang off her untamed curls.

"Didn't even feel it. This hair is pillow-proof." Jesse tugged one strand down, looking wistfully at the auburn locks.

While Bing Crosby crooned "White Christmas," Maggie grabbed the pillow again and pummeled Jesse against the couch.

For all Maggie's petite build, she was a mighty force. They wrestled about, trying to gain control of Santa.

Cold air swept in from the hallway as someone bustled in through the front door.

"Oh yeah! My favorite fantasy!" Officer Marty D'Amato's voice boomed over their laughter. "Two women fighting, and I'll just have to jump in and put them both in handcuffs."

Maggie rolled to the floor, victorious, and held up the prize. "Victory is mine!"

Jesse grabbed the pillow and bopped her on the head. "Beer's in the fridge, Marty."

"You girls always spoil my fun." Taking off his knit cap, he ran his hands through his thick black hair. The result, as usual, was a wildly mussed thatch. He slung his navy pea coat over a coat stand by the front door and slipped off galoshes slick with winter snow. His voice floated behind him as he headed back into the kitchen. "Where's Joe?"

"He's on site today. He'll be over around six. Jim and Susan are joining us for dinner."

He reappeared. "Outta sight. Susan's a great cook."

"And I'm not?" This time, the pillow grazed Marty's cheek before he grabbed it mid-air and hurled it back, a Kris Kringle missile.

"You are, *bella*. Remember? I told you your manicotti was almost as good as Mama's." He kissed her cheek, then turned to Maggie. "Hi, Maggie." The change in his voice was like a gentle rain after a thunderstorm—all the gusting and booming now softened to a tender patter. As if recognizing this himself, he coughed, took a swig of beer, and plunked into the easy chair beside the sofa. "What are you girls up to, besides beating each other with Santa? You know you're on the naughty list now, right?"

"Maggie just informed me that she might not be able to be my maid of honor."

Marty concentrated on his bottle. "Huh."

"Not just 'Huh.' I can't get married without Maggie."

"Uh, I think you can. You actually just need Joe." Marty took a long pull of his beer.

Maggie laughed. "That's what I've been telling her. Thanks for taking my side, Marty."

"Hello! We're here," Susan Riley called as she hustled in from the cold, stomping the snow off her boots on the front hall mat.

Jim Graham followed right behind her. "I've brought champagne! And Susan's brought a banquet." He laughed as he juggled a platter of hors de oeuvres and a full grocery sack.

"Holy crap, Susan. I invited *you* to Christmas dinner, remember? You've got a moveable feast here." Jesse took a grocery sack and a platter of shrimp from her.

"Joe just finished showering and is on his way. He should be here soon." Relieved of her offerings, Susan hugged Jesse then hung up her coat beside Marty's.

Susan's eyes, a deeper shade of hazel than Joe's, were full of fondness.

Jim pulled Jesse in for a hug, and she kissed him on the cheek. He was, literally, the father she'd never had. When she was only five, her mother, Eileen Graham, had divorced Jim and spirited Jesse away from him. Though he'd hired a detective to find them, Eileen had hidden their tracks too well. Jesse had found him during her search for answers to Helen Cavanaugh's death.

As they gathered in the kitchen, a large pot of sauce bubbled on the back burner, filling the room with aromas of garlic, basil, and oregano. Tucked behind white Cape Cod curtains, the windows steamed up with the warmth of the stove, and a friendly growl emanated from the vintage 1940s refrigerator.

Marty helped unload the food while Jim set out the appetizers. Jesse checked the spaghetti sauce that had been simmering all afternoon.

"Mmmm, *bella*, this aroma is straight from my grandma's kitchen." Marty leaned in to inhale the aroma wafting from the large saucepan.

"Hello, all!" A trace of cold air followed Joe into the room, but he grabbed Jesse around the waist, drawing her in for a kiss that warmed her.

"Hello, Just Jesse."

She loved hearing him call her that, a nickname he'd dubbed her the day they met. His hazel eyes held hers; her heart skipped and she understood the word "swoon." For a moment, it was just the two of them in a space surrounded by a soft murmuring of the others' voices. A crooked grin crossed his lips, and he winked.

"Hey, lovebirds, we're starving here." Marty lightly punched Joe's arm, and the voices of the others came back into focus.

"Right on." She reluctantly left Joe's embrace to serve the food. A glance around the room warmed her as her friends—no, her family—laughed and talked while they worked together in her cozy kitchen.

They settled around the round oak table covered with a red-and-white checkered tablecloth, forest-green napkins folded on the mismatched plates. How different from the professionally prepared dinners served in an elegant, if sterile, dining room when she was growing up with her mother. She shook her head. No bad memories. Murder, fear, and ghosts would be banished tonight. She would only look forward to her bright future with Joe.

Marty raised his glass of wine for a toast. "'God bless us, every one.' Just like Little Timmy said in that Christmas story right before he died."

"Actually, it was Tiny Tim, and he didn't die, because Ebenezer Scrooge reformed his ways," Jim fell into English literature-professor mode as he raised his glass.

Jesse barely heard him. Maggie had her full attention. She was ashen, her deep brown eyes round, and when she spoke, her voice was far away.

"We taught my little brother Timmy to repeat that at every Christmas dinner. Before he died."

Chapter One

June 1969

It was the whistle of the train at midnight that signaled another ghost.

Jesse scrunched the pillow over her ears. Though she wasn't quite awake yet, the tug in her gut was a subliminal recognition of what was about to happen. And she wanted no part of it. Through the clothesline-clean smell of the pillowcase came a small voice singing, "I've Been Working on the Railroad."

She snuggled deeper into the covers, hugging the pillow tighter over her ears. The train whistled again.

"Oh crap." She whipped back the bedclothes and sat up.

The noise that had awakened her carried a familiar, disturbing sense that seeped into her blood. She rubbed her arms, squinting through sleepy eyes at the serene décor, so in contrast to the chills she warded off.

Moonlight filtered in through the sheer curtains illuminating the beach-themed room. Starfish sprinkled the bedspread that crumpled along the white footboard. Seashells danced along the wallpaper border tucked just below the ceiling, and real seashells filled the clear glass lamp base beside her bed. The lamp she didn't want to turn on.

Silence.

Damn. Not another ghost. She cocked her head.

Stillness.

She lay back down, pulling the sheet up over her ears. All she wanted to think about was her wedding. And Joe. Not ghostly visitations. Closing her eyes, she inhaled deeply, trying to stem her thrumming heartbeat. Only the rustle of leaves in the maple tree outside her window disturbed the night.

Breathe. Breathe.

She yawned and floated toward sleep.

Sleep, and the hope that what she'd heard was a dream.

THERE WAS something comforting about setting the table. Something precise. Fork on the left, knife and spoon on the right. Nothing surprising. Nothing that threw you off guard, pitching you into a downward spiral and shaking up your world. Nothing that came unbidden out of the darkness. Fork, knife, spoon. Predictable and precise. Jesse hummed as she worked her way around the table in the morning light.

She stopped, the silence in the room deafening. They were staring at her, all of them. Looking up, she almost laughed at the comical picture. It was as if someone had yelled "Freeze," and they all did: Maggie, her parents, her siblings, arms stopped in midair, steps stopped in mid-stride. The only thing moving in the Keegan cottage was the black tail of the cat clock above the sink as it counted the seconds one swish at a time. She would have laughed —except for their faces. Siobhan Keegan's was pale, her husband, Liam's, a mask of sorrow. Courtney's was dark with anger, Sean's simply perplexed.

"What?" She had no idea what had brought this on, but she was the source of their emotional energy. Slowly, she lowered the last spoon to the table. Her simple chore had been so predictable. But now, this.

"You were humming..." Siobhan Keegan whispered.

"Oh, uh, yeah, I guess I was." *Is my voice that bad?* The impact seemed a bit extreme. "Sorry... I didn't realize I was so off key."

Maggie hurried to her side, putting an arm around her shoulders. "It's okay, Jess. You weren't off key at all." She looked at her mother. "It's just, well, *what* you were humming."

She cast her mind back. Was it some evil, satanic ritual song? No, she didn't know any of those. Some misinterpreted Beatles song that, played backward, caused people to become axe murderers?

She frowned. "I was humming—"

"I've Been Working on the Railroad." Mrs. Keegan's shaky voice shimmered above the tension in the room.

Still, no one moved. She stared at them. *What the hell did I do?*

Finally, Maggie squeezed her shoulders. "Finish up setting the table, Jess. We have time for a swim before lunch."

Jesse folded the last paper napkin under the last fork and returned the remaining ones to the counter where Mrs. Keegan worked... worked with shaking hands that swiped at her eyes.

SIMON AND GARFUNKEL sang about going to Scarborough Fair as Maggie sat on the beach of Seneca Lake, tugging at the wisp of hair curling at the nape of her neck. Her hair wasn't usually this long. Her friend, Sister John Mary, who had done a stint in cosmetology before joining the convent, cut her hair short monthly. It was easier, having it cut short. Then it didn't pull against the starched white wimple attached to the black veil she wore as Sister Angelina.

The wisp was long enough to curl around her finger. She had been away from the convent on vacation for a week, leaving the day she had been due for a trim. That meant five weeks of growth, long enough to curl around her finger. Should she keep it a little longer for the wedding?

Sister Therese had finally given her permission to be Jesse's maid of honor. She would wear her habit. So, it didn't matter what her hair looked like. She'd be wearing a veil. Black and white, just like Joe... and Marty.

"Mags, look alive!" Jesse's voice skittered over the waves and across the beach just as a wet, yellow Frisbee landed in her lap. She laughed and flung it back to Jesse, who missed it.

"Man, I'm off my game today. Lack of sleep. That darn train woke me up a couple times last night." Jesse scooped up the disk and tossed it to Sean, who stood waist-deep in the lake.

Grabbing it in midair, he cocked his head at her. "What train?"

"The one that runs along the back of your property."

"Nah, that train hasn't run in, what, ten years, sis?" He swooped the Frisbee back to Jesse.

"Fifteen. Fifteen years." Maggie's voice echoed back to her across the water.

"Whatever. You were dreaming, Jesse." Sean jumped to catch the Frisbee.

Jesse frowned. "I'm sure there was a train."

"Head's up!" Sean called as the Frisbee skimmed Jesse's shoulder. Stretching to reach it, she tumbled into the lake. The Frisbee skipped along the shore landing in the scruffy grass of the neighbor's yard.

"Sis, go grab the Frisbee." Sean skidded his hand along the water's surface.

"Your throw, your recovery. Rules are rules, after all."

Sean shaded his eyes toward the dilapidated cottage. "Seriously. Go get it. That guy still gives me the creeps."

Maggie glanced at the cottage next door. "Shh, Mr. Becker will hear you."

Jesse scanned the yard. Someone had made a half-hearted pass over the lawn, but no further attention had been paid to the landscaping in years. A scrappy yew crept along the front porch, and weeds poked up through the cobblestone walk. The place looked deserted.

Sean didn't budge. Neither did Maggie.

"Geez, I'll get the dang Frisbee." Jesse splashed up to the shore and jogged over to the yard. She scooped up the Frisbee while surveying the porch, then dashed back into the lake. "Hey, somebody's home. The curtain moved in the front window. Kinda gave me the shivers."

"I know what you mean." Sean turned his back on the place.

"How's the water, Jess?" Maggie squinted, the sparkle along its surface alive and shimmering like diamonds.

"Get off your tush and join me. It's warm! Really warm!" Jesse reached back and swept her arm forward, releasing the Frisbee to Sean.

"Right!" He winked at Jesse. "Like bathwater, sis. C'mon in!"

After slipping on her water shoes, she jumped up and ran to the water's edge, splashing water up her legs as she sprinted into the waves up to her hips. The shock of the icy temperature jolted her, and she stopped, planting her feet in the stony lake bottom.

"You guys lied!" she shrieked hopping from one foot to the other. "Sean, it's freezing!"

Lunging to grab the Frisbee her brother arced at her, she lost her balance. Cold water enveloped her, numbing her limbs, stiffening her fingertips. She dove deeper, craving the cold, craving anything that would stop her mind from thinking about Marty.

Surfacing beside Jesse, she blew out the air she'd been holding and splashed her.

"Hey, Esther Williams, no need to be nasty about it," Jesse laughed and splashed her back. Both women hooted, their hands directing frigid sprays toward each other.

Sean joined the battle, scooping his open palm along the surface, sending a wave of water over them. They screamed and joined forces to direct their sprays toward him. Keeping up a constant deluge, they moved in and dunked him, holding his head under the water for a few seconds. He came up sputtering, whipping his Beatles-cut hair around in one defiant last attack.

"Hey! You kids want to go skiing?" The next-door neighbor on the other side of their cottage waved his arm from the nearby dock.

"Hi, Mr. Williamson!" Sean waved back.

The three of them waded over to greet him.

Mr. Williamson's leathery face was a testament to his love of being out in nature. As he beamed at them, his white teeth contrasted with his tanned skin. Though he was close to seventy years old, he moved effortlessly as he uncovered the boat.

Maggie loved to ski off the back of Mr. Williamson's boat. Once he was out of sight of the cottages, he'd punch the gas and whip them around in a dangerously delicious joyride.

As they approached him, he untied the front lines.

"Mr. Williamson, this is my friend, Jesse Graham."

"Hello, Jesse. Do you water ski?"

"I do."

"Climb aboard and we'll take a spin around the lake." He beckoned them to join him.

"We'd love to go skiing, but we're about to have lunch." Maggie shaded her eyes as she looked up at him. "Today is Sean's birthday. Why don't you and Mrs. Williamson join us for cake and ice cream in a bit?"

His grin faded. Removing his railroad engineer's hat, he smoothed his thinning salt-and-pepper hair and looked back at the cottage. He shook his head. "No, Myra's having a bad day. She prefers to stay inside."

Maggie could count on one hand the times she'd seen Mrs. Williamson over the last few years.

A loud bell sounded from the cottage just off the beach. Mom waved a dishtowel at them and yelled something they couldn't hear.

"There's Mom. We'd better go in," she said.

After bidding Mr. Williamson good-bye, they made their way to the towels scattered on the shore.

"Time for lunch and Sean's birthday cake," Mom called.

"Oh, geez. She made a cake," he muttered.

Maggie patted her brother on the shoulder. "Of course she did, Sean. It's not every day you turn eighteen, you know."

"Yeah, you're finally legal to drink... though that probably never stopped you before," Jesse said, giving his arm a light punch.

He turned scarlet.

"He would never take part in underage drinking." Maggie gave him her stern "teacher look" as she bent to retrieve her towel.

She caught Jesse and Sean winking at each other and straightened, frowning at him. "Would you, Sean?"

"No, no, of course not, Sister Angelina." He threw a wet arm around her shoulders.

She hugged him around the waist as they walked to the porch.

When they bundled into the cottage, Courtney was curled up in the corner of the worn plaid sofa, her head buried in a book. She'd often used studying as an excuse for ignoring the family. But that excuse ended when she'd earned her Ph.D. from Cornell University the previous month. Today, her face was buried in a novel.

"Hey, Red." Liam Keegan pointed to Jesse's curls, a crown of spirals after her swim. "You and I got the good old Irish ginger." He rubbed his knuckles on the top of his own wavy red hair.

"Careful, Dad, you'll start an electrical fire," Sean called over his shoulder on his way to the bathroom.

Jesse tamped down her mass of curls, but they sprang back up. "I look like Shirley Temple. Unlike my best friend here, Audrey Hepburn's twin."

"Your hair fits your personality—free and with a mind of its own." Maggie tugged one of her own short strands.

Jesse sat beside Dad, and he winked at her. "Nothing wrong with wild, Irish locks."

Jesse laughed. She smoothed her hair, her eyes crossing as it sprung back into ringlets.

"With that red hair, you could be my third daughter, Jesse."

Courtney shifted on the sofa.

"Well, I'll keep the Irish ginger, but I may cut it as short as Maggie's. Maybe wear a veil to keep it under control."

Maggie laughed. "You could have joined me and taken your holy vows with the Sisters of Saint Joseph."

"I had no intention of heading in that direction. They probably wouldn't have taken me anyway," Jesse said. "But you—you're the perfect nun, Sister Angelina."

Maggie fidgeted with her napkin, keeping her face down, feeling it flush. "Nobody's perfect, Jess."

"Jesse's right. You are the perfect sister, Sister Angelina." Dad patted her hand.

His words stabbed her heart. *No, not anymore.* She pulled her hand away and focused on the table, straightening her silverware, relieved when Mom hustled everyone to the table.

Sean needed no convincing, but Courtney uncurled herself from the couch and sauntered over, the last to be seated.

"Sister Angelina, would you please say grace?" Dad asked softly.

Courtney snorted.

Crossing herself, Maggie led the prayer, and they dug into ground baloney sandwiches and Charles Chips potato chips— Sean's birthday meal of choice. Mom included a salad.

"Mr. Williamson invited us to go water skiing," Sean said around a bite of sandwich.

"We invited them to join us for ice cream and cake, but he said Mrs. Williamson wasn't feeling up to it." Maggie put down the chip she was about to eat, saddened by the change in her neighbor, who used to be so vibrant.

Mom stared in the direction of the cottage. "There but for the grace of God," she said, crossing herself.

"So sad. Myra used to work side by side with Harold in their garden." Dad slathered mayonnaise on another slice of bread then smoothed a thick layer of ground baloney on top. "She's been daffy for, what? Five years or so, Mother?"

Mom nodded and turned to Jesse. "Years ago, they bought the lot behind them and created the most beautiful garden that stretched from the road behind the cottages all the way back to the railroad tracks. Harold worked for the railroad back then, and incorporated that theme. He had working lanterns and railroad crossing signs that lit up. Timmy loved it." Her voice caught.

"Myra kept right up with Harold, hauling dirt, digging holes, planting. Then she just... I don't know, lost her mind." Dad took a bite of his sandwich.

Courtney rolled her eyes. "It's called dementia, Dad. Early onset dementia."

"Whatever happened to her, it's so sad."

The sadness that had taken hold of Maggie sat heavy in her stomach. Forcing an upbeat tone, she said, "Hey, this is Sean's birthday celebration. Let's lighten it up." She pointed her fork at him. "Based on a previous exchange, I have a suspicion that you've been practicing for legal drinking."

Hoots and laughter followed. Sean's face turned scarlet, and he ducked when Dad swatted the back of his head.

Conversation was punctuated with laughter and teasing, except for Courtney, who didn't join in. She tried to excuse herself from the table early, having eaten only half a sandwich, but Mom insisted she stay and wait for birthday cake. She slumped back, arms folded, and glared at the table while the others finished eating.

Outside, the music of an ice cream truck echoed along its path. Sean's head swiveled toward the sound. "Hey, the Good Humor man!"

"We won't be needing the Good Humor man. I have enough ice cream for an army." Mom placed the cake before Sean, who shook his head, giving a half-smile as she lit the candles.

"Mom, please. You don't have to sing to me."

"We always sing on birthdays, sweetie."

"Jesus." Courtney shifted in her seat.

"Courtney." Maggie kept her voice soft.

"Oh, excuse me, Sister Angelina." Courtney's voice dripped loathing.

"Okay, let's sing, everybody. 'Happy birthday to you...'" Mom began the tune.

All but Courtney joined in, laughing and nudging Sean. He beamed.

After they'd all finished their cake, Courtney shot from her seat and left the room.

"Sorry, Jess. Courtney's just so cross all the time. She has been since..." Maggie hushed at a look from Mom, who shoveled a hefty slice of cake off the platter aiming for Jesse's plate.

"Here, have another piece of cake."

Jesse held up her hands in protest. "No," she groaned. "I'll explode if I eat any more."

"We can't have that just a month before your wedding. Your fiancé—what's his name again?" Mom balanced a slice of cake above Jesse's plate.

"Joe Riley." Jesse smiled, savoring the words.

"Joe Riley would shoot me."

Maggie pulled Jesse's plate away before Mom could deposit the slice.

"And then Officer Marty D'Amato would have to arrest him." Jesse stood to help clear the table.

His name was like an electric shock. Maggie stood so quickly, her chair fell backward.

"Careful, Grace," Sean teased as he righted her chair.

"You okay, Mags?" Jesse asked.

"'Feelin' Groovy.'" She busied herself taking dishes to the sink.

Chapter Two

❦

Water lapped the shore as the sun surrendered to the horizon, blazing the sky a fiery orange. Peepers chirped from the nearby wetland. The fecund blend of moist, rich soil, marsh grasses, and a bonfire farther down on the shore drifted to Jesse, and she inhaled contentedly. As twilight closed in around them, she shrugged into her sweatshirt to ward off the growing chill. She reveled in the peace that infused her body, mind, and spirit. A perfect ending to a day at the lake.

"Mags, August 23 is only a month away. My wedding day—can you believe it?"

"Yeah, well, the wedding shower is even sooner, and you still haven't even picked out thank-you cards yet." Maggie cracked open another pistachio and popped it in her mouth, tucking the shell into a paper bag. She sat beside Jesse at the edge of Seneca Lake's shore.

"Don't remind me. Uncle Ben is going to parade me around in front of all his wealthy acquaintances now that I'm an official part of the Wyndham family. One hundred of his closest friends." Jesse took a long draught of her beer. Her relationship with the

Wyndham family continued to be a balance between their demands and her wishes. And she had no wish to be the newly discovered heir to their wealth.

"I thought you came to terms with all of that. Didn't you two smooth things out?"

"Yes, once he accepted that I wanted no part of being the Wyndham heir. At least I salvaged my friendship with my cousin Al. He's the one who knows how to run the estate. And I finally convinced Ben to reconsider putting me in charge when I mentioned I might run the family business into the ground. Cousin Al will captain the Wyndham ship very well." She snickered. "I'm no sommelier. Just give me a Genny Cream Ale." She raised her bottle then swallowed the last of the amber liquid, savoring the cool, effervescent beer.

"Well, I'm going to wear my new modified habit to the shower. What a relief to be free of the wimple, long veil, and long skirt, especially in the summer."

"That will be grah"—Jesse yawned—"great."

"Am I boring you with my limited wardrobe choices, Graham?"

"No, sorry. I just didn't sleep very well last night. That train woke me, and I tossed and turned after that."

"You've got to be dreaming. No trains go by here anymore. The railroad eliminated this line long ago." Maggie sipped her beer.

Jesse considered this as she drained her bottle. "Speaking of the railroad, what was that awkward thing that happened before lunch today? It was weird."

Maggie pulled up her legs, wrapping her arms around them and resting her chin on her knees. "You were humming 'I've Been Working on the Railroad.' Timmy's favorite song. He used to sing it all the time because he was obsessed with trains." She set the shell-filled paper bag on the ground beside her. "He used to sing that day and night while he carried around the engine to his train set." She smiled softly. "Wearing his engineer's hat." Her smile faded, and she stared at the lake. "We don't talk about Timmy. Ever."

"Oh, geez. Sorry. I didn't know." Jesse stared down at her empty bottle. "I've never sung that song before—at least not since I learned it in first grade." A cool breeze swept across the lake and tossed tangled auburn ringlets across her vision. Brushing them away, she fought down a feeling of déja vu... and dread. Maggie had never spoken much about her younger brother's death. "Timmy drowned, didn't he?" From the corner of her eye, she peered at Maggie, who still silently stared out at the calm water.

"Yes. We think he did, anyway." Maggie's voice was barely audible above the lapping waves.

"You think so? You mean you don't know?"

Maggie shook her head. Her mouth arced down. "Sometimes when I come here, it's as if Timmy's still here—I half expect him to come running through the house with his hat on, carrying the engine and singing." She rested her forehead on her hands. "His death still carries a pall here. Mom and Dad have never been the same, and Courtney... well, you see how she is."

"Because of Timmy's death?" She didn't want to cause Maggie more pain, but maybe she needed to talk about this. In all the years they'd been best friends, shared all their secrets, she had never expanded on the circumstances of Timmy's death.

"Courtney was babysitting him when it happened. The rest of us had all gone to town for groceries, but her friend was being dropped off to spend the weekend while her parents went somewhere. I think they took her brother to tour Cornell or something like that. Anyway, she was sunbathing and fell asleep. When we returned, our rowboat was missing... and so was Timmy. We never found his... him."

"Oh, my God, Mags. I'm so sorry."

"I never wanted to talk about it. Like, if I spoke about his disappearance, that made it real. I think we've all hoped it was a dream we'd awaken from and Timmy would be with us again."

Tears glistened on Maggie's cheeks. Jesse looped an arm around her shoulders and pulled her closer, holding Maggie while she wept. Finally, Maggie straightened and wiped at her eyes and nose with the back of her hand. She checked her sweater pocket for a tissue but came up empty.

Jesse held out her arm. "Here, use my sleeve."

Maggie chuckled.

"No, I mean it. That's what friends are for." Pulling the sleeve over her hand, she wiped the tears running down Maggie's face, then swooped under her nose.

"Ugh, Jesse. That was gross."

"But effective. You really looked bad with that snot running down your face."

"Graham, you're a bitch."

"But I'm your favorite bitch, Sister Angelina."

IN THE STILLNESS OF MIDNIGHT, Jesse stood at the bedroom window, trying to locate the voice she was hearing. The lake stretched out like a swath of silk. Fine mist swirled across its smooth surface. Tranquil. Serene.

Still blurry from lack of sleep, she tracked the dusky gray mist as it crept along the water's surface. If she reached out, could she capture that tranquility and absorb it into her life? Was she doomed to be accosted by ghosts whose stories so badly needed to be revealed?

And why now? For the last six months, she'd been consumed with wedding plans, savoring the excitement and anticipation of life with Joe. That was what she wanted to think about—not ghosts. She was almost killed trying to help the last two ghosts. She shouldn't be surprised that another one showed up though. Marty had told her once you let one ghost in, others will follow.

But not now. Not when her life was so perfect, so happy. She smiled, wrapping her arms around herself at the thought of Joe's arms around her.

I've been workin' on the railroad...

Her joy faded, and she dropped her arms as the words drifted to her softly. Did she hear it with her ears or with her mind? Sometimes, she didn't know. She pressed her fists into her eyes as if that could stop what was inevitable. *No, please don't come to me. Please don't ask me...*

A train whistle, soft and insistent. It wasn't coming from the railroad tracks behind the Keegan cottage. It was coming from *inside* the Keegan cottage. And it beckoned her.

She eased open her bedroom door, pausing to listen. The house was still. Warm night air cloaked her, redolent with the scent of the butterfly bush below the hall window. As she moved into the hall, floorboards softly creaking beneath her feet, the young voice sang again. *"... all the live long day."* She rubbed the back of her neck to stem the prickling. She would never get used to this.

The voice was coming from the room across the hall. A room she had never seen because the door had always been closed. *Ah, Timmy's room.* A soft nightlight illuminated a hallway mirror offering her image: auburn hair wildly tossed, pillow wrinkles along one cheek, and fear in emerald-green eyes. She was not afraid to admit to fear. Her last encounter with a spirit had been violent. But this tiny voice didn't seem to threaten as the Seneca woman had. This tiny voice wanted to play. And somehow that chilled her more.

Approaching the door, she pressed her ear against it, waiting. Silence.

Dare she hope that she wouldn't hear anything and could return to her bed and delicious sleep? She edged away, and there it was. The train whistle. She'd have to reach to her toes to pull up enough courage to open that door. Especially now that she could feel icy air curling from beneath it.

Okay, Graham, just do it—open the damn door. Her whole body resisted, frozen. *Do it, for God's sake.*

She turned the doorknob, cold against her hand, and inched the door open. The room was dark, lit only by the half-moon that shone through the upper pane of the window. The moon glow slanted in, illuminating the middle of the floor where a model train engine chugged around a circle of track.

Chapter Three

Jesse hadn't slept the rest of the night. After she'd turned off the switch, the engine had stopped circling and the room had grown warmer. Timmy was gone. She'd tossed and turned, willing sleep that never came. Being sleep-deprived would not help her with final plans for the wedding.

No ghost. Not now. Not ever again.

She yawned as Mrs. Keegan set a plate stacked with pancakes in front of her.

"You need to go to bed earlier, Jesse. You can't sit out on the beach drinking beer all night. You need to be rested for your wedding night." She singsonged the last two words.

Oh, geez. Jesse wished the floor would open and swallow her whole.

"Mother," Maggie scolded.

Mr. Keegan smiled at Maggie. "You wouldn't understand, Sister Angelina. Marital relations are something beyond your ken, as it should be." He made the sign of the cross.

Jesse raised her eyebrows at Mr. Keegan's formal address. Yesterday, she'd thought he was teasing Maggie as she did, but based on the way his eyes shone, he did it out of pride.

As if reading her mind, he turned to her. "I'm the only one in in my family who had a child who took a religious vocation. We always call her "Sister.""

Maggie pursed her lips and sighed.

Jesse remembered that yesterday Sean had called her "sis." Courtney never called her anything.

Mrs. Keegan filled their coffee cups, winking at Jesse. "She's still my baby, religious sister or not. And you look like you need more coffee. Remember—rest up now because, well, you know." Again, she singsonged the last words.

"Red here will understand soon enough, thanks to Joe, eh, Mother?" He nudged Jesse with his elbow.

I need to end this conversation now. "Speaking of Joe, he and Marty should be here soon," she said.

Maggie bent her head over her pancakes.

"We can't wait to meet them, dear." Mrs. Keegan tried to pile more pancakes on her plate, but Jesse held up her hands.

"No, thank you. I can't eat another bite."

"Pre-wedding jitters, I suppose." Mrs. Keegan winked at her husband.

Jesse felt the blush infuse her cheeks, eliciting a loud chuckle from Mr. Keegan. *Lord, I'm twenty-nine years old and blushing like a flipping schoolgirl.*

But wedding night jitters were the least of her worries this morning. *More like post-ghost encounter jitters.* But she knew better than to mention anything about the previous night's manifestations. No, telling the Keegans that Timmy was present upstairs would not only horrify them, it would open wounds they been trying to heal for fifteen years.

Courtney sauntered into the kitchen, looking sleep deprived.

"Morning, sweetie," Mrs. Keegan said as she rubbed her daughter's shoulders.

Courtney shifted away from her and poured a mug of coffee. "'Morning."

"Pancakes?" Mrs. Keegan offered.

"No. I'm fine." She avoided eye contact with her family members, but pierced Jesse with a baleful glower.

Jesse shifted in her chair. What did she do to earn Courtney's wrath? They'd never even exchanged words. Geez, Courtney was so sullen.

"Why don't you tell us about your ability to see ghosts, Jesse?" Courtney sipped her coffee, never breaking eye contact. "You know, at your house, at St. Bart's. Anywhere else?"

Jesse's jaw dropped. *What the hell?*

Mr. Keegan's silverware clattered to his plate.

"Stop, Courtney." Maggie glared at her sister.

"I'm serious. We'd all love to hear about them." Courtney tipped her head, jutting her chin out.

Jesse glanced at Maggie, unsure what to say.

"Jesse has the ability—a gift, really—to see people who have passed on." Maggie's "teacher voice" was calm and reassuring; however, she kept her gaze on the table as she spoke. "She has encountered her mother and the Seneca woman who haunted St. Bartholomew's."

"Stop, Sister! We don't want to hear any more about these things." Mr. Keegan turned to Jesse, his face crimson, mouth turned down. He jabbed a finger in her direction. "You need to go to confession, young lady. You should not be meddling in the spirit world—it's against our religion!"

While he was scolding Jesse, Mrs. Keegan went into the kitchen and came back with a glass jar sealed with a black screw-on lid. Opening it, she dipped in her index finger, then made the sign of the cross on Jesse's forehead.

Jesse prayed it wouldn't hiss and steam.

AFTER CLEANING up the breakfast dishes, Jesse and Maggie headed to the beach. Maggie hefted the blanket she carried under her arm. Jesse kept looking toward the road—where were Joe and

Marty? They'd expected to arrive around 10 a.m. She noticed Maggie glance in that direction again, too.

"Before Joe and Marty get here, I have to tell you something." She stopped in her tracks. "Mags, are you blushing?"

Maggie halted and glared at her. "Stop, Jess." She turned and walked toward the water.

"You're blushing. It's Marty, isn't it?"

Maggie quickened her pace.

"It's okay, Mags. You have feelings for him? So what."

"Shh!" Maggie looked back at the porch where her parents sat reading the morning paper. "Hush, please," she begged.

"Sorry. But, so what—"

"So what? It would kill my dad to know I had feelings for... someone. Anyone. I'm so afraid I will betray myself. Dad can see right through me." She slapped out the blanket and let it float to the ground. A pair of seagulls pecking in the stones soared into the sky, squawking at her intrusion.

"They're feelings, Mags. You can't control your feelings. It's not as though you've acted on them." She took her friend's shoulders and turned her till they faced each other. "You haven't acted on them, right? I mean, you would have told me, right? Every delicious detail?"

Maggie sighed and flopped down on the beach blanket.

"Have you?" Jesse scrambled to sit beside her, locked on Maggie's expression.

Maggie stared at the water.

"You haven't, but you'd like to." She whistled softly. "Oh, Mags."

"I've never felt like this before. I feel like a tiger lives in my chest, ripping me apart." She pulled at a loose thread of the fringe of her jean shorts. "I'm a sister of St. Joseph. I took a damn vow."

Normally, Jesse would have laughed at the oxymoronic expletive, but her heart ached for her best friend.

Jess—it's destroying me." Her voice caught.

"Aw, geez. I'm sorry. You should've told me." She gave her a hug.

"I guess it's my cross to bear."

"You've been trying to deny it." She didn't want to sound harsh, but one thing that had sealed their friendship had been their honesty over the years. While Maggie was a gentle soul, she never backed down from making Jesse face the reality of life's events. She wasn't going to cheat her friend out of the same consideration.

Maggie gave her a half smile and nodded.

"I'll help in any way I can. If you need me to provide constant distractions, I can do that."

"I have no doubt." Maggie laughed. "So, back to what you wanted to talk to me about."

"Oh, yeah. Well, speaking of distractions, I need to tell you about what happened last night—"

"Should we throw these two mermaids back into the sea, Joe?" Marty's deep bass voice echoed off the water.

"Absolutely! Throw 'em back where they belong!"

Jesse's heart soared at the sound of Joe's voice. How could one person make her feel like it was Christmas? Or Disneyland? Or maybe heaven?

Maggie squealed as Marty scooped her up, crossing the beach and running toward the water. Joe followed suit with Jesse.

"You jerks! Put us down!" Jesse loved the feel of being in Joe's arms, even if the end result would be a soaking. Water sprayed up from his feet as he ran into the lake. "I'm getting drenched!"

"That's the idea." He laughed.

"Put my daughter down!" Mr. Keegan's voice thundered from the porch.

Joe and Marty froze, turning slowly.

Mr. Keegan strode down the walk to the beach, his fists clenched, his brows angry slashes above his eyes. Purple veins pulsed against his red face, and Jesse feared he'd have a heart attack on the spot.

Marty slowly lowered Maggie into the shallow water, the arm she had thrown across his shoulders slipping down and away. He straightened and stared down Mr. Keegan. "What the hell?" he muttered.

"Dad, it's okay—"

"No, I don't think it is."

"Dad, these are my friends, Marty D'Amato and Joe Riley."

Mr. Keegan rocked from foot to foot. He didn't seem to know whether to punch Marty or shake his hand. Clearly, the urge to punch was his preference, but, always a good host, he resisted that urge. But neither did he shake his hand. He gulped two deep breaths, and his face returned to its normal hue.

"How do you do, Mr. D'Amato?" His nostrils flared as he forced the greeting.

Marty extended his hand. "Please, call me Marty."

Ignoring his offered hand, Mr. Keegan shot him a disdainful look and turned to Joe. He nodded. "Mr. Riley."

By now, Mrs. Keegan, Sean, and Courtney had followed him to the beach. Mrs. Keegan fluttered her hands and pressed them against her heart. Sean crossed his arms, watching the exchange with interest. Courtney smirked.

Maggie stepped to her mother. "Siobhan Keegan, may I present Marty D'Amato and Joe Riley?"

Maggie's face glowed, though she never looked at Marty while she introduced him.

"How do you do? Please come inside and have some lemonade." Mrs. Keegan gestured toward the cottage as if no one knew where to go for the lemonade.

"I think they'd prefer a beer at this point," Jesse muttered to Maggie.

"I know I would," Maggie said, glaring at her father as she passed him.

"Quite a welcome," Joe whispered.

"Oh, just wait. There's more." Jesse took his hand and led him to the cottage.

MAGGIE SLICED banana bread while Mrs. Keegan stirred the lemonade.

Mr. Keegan sat at the head of the table, his arms spread flat on the surface, hands splayed out, as if marking his spot. Joe and Jesse sat on his left, Marty on his right with an empty chair between them. "Sister Angelina, we need more napkins over here."

"Dad, I've told you, you can call me Maggie here." Her gaze flicked to Marty then away.

Her face was the color of the rosy hydrangeas in the vase on the counter beside her. Was it embarrassment or anger? Jesse wasn't sure. Her bet would have been on "ticked off."

Marty shifted in his seat. If he'd had a tie on, he'd be loosening it right now. He caught Jesse's attention and widened his eyes at her. She could almost hear the string of Italian expletives parading through his mind.

"What exactly do you do, Mr. D'Amato?"

Marty's head snapped to attention. The words were more an accusation than a question.

"I'm a police officer, sir."

"Law enforcement, eh?" He nodded as if weighing the nobility of Marty's job with the blasphemy of touching his daughter. "Where?"

"Seneca Corners, sir. Not far from here."

"Hmmph." He scowled at him. Apparently, blasphemy had won.

Maggie set the platter of banana bread and a bowl of strawberries on the table and took her mother's usual place between Marty and her father. She looked him in the eye as if daring him to tell her to move.

Go Maggie. Jesse loved to see her friend's spunky side shine through. As gentle as Maggie was, getting on her bad side was never a good idea. She had a will of iron.

Mr. Keegan turned his attention to Joe. "You own Riley Construction, right?"

"Yes, sir."

"Knew your father. Contracted with him for the addition on this cottage. Quality workmanship." He grunted.

Joe always examined structures when first entering, and Jesse had seen him do so today. He studied the kitchen area and entrance to the master suite beside it. "Nice design. Did you have it drawn up?"

"Drew it up myself. Fifteen years ago, after—" He shot a glance at his wife. "Knew exactly what we wanted. Updated kitchen and enough bedrooms so no one had to use—"

The air was charged, just as it had been when Jesse was humming as she set the table. She glanced at Mrs. Keegan, whose haunted eyes stared down fifteen years of sorrow. Maggie was looking down at her plate, hands folded in her lap.

"Hurrumph." Mr. Keegan cleared his throat and buttered a piece of banana bread as if he were trying to sand it down. "So we could all have a room on the first floor."

Geez. Timmy isn't just appearing to me. He's still alive in the sorrow of every member of this family. Her presence here conjured more than just the actual ghost of Timmy. It opened a long-festering wound. And grief that had been buried this long resurrected with a bang.

She and Maggie had planned to stay at the cottage to work on wedding plans while they had some fun in the sun. *My wedding is far from the first thing on her mind right now.*

Were they all in a tempest that could rip her wedding plans to shreds?

Chapter Four

J oe and Jesse held hands as they walked along the stony beach that narrowed and surrendered into rocky boulders. Balancing on the rocks, they climbed up and found a large flat boulder and sat down. Clouds floated in from the west, easing the heat of the summer sun. Muffled voices carried across the water from passing boats whose occupants waved with glee, full of the joy of a cooling ride.

"Maggie's father is pretty protective." Joe glanced back at Maggie and Marty, who still strolled farther down the beach.

Joe's hair gleamed coppery red in the afternoon sunlight. She could look at him all day and never tire of the view. Unable to resist, she ran a hand through his hair, tousled by the breeze off the lake. She leaned in for a kiss, and he complied, his lips soft and inviting against hers.

A smile broke across his face. When she pulled back, he waggled his eyebrows and hooked a thumb toward tall grass. Swatting his arm, she kissed him again.

"I'm glad Maggie and Marty were so considerate to give us some 'alone time.'"

Joe winked at her. "Was it for us or for them?"

"Ah, you're aware of their feelings for each other, too."

"Hard not to be. Plus, Marty has talked to me about it. A lot."

"Maggie finally opened up to me, too. And, yes, it's pretty obvious."

"It sure was to her father today. That was weird, him calling her 'Sister Angelina' like she's some saint he doesn't know."

"He always calls her 'Sister Angelina.' Wants the whole family to do the same. That's a lot of pressure on Maggie. She can't even swear around him."

Joe threw his head back and laughed. "Somehow, I don't think that's a problem for Maggie, unlike it would be for someone else I know."

She gave him the side-eye. "Oh, really? You think I swear a lot?"

"You've been known to string colorful words together at times." He glanced down the beach. "No, I don't think it was for our sake that they've slowed their pace."

MAGGIE BUNCHED HER FISTS, stuffing them into the pockets of her shorts lest she accidentally brush against Marty's hand and grab it. She would not be able to resist.

Gentle waves lapped over their feet. Seagulls swooped above them searching for dinner, others floating on the surface eyeing the delicacies that waited below. Along the border of someone's property, honeysuckle wildly offered its blossoms, the heady scent seductive.

"I guess we need to talk about last-minute details for the wedding," she said. "At least that's the reason for you being here."

Marty shrugged. "I don't know the first thing about wedding plans."

She nodded. "Well, neither do I. Obviously."

"I guess I have it easy. All I have to do is show up with the ring."

"A responsibility of major importance."

"Yeah, but you have all the other stuff, like buying flowers and fixing her veil, and... hell, I don't know what you have to do."

"I think it's pretty clear-cut what we have left to do. Jesse is so organized. She and I pretty much crossed all the t's and dotted all the i's one night over a bottle of wine. I know she mainly wants exactly the opposite of what she and Robert had planned for their big bash. She just wants a quiet wedding, a few friends..."

"But the Wyndhams won't put up with that, will they?" Marty asked as he skipped a stone along the glassy water.

"The compromise was a small, intimate wedding in exchange for an extravagant reception. Jess figures she has to be there for the entire wedding service, but she can skip out whenever she likes from the reception."

"Not if it's anything like my family's receptions. Italians know how to do it up right. The bride's there till the end. There's always at least fifteen bridesmaids because you're screwed if you leave any relative out. Everybody gets these little almond candy things stuffed in fishnet or something."

She laughed.

"They play the 'Tarantella' and 'Volare' all night while people stuff money down the bride's dress while they dance with her. The ladies seem to compete for whose neckline plunges the lowest and whose stilettos are the highest. I've always gotta dance with my grandma at least once, and I always know what she's going to say: 'Martin. Don't let me die before I dance at your wedding.'" He stopped, crimson starting at his neck and spreading to his face. He picked up a stone and threw it with too much force to skip.

She pushed her fists deeper into her pockets. "Well, I won't have to worry about my neckline or my stilettos. I'll be wearing my habit and sturdy thick-heeled shoes like my great-aunt Mary wears."

Marty stopped again, touching her elbow and turning her to face him. "You look beautiful no matter what you wear, Maggie.

You're beautiful inside and out. When I'm with you, I feel so... I don't know... good. We have such great conversations, you know?"

His words washed over her like a summer rain shower. "I know, Marty. I enjoy talking with you, too." *Please, let this conversation end right here. Please.*

"Maggie, I need to tell you how I feel."

"No. Marty, please don't." Surely, he could hear the frantic pounding of her heart threatening to burst through her chest. Oh, God, she wanted him to continue. Dear God, she needed him to stop.

He took her hand. "I need to."

"Marty, don't do anything to ruin our friendship."

"Is that all you want? Friendship?"

She dropped his hand. "That's all I can have, Marty. After all, I am—"

"Yeah, I know. A Sister of St. Joseph. Geez, even your father treats you like some holy relic."

She turned and started down the beach again.

"I'm not a holy relic. I'm just a woman who answered a call to do God's work. Dad was so proud when I entered the convent and took my vows. Mom was, too, but for Dad, it was as if it somehow made up for losing Timmy. I don't know, I guess that's a silly thing to say." She smiled up at him. "See, when I'm with you, I talk about things I haven't even said to Jesse."

"Don't you think that's significant? Don't you think that means we have something special?"

Oh, I know we have something special. Her legs trembled as if she stood atop an earthquake, and she struggled to maintain her balance. Inside, emotions waged a fierce battle: desire vs. dedication. She had sensed a call from God, a life of easing the suffering of others, of helping children find their way. When she had taken her final vows, life made sense, she knew her purpose. And she loved her life with the sisters and her work with the girls at St. Bart's. But since she'd met Marty, an empty place within had opened up and grew emptier with every encounter.

She stuffed her fists farther into her pockets, pressing down the longing that enveloped her as it always did in his presence. Not only longing, but a physical pain that lodged around her heart, and she understood in that moment that heartache wasn't just a romantic term. The pain was real. She sighed.

"Please don't make it difficult for me to be with you. Please, can we preserve this friendship as it is? No pressure, no expectations?"

Marty brushed his hand along her arm. "*Cara mia.* We can keep things the way they are for now. But we can't live our lives in limbo. Sooner or later, we have to deal with this."

Chapter Five

Jesse searched the jigsaw puzzle pieces spread across the card table for the silvery white of the snow-capped mountain. The only sections of the puzzle she could manage under the dim light of the screened-in porch were the mountains or the clouds. The other colors were too dark to see.

The cool breeze off the lake sharpened the cool metal of the lawn chair against her legs and back. The moon, waxing toward full, cast silvery light along the grass and out onto the pebbles on the shore. Its reflection draped a gently undulating ribbon of lemon yellow atop the inky lake.

"Aha!" She snatched up a puzzle piece and positioned it near the peak of the mountain. She grinned triumphantly at Maggie. "Step it up, Mags. You haven't found a piece in the last fifteen minutes."

"I'm not the puzzle ace you are, Graham." Maggie leaned forward and studied the pieces. She had been subdued since Joe and Marty had left after supper.

The meal had been punctuated with awkward silence and stilted conversation. Mrs. Keegan had that ensured Maggie sat between her and Sean, though it wasn't her usual seat. Perhaps

Maggie hadn't noticed since the table included two extra places. Courtney actually had seemed a bit animated at supper, even contributing to the conversation. She'd sat directly across from Marty and never took her eyes off him.

When Joe had suggested he and Marty should head back to Seneca Corners, there was no Keegan hospitality offered like, "No, stay for a game of cards" or "You don't have to hurry off. How about some more dessert?" Instead, Mr. Keegan stood and shook Joe's hand bidding him safe travels back. He'd welcomed Jesse so warmly when she arrived and made her feel right at home. This coldness seemed unlike him. Had he always been all Papa Bear like this?

Now, she glanced at Maggie's somber, moonlit face, noticing sadness etched there, a crease between her brows. Knowing Maggie as she did, probing with questions would be useless. Maggie would tell her what brought on this sadness when she was ready. But Jesse guessed she already knew. She inhaled deeply.

"That honeysuckle is downright sexy."

One corner of Maggie's mouth lifted. Usually, she'd have a smart-ass comeback like, "Wow, how long has it been for you and Joe?" But she said nothing.

She doubted this was the time to tell her about Timmy. Maggie appeared fragile tonight. She didn't want to cause her more distress.

As if reading her mind, Maggie said, "What were you going to tell me about today? Before we were so"—she smiled the saddest smile Jesse had ever seen—"rudely interrupted?"

"Oh, nothing. Nothing important."

Maggie focused on her. "Tell me anyway."

She waved her hand dismissively. "Oh, just some wedding plans."

"If it's about the wedding, why not tell me? Isn't that why we're here right now? 'Fess up, Graham."

"I don't think you need to add this to your worries tonight."

"What worries? I'm fine."

"Right. And yonder moon is made of Swiss cheese. Mags, I can see you're upset about something. Is it what we talked about earlier? Is it about Marty?"

"Shh." Maggie pressed her index finger to her lips, looking toward the open window beside them. Her voice was so soft, Jesse could hardly hear it above the crickets.

Jesse cocked her head toward the lake, and they walked toward the shore. The stones crunched beneath their feet as they walked along the water, and she liked the harmony that created against the rhythm of the choppy waves. They turned in the opposite direction from the one they had taken that afternoon, now heading toward the Williamsons' cottage.

Just as they reached the edge of the water, a figure dressed in black appeared in front of them. He brushed by Jesse, almost pushing her into the water.

"What the heck?" She stopped just in time to keep her shoes dry.

Maggie called after the man. "Good evening, Mr. Becker."

He strode on in silence, past the Keegan cottage to his own.

"So that's Sean's boogey man. Rude as hell." Jesse watched him retreat into his cottage.

"Always has been." Maggie looped her arm through Jesse's and they continued their walk. Stopping in front of the Williamsons' boathouse, they hoisted themselves on the seawall.

"Remember the summer we came out here to smoke? What were we, sixteen?"

Maggie chuckled and pantomimed taking a deep draft. "Yes. I was sweet sixteen and never been kissed. You were sweet sixteen and never been missed."

Jesse slapped her arm. "Hey! I was seventeen before I gave it up."

"Behind the home ec building." Maggie's laugh lit up her face.

There's my Maggie. Stay with me. This will be tough.

"Do you want to talk about Marty?"

Maggie sighed. "I don't know if I'm ready. I have so much thinking—and praying—to do."

"To know what to decide?"

"To know how to deal with this. With my feelings. There is nothing to decide."

"Did you ever stop to consider that maybe your feelings are a message from God? Like maybe God wants you to follow your feelings?"

"Stop, Jesse. That's why I can't talk about this yet. Your opinion, Marty's opinion, even Dad's opinion of what I should do will only confuse me. Please, I can't talk about it right now."

"I understand."

"So, let's change the subject back to what you were going to tell me."

"Mags, tonight's not the time."

"Spill it, Graham."

She liked hearing the old fire in Maggie's voice, but this revelation would douse it for sure. How to begin?

"Remember how you were a bit skeptical of Helen's ghost until you experienced her presence yourself?"

"Yesssss."

"And how you believed in my encounters with the Seneca woman even though you never saw her?"

"But I saw the evidence of what happened to you because of her. My God, you almost died! What's this about?" She grabbed Jesse's arm. "Oh, no. Are you being visited by another ghost?"

"Yes."

"Where? At your house again? At St. Bart's?"

"No, Mags. Here. Here at your cottage."

Maggie's eyes grew wide, reflecting the moon in an ethereal light, as if they glowed from within. Jesse didn't want to say it, and Maggie didn't want to hear it.

"No." Maggie's voice was clipped, abrupt. As if cutting off her words would cut off the reality of what she was about to hear.

Jesse waited.

"We'd better get back; it's getting cold out here." Maggie dragged her arms through the sweatshirt she'd had draped over her shoulders.

"Maggie—"

"No. Stop talking." She covered her ears and slid down off the seawall.

Jesse hopped off, too, landing on a sharp stone that cut into the sole of her shoe. She scraped her foot over the pebbles to dislodge it, wiggling her foot to test for injury.

Maggie slumped back against the seawall. "It's Timmy, isn't it?"

"Yes, it's Timmy."

She dropped her head in her hands. "So many of my beliefs are being assailed at the same time. I don't think I can bear it."

"I'm here for you, Mags."

"Here for me? You're the one who keeps bringing all this confusion to me, Jesse."

SLEEP WOULD NOT COME. The look on Maggie's face had stabbed Jesse through like an icepick, and when she closed her eyes, Maggie was glaring at her. They'd had their fights, true friends always did, but never had she seen such anger combined with fear in Maggie. As they'd walked back to the cottage, only the grating sound of their feet on the stones deep in the night had surrounded them. Maggie had been silent, and it would have been futile to attempt to change that.

Clouds blanketed the night sky, blotting out the moon and stars. With the room so dark, she had to blink to ensure she was awake. Try as she might, she could not go to sleep. She named all the states in alphabetical order, which normally would have her nodding off by Michigan, but to no avail. All she could think about was how to make it up to Maggie. The last thing she ever wanted to do was cause her pain.

But Maggie needed to know about Timmy. His death was a

festering wound; it would never heal. Her whole family had ignored dealing with this pain for fifteen years. Timmy needed peace, but maybe the Keegans needed it even more. She couldn't let her dearest friend continue to suffer.

As if on cue, the small voice chanted. Chills prickled her scalp and flooded down through her body to her toes.

I've been working on the railroad... Singsong and innocent, the sound chilled her.

She rubbed her fists into her eyes, trying to block out the vision she expected to see. The train whistled into the silent darkness, urging her to come. Reluctantly, she pulled the covers back and slipped out of bed. She tried to picture the layout of the downstairs. Who might be hearing this? Which room was directly below Timmy's? She wasn't certain, but it could be Sean's or maybe Courtney's. Could they hear Timmy's voice or the train, too?

Sometimes she wondered if these ghosts were a figment of her imagination. But both Maggie and Joe had seen or felt Helen's presence. And her student Becky had been threatened by the Seneca woman, just as she had. So, others could see, and hear, and sense them. Had Timmy been appearing all along? Or was it just her presence that evoked him?

And why now? Marty's voice echoed in her mind. "Once one visits, they all start to come to you." Helen had opened that portal, or whatever it's called, and now Timmy was coming through.

Reaching his bedroom door, she paused to press her ear against it. His singing had stopped, but he was still there because tendrils of icy air swept out from beneath the door to lick at her feet. *Oh man, I don't want to do this.* She eased open the door. The train clickclacked around the track, the engine light casting an eerie shaft of white stabbing into the dark.

Like a gentle shower, her fear washed away, replaced with a sensation of exuberance. She wanted to sit cross-legged beside the toy. Laughter bubbled up, and she hugged herself with glee. As he began to sing again, Timmy's voice drifted to her across the still bedroom, and she hummed along.

No, stop this. Her mind seemed split in two, one half gaily light-hearted and the other starkly aware that she was taking on Timmy's emotions. With the other ghosts, she had experienced their feelings, too, but not so intensely. Tonight, she was being sucked into Timmy's untroubled state, in a way far more overpowering than she had ever experienced. She was slipping into a blithe sensation that wrapped her in its seductive arms, making her want to stay. This panicked her more than any danger the other ghosts had offered.

"Stop, Timmy." She hissed out the demand.

His voice faded. The train stopped immediately. The engine light clicked off.

Standing in complete darkness, her body trembled, her soul hollow with fear. Jesse remembered being teased by clowns at the circus once, their painted, gaudy smiles antithetical to her terror. Like the terror that seized her right now. The carefree, light-hearted sensation morphed to dread. She wanted to run. But she couldn't. For all her aversion, for all her fear, one thing was certain.

Timmy needed her.

Chapter Six

꧁❀꧂

R olling to her other side, Jesse watched the glow of dawn
seeping into the night sky, and with it came a sense of
relief. Lying here all night, tossing and turning, had been
misery.

Hearing noise down in the kitchen, she threw back the covers
and padded out to the hall. Timmy's bedroom held an eerie silence
she hadn't noticed before. Perhaps that was because of how full the
room had been last night—full of noise, full of movement, full
of peril.

As she undressed in the bathroom and turned on the shower,
she wondered how Maggie would be this morning. Would she still
be angry? Would she be able to get past her anger?

With the water turned to steaming hot, she again recalled her
conversation with Marty in her kitchen. He'd said she had "the
gift" like his grandmother. Marty understood her better than
anyone because he'd witnessed one of his grandmother's ghostly
encounters. And he was right—after one connected with her,
others would follow.

"Geez, is my life going to be like this forever?" Her eyes flew open at the thought. "Owww!" She let the shower pelt her face, trying to rinse off the shampoo that stung her eyes.

Finally soothed by the hot water, she yawned and scrunched her shoulders forward and back trying to wake up. Once her muscles loosened, she switched the water to cool, which woke her up and invigorated her. She was going to need to be alert today.

She took her time getting ready, taming her hair in a ponytail, putting on her makeup, trying to hide the dark circles beneath her eyes. If she didn't start getting sleep soon, she would look like a zombie in her wedding photos. She grimaced. So much for taking care of last-minute wedding plans while she was here. Between an earthly visit from Marty and an otherworldly visit from Timmy, Maggie was too distracted to help plan her wedding.

She sighed. How could she face the Keegan family, knowing Timmy was here, among them? And how would they react to that knowledge? Surely, it would inflame their sorrow. Unable to think of another delay tactic, she headed downstairs, unable to avoid peeking into Timmy's room as she passed.

Which was weirder: her encounter with Timmy last night or the cheerful appearance of his bedroom this morning as it had been the last time he'd been present in it... at least, alive and present?

When she entered the kitchen, Mrs. Keegan was cooking, as usual. *Ah, the aroma of coffee! This day might turn out well after all.* She poured a cup and held the steaming mug in her hands against her internal chill.

"How did you sleep, dear?" Mrs. Keegan laid a slab of bacon slices in the frying pan. The grease sizzled and spit, emitting a smoky maple aroma.

The better question is "did I sleep?" She took a sip of her coffee. "Fine, thanks, Mrs. Keegan. How about you?"

"Oh, you know how it is." She bustled about, clearly finished with that line of conversation.

Did Timmy's train awaken you? Keep you up until dawn? she wanted to ask, but what if it hadn't? A shock like that wouldn't help anyone.

Stepping out on the porch, she inhaled the clean, pine-scented air. A flock of gulls stood guard along the dock while others swooped toward the water, claiming their breakfast. Down by the point, boats bobbed in the middle of the lake as fisherman tried to catch walleye, perch, and lake trout. The lake was choppy this morning, waves chasing each other to the shore in an eternal race. The sun tried to find its way around the clouds, but never quite succeeded, casting the morning in silvery light.

She wandered down to the beach, automatically turning in the direction she and Maggie had walked the previous night. She studied the pebbles as she walked. How could she help Maggie understand that Timmy's presence meant he needed something?

"Hey there, Jesse."

She jumped, startled by the deep bass voice. "'Morning, Mr. Williamson." She waved at the man wiping his speedboat down with a chamois. She imagined being towed by that speedboat, skimming along the water's surface on skis, fighting the pull, fighting for balance. And the speed—she loved the speed.

"When are you and Maggie coming along to ski?" His warm, brown eyes crinkled at the corners when he smiled.

"I'll check with Maggie. I'd love to go skiing."

"Just let me know. Happy to oblige." He waved and returned to his chore.

She waved and ambled on as far as possible, until the beach merged into a marshy area. She had to admit, she resented Timmy's appearance. Right now, she wanted to be consumed with wedding plans and thoughts of her future with Joe. Instead, she was exhausted from nights spent dealing with a ghost, leaving her fuzzy-brained and emotional.

Swatting at flies, she turned back toward the cottage.

Her throat tightened at the memory of Maggie's pain last night. But Maggie needed to know that Timmy was still in need of release. Something unfinished needed to be set straight so he could rest peacefully. It was evident in the pall that hung over the entire family that they all needed to find peace.

MAGGIE LAY in bed listening to the morning sounds at the Keegan cottage. Mom cooking breakfast, Dad slapping the pages of the morning paper as he turned them, the bubbling percolator teasing the air with the scent of freshly brewed coffee. Sounds that should be comforting. But though their routine had seemed serene over the years, beneath the serenity had been the thousand-pound weight of the mystery of Timmy's disappearance.

She listened for Jesse's voice, unsure if she was ready to face her yet. The ache in her chest had persisted for weeks, months. Added to the ever-present ache of Timmy's death was the guilt she carried over her feelings for Marty. Feelings a religious sister should not have. With Timmy now appearing to Jesse, the heaviness was crushing her. She was as fragile as a butterfly right now, almost unable to move from her bed. How much more could she take?

After showering, she could think of no excuse to stay in her room. Her head throbbed at each temple, and she had to command her legs to move. *Step. Step. Step.* When she entered the kitchen, only her parents were there. The picture of normalcy and peace.

"Good morning, dear." Mom handed her forks and nodded toward the table.

That's it. Keep busy. Keep moving. Keep pretending.

Sean yawned his way to his seat still in his pajamas, and she and her parents joined him at the table. Jesse entered from the beach, and Mr. Keegan pulled out the chair beside him.

"Come on, Red. Time to eat—we're starving!"

Jesse looked as exhausted as she felt, and the heaviness draping her like a shroud increased. Jesse smiled at her, but Maggie just nodded and looked down at her plate. If someone touched her, she was afraid she'd dissolve into a million pieces.

Jesse sat down, and Mr. Keegan patted her shoulder.

"Hey, you okay?" He frowned.

"Yeah. Just tired," Jesse said.

Courtney entered and sat across from Jesse, staring at her as if no one else were in the room.

"Good morning, dear." Mrs. Keegan planted a kiss on top of Courtney's head. She shrugged it off.

"Tired?" Mr. Keegan picked up his thread of conversation. "How can you be tired, sleeping with this fresh, lake air blowing through your window?"

Jesse shrugged. "Mags, I saw Mr. Williamson this morning. He wants to take us water skiing."

Maggie pushed scrambled eggs around her plate. "Not today. I'm pretty tired myself."

"What's with all this 'tired' business? The lake is the place to rest and rejuvenate." Mr. Keegan stabbed at a piece of bacon, breaking it so one end flew off, landing on the table. He picked it up and popped it into his mouth. Then he snatched up two more pieces and tossed them on his plate.

"I didn't sleep well either." For a split second, everyone stopped to look at Courtney, surprise registering on their faces. But Courtney's gaze burned into Jesse.

Maggie looked up. *What's with Courtney? She never makes eye contact with anyone.*

"What the hell is going on?" Mr. Keegan exploded, as if their not sleeping was a personal affront.

"Tell him, Jesse." Courtney raised an eyebrow, daring her to speak.

"Tell me what?" Mr. Keegan demanded.

"Why Jesse isn't sleeping." Courtney looked at her father.

Maggie's blood ran cold. *Oh God, no.*

"So? What? Wedding jitters? Cold feet? What?"

The cat clocked swished, mocking the silence.

"She hears Timmy." Maggie's voice was soft, but its impact sucked the air out of the room.

Mrs. Keegan stood, slapping her hand to her breast.

"What?" Mr. Keegan's voice was incredulous.

"Tell him, Jesse." Maggie couldn't control the roughness in her voice. She was shattering like a broken mirror. Pieces of herself falling to the floor, sharp and pointed. She grabbed the tabletop to stem her shaking.

Courtney's lips rose in a half smile. "Yes, tell him, Jesse."

"As you know, I seem to have a gift—" Jesse began.

Mr. Keegan leapt up. "Are you talking about that ghost at St. Bartholomew's? The one you supposedly saw? Sister Angelina told us about that. No, it's not a gift—it's a curse, and I don't want to hear about it. Don't you dare bring that ghost crap into my house. Don't you dare taint the memory of my son with that bullshit."

"But it can't be Timmy. He may still be alive." Mrs. Keegan's voice shook. "He may have been kidnapped like the other boys." Her voice grew stronger and she looked out the kitchen window. "He could be living with another family right now." She looked at Jesse. "You must be mistaken. There is no ghost."

Silence captured them as they stared at her. Maggie slumped back in her chair, wiping her hand across her eyes.

"Dad, denying it won't change—" It took every ounce of energy for Maggie to speak.

He held his hand up to her, signaling silence.

"Dad, stop! Let Jesse tell us what—" Courtney added.

He pointed at Courtney. "Shut up! You don't talk to us for years, and now you want to talk? Just shut up."

He turned on Jesse. "Get out. Pack your things and get the hell out. And never come back."

Jesse's gasp pierced the air. "What?"

Maggie stared at her plate, tears running down her cheeks. She was so tired, she couldn't say another word. She was shattered; she was falling.

"Dad!" It was Courtney, not Maggie, who objected.

"Now!" He pointed to the stairs.

Jesse rose like someone who was sleepwalking. She

dropped her napkin on the plate and when their eyes met, Maggie just stared at her. Her voice wouldn't work. Her limbs wouldn't be still. She gripped the table lest she topple to the floor.

Jesse turned to the stairs, but not before Maggie saw the tears filling her eyes.

JESSE BARRELED ALONG ROUTE 5 & 20 toward home. She'd had to pull over soon after leaving the Keegans' cottage because she couldn't see through her tears. After weeping for fifteen minutes, she'd recovered enough to drive, and then her secondary emotion, anger, took over.

Damn you, Timmy! You're dead. You can't hurt anymore, but what you've done is causing me incredible pain.

She shook her head. *Timmy can't help it. He's a little kid. A little kid who needs help.*

Didn't Mr. Keegan see that Timmy's appearances were a cry for help? No, he wouldn't. He thought there was something evil about spirits who manifested, and he was afraid. She couldn't blame him —Helen's first appearance had scared the crap out of her. But Maggie understood. That was what hurt the most. Mr. Keegan throwing her out was bad enough, but Maggie didn't even defend her.

Jesse turned the corner into her street, catching sight of what locals called the Cavanaugh House. Her house. And the site of her first ghostly encounter with Helen Cavanaugh. But she had never heard the voices of Helen or the Seneca woman, though sounds were the first indication of Helen's presence. They both had appeared to her, and she sensed their emotions, but they never spoke—at least not audibly. With Helen, she'd sensed pure love and tenderness; with the Seneca woman, rage and desperate sorrow.

Her shoulders relaxed, and her grip on the steering wheel loosened at the sight of her home. Being here was like putting on her favorite sweater, warm, and safe.

She loved this old, dilapidated house—no longer as dilapidated as when she'd first entered it. She was trying to maintain its original décor while updating and repairing the structure. New dark, moss-green shutters flanked each window, and the fresh laurel-green paint on the wood siding gleamed in the late morning sun. Joe had helped repair some of the deteriorated gingerbread moldings and built sturdy new front steps leading up to the porch.

Together they had yanked out the old overgrown shrubbery and planted neat yews across the front of the house, punctuated with a couple of hydrangeas whose bright blue blossoms greeted her merrily, bowing on the breeze.

She unlocked her door and entered the front hall, welcoming the sense of peace that enveloped her. Dropping her car keys in the ceramic dish on the hall table, she caught her reflection in the mirror. Her mascara smeared in a raccoon effect beneath her dull, green eyes. Her mass of red hair fell around her shoulders, released of the elastic that had held it neatly in place this morning. *I look like a feral Lucille Ball.* As she puffed out a sigh intended to be dismissive, her heart hitched again. Though she stared at her reflection, she was numb and detached from it, as if observing someone else.

"Hey there, glad you're here. I brought over the..."

She jumped, heart thudding in her throat. "Holy shit, Joe!"

He stood in the open doorway, thumbs hitched in his jeans pockets.

"Nice welcome. A bit too flowery for my taste, but..." He stepped closer, tipping her chin up. "Are you all right? I thought you were staying at Maggie's until the end of the week."

She shot him a rueful smile. "I got kicked out."

"Kicked out? Okay, I didn't feel the love there, but I thought you were enjoying your time getting to know Maggie's family. Making plans for our wedding."

"I was."

"And?"

"And I met Timmy."

Joe frowned at her. She recognized the look. He was trying to make sense of her statement.

"Maggie's little brother, Timmy. He drowned fifteen years ago. At least they think he did. No one ever found him."

"But he found you." Joe brushed his fingers across her cheek. "So, you're dealing with a ghost again." He dropped his hand, walked to the living room, and flopped on the sofa. Leaning his elbows on his knees, he dropped his head in his hands.

"Are you going to be mad at me, too? Geez, I don't invite these people. I haven't hung out a shingle that says "Ghost empath for hire. Please come in and destroy my life."

Now she was shaking. Did she somehow beckon spirits to herself? Was she even unaware that she did? Regardless, having Maggie and Joe both desert her right now would be devastating.

"Come here, Just Jesse. I'm not angry with you." He held his hand out to her.

She burst into another fit of crying. That nickname was love. "Oh, God, Joe, you had me scared for a minute."

He pulled her down beside him on the sofa and wrapped her in his arms. She nestled into him, crying against his shoulder. "I don't want any more ghosts. I don't want Maggie to be hurt or angry with me. All I want to think about is our wedding and our life together. I feel so blindsided right now."

Joe kissed the top of her head. "Tell me what happened."

She related her encounters with Timmy, including her out-of-control happiness, and her attempt to explain them to Maggie. "She blew up at me, Joe. She said I'm the one who brings all the confusion to her."

"What confusion?"

"She said all her beliefs are muddled and I'm to blame."

"Maybe for one, but I doubt for the other."

"Marty?"

Joe nodded.

"Yes, though she did meet him through me when I was investigating Helen's murder."

"It's not as though you threw him at her."

"I know, but I feel so bad that she's hurting."

Joe pulled her closer. "I feel bad that you are hurting."

Despite her dismay at the morning's events, she sank deep into Joe's arms, savoring his love, allowing his strength to surround her.

She was home. She was safe. She was loved. And now that she was out of the Keegan cottage, she was finished with Timmy.

Chapter Seven

Lying on her stomach, Maggie floated on an inflated raft secured to the dock. She dangled one arm in the cool water, not even flinching when a sunfish teased her fingers. Though the sun beat down on her, she didn't relish its warmth. Her body ached as if she had been pummeled by a novice boxer who wasn't sure where to land the punches.

She tried to banish Marty from her mind, as she had been trying to do for months now. But he wouldn't go away. She allowed a smile to play at her lips. She so enjoyed being around him. When he appeared, her world became lighter, she became expansive, as if her arms were open to love and accept everyone, to embrace all of nature's beauty, to accomplish anything. To her, colors were brighter, people were friendlier, she became more loving, warmer... sometimes too warm.

What wasn't warm was how she felt about Jesse. Everything that tormented her right now revolved around Jesse. She'd met Marty at Jesse's. These damn ghosts kept appearing to Jesse. And now her own little brother was appearing to her. *Damn.*

No, none of this was Jesse's fault. Jesse didn't make her fall in love with Marty. And Jesse certainly didn't ask for ghosts.

"Nice way to defend your best friend." Courtney's voice cut into her reverie.

Courtney's shadow brought a chill; Maggie shaded her eyes to look up at her sister, who stood in the water beside her. Courtney never entered the lake. Ever since Timmy's drowning, she barely even came to the front porch of the cottage.

"What are you doing out here?" Maggie asked.

"I have as much right as you do to be in the lake."

"I know that, but, Courtney—"

"Don't change the subject. Why did you leave Jesse hanging out to dry? Dad was all over her ass, and you just sat there."

"You don't understand."

"I understand that she's your best friend.

"Courtney, please. Just let it go. Honey, you don't have the whole picture. You have to have faith."

"Don't use your religious platitudes with me, and don't call me honey. You can barely stand to look at me. And now you've deserted your best friend. What kind of nun are you, anyway? Where's all that charity and love you profess to live in?"

Maggie sat straight up on the raft so quickly she almost fell into the water. Courtney rarely spoke to her, and when she did, her remarks were clipped and insolent. But this accusation, this attack, was beyond her usual rudeness. Had Courtney slapped her, it wouldn't sting this much. Sliding off the raft, she stood, facing her sister, arms akimbo. Why was Courtney so defensive about Jesse when she'd ignored her since she'd walked through the door?

"What's going on?" Maggie stifled the urge to defend her actions, instead trying to understand.

Courtney backed away, waving her hands in front of her. "Oh, no. You're not going to turn this back on me. You own this fiasco, Sister Angelina." She sneered the name. "You were cruel and disloyal. I wouldn't blame Jesse if she never spoke to you again." She turned and splashed back to shore.

Maggie untied the raft, slumped across it, and kicked out past the dock. She pumped her legs, trying to work off the hurt and anger, trying to beat away the guilt that had been eating at her all morning. *Damn it.*

"Let it go, sis." Sean swam up beside her. "You know how Courtney is. She hates everyone and wants people to be as miserable as she is."

"She's right, though. I didn't come to Jesse's defense."

"What difference would it have made? Dad's mind was made up. He doesn't want any part of Jesse's woo-hoo voodoo around here."

"It's not voodoo. I can't believe you'd even say that." She kicked her feet, steering the raft away from him.

"You can't believe that crap? You're a stinking Catholic nun, for God's sake. It's against our religion." He followed her out to the deeper water. "Dad'll kick you out of the house next."

"Dad kicked me out long ago."

Where did that come from? She had never consciously thought that before. She'd never felt like her father kicked her out.

She'd been seventeen, in her senior year, when she'd made the decision to enter the convent, but the groundwork had been laid for several years. It started right after Timmy died... disappeared. Mom had fallen apart completely, Courtney withdrew and would not speak to anyone, Sean had only been three years old. Dad had believed what happened to Timmy was payment for some past sin.

A few months after Timmy disappeared, she and Dad sat by a bonfire on the beach, huddled in sweatshirts and blankets against the cool September evening. The grief on his face flickered in the shadows cast by the flames. He hadn't talked about Timmy since the day he went missing two months earlier. Now the words poured out.

"I should never have left him with Courtney. Just the two of them here all alone."

She listened, accepting his grief like a sacred gift, merging it into her own, willingly, if that would help ease his suffering. But his words were difficult for a thirteen-year-old to hear.

"She should have minded him better." He threw a stick into the fire.

"Dad, you can't blame Courtney. She's only twelve years old."

"She was supposed to watch him, not fall asleep while she was sunbathing. She should have—"

"Stop." She had never spoken to her father like that, but the fury rising within her wouldn't abate. "You cannot blame Courtney. It could have as easily been me."

A reflection of the flames flickered in shadows across his face. "Never you, Maggie. You are too special, too good. God has something important in mind for you."

She was silent.

"Maggie, have you considered entering the convent?"

She stared into the flames, mesmerized by their dance. She had, in fact, contemplated religious life, mainly because the nuns at school often talked about it.

"Give your life to God, Maggie. Give your life to God."

She had always believed her father's words were a sign. She entered the novitiate of the Sisters of St. Joseph immediately after high school.

Now, as she stared into the depths of the lake, she wondered if she had been a sacrificial offering. Her life as atonement for Timmy's. Shifting her focus to the surface, she watched the reflection of Sean's scowling face contorted by the ripples in the water.

"What do you mean, 'Dad kicked you out'?" His voice was harsh, defensive.

"Nothing. I don't know why I said that."

"So, you believe Jesse saw Timmy's ghost? You believe that crap?" He glared down at her, hands on his hips.

"Yes."

"Then maybe you ought to leave, too." He dove into the water and swam back to shore.

Leave? Leave what? The cottage? The convent?

Were Sean's words a sign?

Chapter Eight

❧

J esse pulled the covers over her ears, but the annoying sound persisted. Dragging herself up from a sound sleep, she frowned, trying to make sense of what was waking her up.

A train whistle.

Squinting into the dark, she struggled to grasp a clear thought from her muddled brain. She was awake enough to know she was home, not at the Keegan cottage.

The train whistled again.

Rolling on her back, she threw one arm across her forehead. Since living here for a year, she had grown accustomed to the sound of the night train that ran past her house a quarter mile away. She never even noticed it anymore. Yet it woke her tonight. Why?

As if in answer, Timmy's young voice floated from the attic room.

What is it about that room?

She flopped her arm on the blanket. *I thought I was finished with Timmy.* Heaving a sigh, she threw her legs over the side of her bed and stumbled down the hall to the attic room.

Pausing outside the door, she pressed her ear against it. Silence.

She gripped the handle and waited. Nothing. When Helen Cavanaugh had been on the other side, Jesse had been stunned by the deep sense of being loved. She stared at the ceiling, trying to define what emotion enveloped her at this moment. Not fear. Not dread. Anticipation?

She opened the door and studied the room. No longer was it the empty attic room with exposed rafters where Helen had introduced herself. Joe and Marty had drywalled it and helped her sand and refinish the broad-planked oak floors. While the armoire still stood against the wall where it always had, now a desk with a chair sat with a view out the front window, and an overstuffed chair with an ottoman nestled in a corner with a reading lamp beside it. Books filled the built-in shelves Joe had constructed on the wall opposite the armoire, and a floral rug unified all the furniture pieces into a cozy study. Jesse examined the room. All was in order.

Except the train engine lying in the middle of the rug.

She gaped at the toy. How could this be? But even as she wondered this, and against all logic, she sank into pleasure at seeing the toy. She knelt on the floor and picked it up.

I've been working on the railroad... Timmy's voice floated in the air like a feather drifting from above. The room became frigid.

She hummed along with him and searched the room for a young boy. A boy to play with. She wanted to play. Kneeling on the floor, she rolled the engine along the rug. Where was he? She could hear him.

Shivering, she rubbed her arms. "I'll be right back. I need my bathrobe." Her voice was light and young on the night air. She scanned the room for Timmy, but he didn't answer.

"Timmy? Timmy, where are you? I'll be right back."

Unfolding her legs, she stood and skipped out into the hall. The icy chill and childish emotions slid away like melting snow. What just happened? Yanking the door closed, she leaned against it, trembling. She had never succumbed to the other ghosts so completely. With Timmy, she seemed one with him.

She'd left the train engine on the floor in the study. Had there even been a train engine? Was she hallucinating? She had never taken LSD, so this wasn't a flashback. She wrapped her arms tighter around her waist. *Am I going crazy?* She had to be sure. Slowly opening the door, she peeked into the room. The air was no longer icy, but the train engine lay on its side in the middle of the rug.

I'm not crazy, but I'm trapped.

Chapter Nine

❦

S harp raps on the front door jolted Jesse to consciousness. She was sleepily aware that this was not the first attempt.

"*Bella*, I know you're in there. You can't hide this yellow Volkswagen Beetle. Open up, it's the police," Marty bellowed as he began another round of knocking.

She stood, stretching and yawning, trying to get her bearings. She vaguely remembered coming down to sleep on the sofa in the hopes of not being awakened by Timmy again. Her foot caught on the planner splayed out on the floor. As she stepped over it, she glanced at the clock on the secretary. Nine o'clock. Well, at least she'd gotten a little sleep.

When she opened the door, Marty's fist was poised for another round, and she ducked just in time to avoid his knock. She glanced at her Beetle, which she had christened "Bert."

"So, Bert gave me away? Hey, Marty, come on in."

"You look bad."

"Why, thank you. And a pleasant good morning to you."

"No, I didn't mean that in an insulting way, just, you know, concerned." He hooked his hat on the coat rack and closed the door.

"Come on, I need coffee." Glancing in the mirror, she agreed with Marty's observation. A tangled mass of auburn curls surged up like a tsunami from the left side of her head. She wrangled the nest into a more balanced coif, but the curls coiled out again. She tugged one. "If these were snakes, I could be Medusa."

"Then don't look at me!" Marty's laugh cheered her. "So, what's up, *bella?*"

In silence, she put on a fresh pot of coffee and set an empty mug in front of him.

"It must be bad. You're never this quiet."

She sat across from him. "You don't know the half of it. Maggie's not speaking to me."

A faint blush colored his cheeks but dissipated quickly. "What? Why? You two are best buds."

Raking her hands through her hair, partly out of frustration, partly to tame it again, she related the encounters with Timmy and their effect on the Keegan family.

"Whoa, I didn't get any warm fuzzy vibes from Mr. Keegan, but he seemed to adore you. That's cold."

Nodding, she blinked away the sting from the still-fresh wound. She gulped hot coffee past the lump in her throat. "Well, no more. He's furious with me. But the hardest part was that Maggie wouldn't even look at me."

Marty took her hand. "Geez, that's gotta hurt."

His sympathy opened the floodgates, and she blubbered, "It... it does... a lot." She wiped at her tears and swept her hand under her nose. "I'm a mess."

Marty grabbed a paper napkin from a ceramic holder on the counter and handed it to her.

Nodding her thanks, she dabbed at her eyes and blew her nose.

"You just need to give Maggie time. She'll come around."

But what if Maggie didn't come around? What if she never spoke to her again? She pressed her hand against her chest, trying to stem the ache that gripped her heart. Marty grabbed another napkin.

"Do you want me to talk to her? Explain how you're feeling?"

His offer brought a glimmer of hope. She opened her mouth to speak, but was interrupted by the doorbell.

"Who could that be?" She looked at the clock as if it held the answer.

"Could be a Fuller Brush salesman. Want me to get it?"

"That'd be great. I'll pour us some more coffee."

While she filled their mugs, a woman's voice floated back to her. Could it be Maggie? With hope, she turned. Her mouth fell open.

"Courtney?"

"Hi, Jesse."

Trying to gather her thoughts, she snapped her mouth shut. This morning was turning out to be as crazy as last night.

"Coffee?" She held up the carafe as if to explain.

"Sure. Thanks." Courtney smiled at Marty as he held a chair out for her. "Thanks."

After setting a steaming mug in front of her, Jesse pushed the sugar bowl and pitcher of cream in her direction. With a shaking hand, Courtney scooped a teaspoon of sugar into her cup and added a dollop of cream, spilling a little along the side of her mug.

Courtney looked from one to the other. "You're probably wondering why I'm here."

"Yes." *She's in as bad shape as I am.*

"I need to know what you saw... or heard the other night at our cottage."

"Why?"

Now Courtney's whole body trembled. "I need to know that I'm not crazy."

"Why would you think that?"

Courtney slammed a fist on the table. "Stop!" She leaned forward, her fists set firmly on the table. "Please. Stop answering my questions with a question."

Though she didn't dislike Courtney, Jesse didn't particularly like her either. Courtney had shunned her from the time she arrived at the cottage, exiting a room when she entered, never greeting her, answering any attempt at conversation with one or two words. Always appearing superior and disapproving. Now she appeared desperate and fragile.

Jesse nodded. "Okay. I awoke to a train whistle. Then I heard a little boy's voice singing. When I went into Timmy's room, his model train was circling the track, the engine light was on."

Courtney fixed her gaze on the table. "The room. How did it feel?"

"Icy cold."

A tear escaped and ran down Courtney's cheek. Her trembling increased. She nodded. "Yes."

"You've experienced Timmy's presence, too." Jesse's heart went out to her. She wanted to pull her into a hug and hold her, reassure her. But she didn't seem like a hugger.

Courtney blinked at her. Gone was the cold, hard stare she was used to. "Yes."

Jesse reached across the table and took her hand. Courtney grasped it like a lifeline.

"How often?"

"Off and on since he vanished. At the time he disappeared, some boys around his age had been abducted. For a long time, I believed he wasn't dead. That he'd been abducted like the others. But one night I heard the train. My room is right below his. I went upstairs." Her voice quavered. "Like you said, the room was icy cold. The train was running..." She covered her face with her hands. "I was only thirteen. I thought it was Satan. I never told anyone. I thought it was because of my sin. Timmy died because I fell asleep." She crumpled toward the table. "When it happened again, I didn't go up. I never went back up. But I've heard it ever since."

Kneeling beside her, Jesse gathered her in her arms. "Oh, Courtney, how awful for you to have carried this burden all these years." She rubbed Courtney's back as the girl sobbed against her shoulder. "You're not crazy. And you're not sinful. Just put that right out of your mind." She bit her lip to hold back her opinion of religion that sprinkled condemnation over people like contaminated holy water.

Courtney leaned back to look at her. "But I was supposed to be watching him."

"Honey, even parents can't watch a child every single minute. What happened wasn't your fault. You need to let go of that guilt."

"Dad said—"

"I don't care if the damn pope said anything."

Marty winced.

Courtney grinned. The pall she carried seemed to ease just a bit.

"Tell me about these boys being abducted." Jesse returned to her seat.

"I don't remember all the details, and my parents didn't want me to know about the situation. But at school, my friends suggested Timmy was abducted like some other boys."

Marty filled her coffee cup. "Yeah. I remember that case. Three boys from the area went missing within five months of each other back in... what was it,1953 or '54?"

"Yes, fifteen years ago. That's when Timmy drowned."

Jesse shook her head, trying to understand. "If Timmy drowned, why would you think he was abducted?"

"We assumed he drowned because our rowboat was gone. It had been tied to the dock. Timmy liked to sit in it and pretend he was out on the lake. He'd use the oar on the side away from the dock." She smiled. "He loved it when a speedboat went by and stirred up choppy waves. As the rowboat rocked, we could hear his giggles all the way up on the porch." Her smile faded. "The boat was gone, the mooring lines lying loose in the water." Her eyes glistened. "That's how they found it. And me asleep on the lounge chair."

"So all of you assumed Timmy untied the boat and floated away."

"Yes." Courtney choked out the word. "They found the boat over in a cove. But they never found his... found Timmy."

Marty nodded. "They never found the boys either."

Jesse turned to Marty. "What else do you remember about the abductions?"

"Just what I've told you. Three boys, pretty young—all about seven or eight years old in the area of the Keegan cottage. They never found the kidnapper."

Courtney rubbed her arms as if warding off a chill. "I don't know what's worse, feeling guilty about Timmy or thinking he'd been abducted by some weirdo." She covered her face and wept into her hands. "Oh, my God. If Timmy was abducted because of me—what would he have suffered?" Her frame shook.

Jesse stared at nothing, remembering her ghostly encounter just hours ago. "Timmy is sending a call for help. Whatever happened to him, there is business that must be settled before he can rest peacefully. I think it might have to do with these abductions." She patted Courtney's arm, trying to soften the idea.

Marty scowled at Jesse. "You've got that look in your eye."

"Marty, it's time to visit the Archive Room again."

"*Mannaggia.*"

Chapter Ten

M aggie folded her last swimsuit, still a bit damp, and tucked it into the zippered, plastic pocket of her suitcase. Each movement sapped energy, her movements slow. She strapped her clothes neatly inside and lowered the suitcase lid, snapping the buckles closed. She wore capris and a crisp, sleeveless white blouse. She wouldn't need to put on her habit until she arrived at the convent.

The incessant headache pounded in her temples, as it had since Jesse left the day before. Maybe when she returned to the convent all the misery would disappear. She would find peace in the serene atmosphere among her sister community. Perhaps a silent retreat would be a good idea right now. She crossed herself and tried to pray, but prayers hadn't been coming easily lately.

She lay on the bed and closed her eyes. Even with the curtains drawn, the soft glow of the afternoon sun blinded her. Life had been somber here the since yesterday. Her mother took frequent naps, and when she was with the family, she kept her head bowed over her latest knitting project. More than once Maggie had caught her weeping.

Her father stormed around, getting angry at little things like the porch light being left on overnight. He railed at Sean even though she had been the one who'd sat on the porch until after midnight. He never railed at Sister Angelina.

She rolled on her side away from the sunlit window. Slowly opening her eyes, she studied her dresser. She'd always been a neat freak, so all the items on her dresser lined up perfectly. Brush, comb, dusting powder, hand mirror. All in a row. One thing in life she could control. She had the urge to get up and sweep it all to the floor.

A soft rap sounded on her bedroom door.

"Sis?" Sean's voice was subdued. It was like living in a funeral parlor.

She rose and opened the door slightly. "Yes?"

"There's someone here to see you." He turned and walked away, his pace slow and deliberate. For the last day, her whole family moved that way.

Her heart surged. Did Jesse come back? Even though she was still angry, she missed her terribly. Her words the other night—how they must have hurt Jesse. How had this wonderful vacation they'd shared end on such a sour note? She pressed her fingers to her temples. But facing Jesse today with this piercing headache could lead to more harsh words. A coil was wound tightly inside her, and one wrong word could unleash it to spring out and attack whoever was closest.

She checked the room for any wayward items she might have missed. Nothing. She was ready to leave. She might as well bring the suitcase out with her since Dad was waiting to drive her back to the convent. She hefted the luggage and headed to the living room. Despite her anger, it would be good to see Jesse.

Reaching the front room, she stopped.

"Marty?" Her heart leapt to her throat.

"Hi, Maggie." His voice was soft, as if he wanted only her to hear it. He gripped the back of a kitchen chair, his hands sliding back and forth. His hair was neatly combed, evidence of the care he'd taken to look presentable.

Dad stood, glowering at him from the living room. "Make it fast, son. I'm taking Sister Angelina back to the convent now." He folded his arms, his stance wide.

Marty glanced at him then turned back to her. "Can we talk?"

"Didn't you hear me, D'Amato? Sister Angelina is going back to the convent now."

"Liam, Officer D'Amato just wants to talk—" Mom looked up from a sea of pink yarn that billowed about her lap.

"No!" Dad's voice boomed.

"Dad, please." Maggie's gut twisted with a confusing mix of guilt, delight, and anger.

Marty stepped toward her. "I'd be happy to take you back, Maggie. I'm heading right past St. Bart's."

"No. You won't be taking her anywhere. Speak your piece and be done with it." Dad's face flushed with rage, his lips curled down, his nostrils flared.

Would he raise his fists, inviting a brawl? The intensity of Dad's fury colliding with Marty's tenderness swirled in the room like a tangible, emotion-packed tornado that made her head throb harder than it had been.

Marty looked at her, his gaze warm, inviting. A comforting balm soothing her ragged nerves.

"Dad, it's fine."

"No, it's not fine." He strode over to Marty. "Look, I don't know what your intentions are here, but I think you're up to no good. Get away from my daughter."

Marty straightened to his full height, silently boasting his two-inch advantage. He leaned toward the man. "My intentions are to talk to Maggie. Now, I can do that here or I can take her to the station."

"The station! She hasn't broken any law!"

"Resisting an officer."

"You goddamn pigs. Can't you leave decent people alone?"

Her headache had reached volcanic proportions and was about to explode.

"Stop! Both of you!" She rubbed her temples. "Marty can drive me back. It's silly for you to drive all the way over there if he is going right by the convent."

"Sister—"

"Maggie!" she shouted. "My name is Maggie, Dad." She glared at him; his eyes shot open, anger shifting to pain. She didn't intend to hurt him, but something inside finally cried out "enough." Exhausted, she kissed Mom goodbye. When she approached Dad, he turned away. She picked up her suitcase and walked out the door.

"YOU OKAY?" Marty cast her a sideways glance then returned his attention to the road.

Maggie leaned her head against the headrest. "Yes." She tipped her dark sunglasses down and looked at him. "No. Splitting headache." She replaced the glasses.

"I didn't mean to upset your father like that."

"It wasn't just you. Things have been upsetting him for a couple of days now."

"Yeah. I saw Jesse this morning. She told me what happened. With seeing your little brother and all."

She concentrated on the woods along the road.

"That's gotta be tough. Having Timmy show up like that."

"I can't talk about it right now." Her voice was sharp.

"Okay. Got it."

Marty didn't do anything wrong. Why bite his head off?

"Sorry. I just have this wretched headache."

"Mama gets them. She taught me how to massage them away. I could try."

Her heart beat faster. How would it feel to have Marty's hands on her? She shivered.

"You cold?" He fiddled with the air vent.

"No. I'm fine." The pain in her head went into overdrive; she could barely squint the sun was so bright. One hundred men with hammers and anvils were pounding them in her skull. She clutched her forehead.

He pulled over and parked the car. He took her hands from her face. "Turn toward your window."

She did as he said, squeezing her eyes tightly to block the piercing daylight. His hands were cool against her skin, his fingers surprisingly smooth. He gently touched her temples, two fingers tracing slow circles on either side. Relaxing, she surrendered to his touch, feeling tension begin to slip away like waves at ebb tide. After a while, he pushed his thumbs gently along the nape of her neck. She automatically cranked her head to the left then the right. Finally, his fingers moved to her forehead, gently massaging, directing the pain away from her face. While the headache remained, the intensity slackened.

"May I touch your shoulders?"

His voice was tentative. At this point she wasn't sure what she might surrender to. She nodded.

His hands kneaded the muscles along the top of her shoulders, relaxing them from rock hard to supple. He guided her to sit forward and worked down to her shoulder blades, thrusting his thumbs into the taut muscles.

For the first time, she appreciated the perfection of this summer afternoon from the warm sun to the smell of blossoms in the trees that surrounded them. Just over the ridge, Seneca Lake sent up the music of her waves. Maggie eased back against his hands. When had she ever enjoyed such bliss? She wanted to feel his hands on her for the rest of her life.

Her eyes flew open and she bolted upright. His hands dropped away. She edged closer to the passenger door.

"Thank you." Her voice was clipped. "My headache is just fine now." She stared straight ahead out the window.

"Maggie, I wasn't trying to seduce you or anything."

"I need to get home."

He started the car. "Sure thing."

As they drove, she sat rigidly, teeth clenched, hands clasped around her purse like it was an anchor holding her secure in her life at St. Bart's.

No longer incapacitated by a headache, she now had to deal with desire that filled her to bursting. She wanted to tell Marty to stop the car and place his hands on her back again. To sink into his arms. To feel his mouth on hers. To soak up his comfort and the love for her that he was so bad at disguising.

The question was, how good was she at disguising hers? Surely, her resolve would crumble if she broke the awkward silence that sliced the air between them.

Chapter Eleven

꧁꧂

Musty air greeted Jesse as she entered the stacks in the local history research room of the library. Bookshelves marched along either side of the aisle, and file cabinets lined the far wall. As she headed toward the back, she hoisted the tote bag on her shoulder. Relieved to find the one microfilm machine available, she claimed the plastic chair, letting her tote slip to the floor, the notebooks and pens that stuffed the bag clacking as they settled.

Marty hadn't been sure of the dates of the disappearance of the young boys, but, like Courtney, he guessed it was fifteen years earlier. She'd put in a request for reels from the *Seneca Corners Sentinel* for 1953 and 1954. Flipping on the machine's light, she slipped in the first reel and skimmed it. Because the *Sentinel* was a small, local paper, it wasn't indexed. That meant the only way to search was to inspect each edition. At least she could skip all sections but the local news. Even so, it was good she'd prepared dinner ahead of time and cleared her calendar for the day. This was going to be a long, arduous process.

After skimming articles for an hour, she sat back and rubbed her eyes. Standing to stretch, she walked a couple circuits around the room, rolling her shoulders and reaching for the ceiling.

Just as she was about to sneak a candy bar to appease her rumbling stomach, the librarian entered.

"How is the search going?" The librarian was a pleasant woman in her early fifties. If she noticed Jesse's contraband, she gave no indication.

Jesse eased the wrapped bar into her pocket. "A needle in a haystack."

"What exactly are you searching for? Maybe I can help."

"Back about fifteen or so years ago, three young boys were abducted. The kidnapper was never found. Neither were the boys."

"I do remember that. Parents were so frightened they formed neighborhood watch groups. One turned into a vigilante group that started to accuse neighbors. It got pretty ugly."

"Do you remember what year it happened?"

The librarian tapped her index finger against her lips and stared into space. "Hmm. My sons were older than the victims, in middle school, I think. The kidnapped boys were young—maybe eight or nine. So, it would have been about fifteen years ago."

Jesse's shoulders slumped. "Yes, that's the closest I can get to pinpointing the time frame."

"If it helps, I remember that the abductions took place in the summer. School was out, so none of the boys were taken on their way to or from school. In fact, if I recall, they seemed to be taken from right under their parents' noses. It was so bizarre."

Timmy went missing right from under Courtney's nose, too. True, she'd been sleeping, but if some stranger tried to grab him, wouldn't he have cried out? Yelled for help? And wouldn't a stranger be recognized as such, lurking around the cottages? Though, if some were rentals, there could be new people arriving and leaving all through the summer.

"Thanks. Knowing it was summer will narrow my search. Did all the abductions occur in the same place? At the same location?"

The woman tilted her head, trying to remember. "Gosh, I guess

I don't remember that. I mean, they all took place in the area of Seneca Corners, but I can't narrow it down more than that." She looked at the microfilm machine. "Good luck with your search."

"Thanks." Jesse returned to her seat. When the door closed, she pulled out her candy bar.

Chapter Twelve

✤

Maggie stared at the pink memo. The edges were fluted from her holding it for so long. She reread the message from Jesse. "Dinner at my place tonight. 6:00 p.m. Please come."

"Excuse me. I'd like to get my mail." Sister Alphonse squeezed past her, reaching into a cubby hole that held two educational catalogs and a letter.

Maggie stepped back. "Oh, sorry."

"What's wrong with you these day, Angelina? You've been walking around in a daze."

"I'm fine. Allergies." *Dear God, I just lied.*

Sister Alphonse studied her. "Yes. I see how irritated and red your eyes are. There's medicine for that, you know." She turned brusquely and strode off.

There is no medicine for what ails me.

"Sister Angelina, I'd like to speak to you... about your allergies." Sister Therese beckoned to her from her office.

Her heart pounded. Whatever Sister Therese really wanted to talk about had nothing to do with stuffy noses. She had finished teaching a summer math course last week, and she hadn't been on top of her game. Her instruction had been solid, but she hadn't included some of the more creative projects she often added. Was she about to be reprimanded?

As she entered the office, Sister Therese sat and nodded for her to do the same. She had always enjoyed visiting with Sister Therese in her office. Their discussions usually centered around enhancing the math curriculum and student achievement. The only difficult time in here had been when Sister Catherine had been murdered. She shuddered at the memory.

"Are you ill?" Sister Therese's voice brought her back to the present.

She sat up straighter. "No. I'm fine, thank you."

"You're shivering." Sister Therese studied her.

"I just remembered being in your office when Sister Catherine... and Jesse was hiding from the murderer under the desk in the outer office."

"Yes, such a tragedy. There are so many unexpected events in life, aren't there?"

"Indeed."

"How we deal with those events is certainly a sign of character, don't you agree?"

"Yes."

"As I recall, we gathered in here to pray for the repose of Catherine's soul. And, of course, we discovered she wasn't a sister at all but a very brave woman nonetheless. There are so many courageous women who serve in many roles outside the religious life."

Trying to sound noncommittal, she kept her voice light. "Yes, yes there are." Where was this going? Sister Therese didn't have time to invite her into the office for a casual chat.

"But for you and I, our highest calling is our religious vocation. Wouldn't you agree?"

"Of course." Maggie shifted in her seat, smoothing her skirt. What she really wanted to do was rub her temples, maybe lay down for a nap with a warm washcloth over her eyes. Take a couple of aspirin. But not sit here waiting for Sister Therese to get to the point. They sat in silence for a moment.

"Tell me about your allergies. I don't remember you suffering from them in the past."

Now, she was silent. She couldn't lie again.

Sister Therese leaned back. "Speaking of Jesse, how was your vacation at your family's cottage?"

They hadn't been speaking of Jesse—well, she had mentioned her once. It was too painful to speak about. The sharp stinging brought on by her own lack of support for Jesse at the cottage had descended into a dull, constant throb. Her face flushed.

"It didn't end well."

"Do you wish to tell me about it? I don't mean to pry, but Alphonse is correct—you haven't been yourself since you returned. Are your parents all right?"

"Yes, they're fine, but my father and I had a fight."

"As I said, I don't wish to pry, but you seem quite miserable. Would it help to speak with Father Steve?"

She twisted her rosary beads through her fingers. How to explain her father's anger without bringing up Timmy's ghost or Marty? Sister Therese would frown on both. She had not been sympathetic to Jesse and her student, Becky, when the Seneca woman's ghost appeared to them, so she wouldn't understand about Timmy. And she would never understand about Marty.

"We fought about my little brother, Timmy." That wasn't a lie.

Sister Therese sat forward and tapped a pencil on the desk blotter. A crease appeared between her brows. "But didn't your little brother die many years ago?"

"Yes." All she could manage was a whisper.

Sister Therese continued to tap and then her face clouded. "Jesse Graham was there with you?"

She nodded. "Yes."

"I see. She didn't bring up any of that ghost business, did she?"

Maggie stood, pressing her fists down on the desk. As upset as she was with Jesse, she would not listen to Sister Therese speak of her like that. She struggled to keep her voice low. "Jesse doesn't 'bring up ghost business.' She has a gift."

"Gift or curse? She shouldn't be dabbling in the occult."

"Now you sound like my father..." She sat back down.

"Then you should listen to him."

Maggie threaded her rosary, slipping it, bead by bead through her fingers. Arguing with her superior would get her nowhere. "Was there anything else, Sister Therese?"

Sister Therese leaned her forearms on her desk. "You tell me, Angelina. Is there anything else?"

Sister Therese's scrutiny nailed her to the chair. She squirmed and her rosary beads clacked and jangled as she handled them. *Nothing that I want to discuss with you, or anyone else for that matter. Except maybe Jesse, if I were speaking to her.*

"No."

Sister Therese did not immediately dismiss her. Finally, she nodded. "Good day."

Hardly.

JESSE'S HEAD spun as she finalized dinner preparations. She'd put the lasagna in the oven and was tossing the salad. Tossing it hard. Absentmindedly, she brushed the nape of her neck.

While she'd searched for coverage of the abductions, she also hunted for Timmy's obituary but found nothing. There was a brief article about his suspected drowning, but no follow-up that even mentioned his body was never recovered. The Keegan family had been living in an anguished limbo.

"Hey, Just Jesse!" Joe's voice boomed from the front hall. "Smells good in here!"

Entering the kitchen, he swept her into his arms. His kiss was long and languorous, and she sank into it, clinging to him for safety... for sanity. Her arms circled his neck. For a moment, she let go of all her anxiety and sadness, then she pulled away.

He didn't release her but ran his fingertips along her cheek. "I hope I got here early enough for some make out time. Hey, what's wrong? Didn't your research go well today?"

"Joe, I can't believe what I found out. I—"

"*Mama mia*, I must've died and gone to heaven! The aroma in here takes me back to my Grandma Rose's kitchen!" Marty called from the hallway. Entering, he heaved a case of beer onto the table. "Jim and Susan are right behind me. Hi, *bella*." He kissed her cheek, then landed a soft punch on Joe's arm. "Hey, man." All the time, his gaze traveled the room, resting on Maggie's usual seat.

"Hello!" Jim called from the hallway. "We're here!" He brought in two bottles of Chianti, and Susan followed with a vegetable casserole.

"I see we have enough beer and wine to get us through the night," Joe said, laughing. He grabbed a church key and a corkscrew from a drawer.

"Good, 'cause I may need a case all my own." Jesse set the salad bowl in the middle of the table.

"What's wrong, Jesse?" Susan placed a hand on her arm.

She slumped into a chair and rested her head on one hand. "It's been a hell of a week. Let's get dinner on the table and I'll explain."

Marty handed her a cold beer, and she nodded in thanks.

Joe pulled the lasagna out of the oven and slid the cookie sheet covered with buttery garlic bread slices under the broiler. Jim poured wine while Susan set the vegetable casserole on a trivet next to the lasagna pan.

When everyone sat down, the place set for Maggie bellowed with emptiness. Marty looked at it and pursed his lips to the side.

"Shouldn't we wait for Maggie?" Susan asked.

Jesse glanced at the clock. Six-fifteen. Maggie was always punctual, usually early.

"I don't think she's coming tonight." Jesse straightened her napkin on her lap. She looked up. "I have a lot to tell you."

While they ate, she filled Jim and Susan in on the events at the Keegans' cottage and the subsequent fallout with Maggie. She added the visit from Courtney, including the information she and Marty had provided about the boys' abductions.

Susan nodded solemnly. "I remember that so well. The whole community was on edge—and on high alert. People demanded the police do more to find the kidnapper. There was a lot of ill will toward the Seneca Police Department back then. Sorry, I don't mean to be negative, Marty."

"No need to apologize. I was in high school back then."

"Yeah. We both were," Joe said. "But, Mom, I remember you telling me about the abductions. You were pretty shaken up."

"I was. For the boys, but also for what happened to Seneca Corners and the surrounding county. At first the community came together, people formed neighborhood watch groups and searched for the boys, helping the police as much as possible. As time passed, people became frustrated with law enforcement and suspicious of each other. Some of the groups became almost militant."

Jesse shivered. "Yes. That's what I learned today when I looked at old newspaper clippings about the case. The boys were taken within a three-mile radius of each other. Two were local boys, one was vacationing on Seneca Lake with his family, not far from the Keegan cottage." She rotated her wineglass as she spoke. "One vigilante group went after Mr. Keegan. They said they'd traced a trail from the vacationing boy to him." She folded her arms and hunched forward to stem her trembling. Joe rubbed her back, and she leaned into his touch for strength. "The group convinced the police to take him in and question him about the kidnappings."

"Oh, my God." Susan said. "The department was under so much pressure to act, they probably grabbed at any possible lead they could."

Marty scrubbed his hand across his face. "But they never found anything on him, right?"

"Right. They held him for several hours, then released him due to lack of evidence. Maggie's never spoken of it to me."

"Perhaps it was too painful," Jim said as he refilled wine glasses. "Or perhaps her father forbade her to talk about it."

"That could be; the guy's a like a drill sergeant." Marty took a long sip of Chianti. "And no wonder he wasn't thrilled to have me around—I'm a damn Seneca Falls cop. *Aye-yi-yi.*" He cast a sorrowful look at Maggie's empty seat.

Susan patted his hand.

Jesse nodded. "That's not all. Mr. Keegan wasn't their first target. Two other men who live in that area caught the wrath of the group. One was the son of the owners two doors down from the Keegans. His name is Bruce Becker. He still lives there now. Never married. The other guy is Cordell Jefferson, who owned a van that taxied vacationers from the Geneva Airport to their cottages. He also offered a shuttle service, taking vacationers to the general store just a couple miles down the road. He was probably targeted because he was black. There was talk of lynching him."

"Jesus." Joe slammed the table. "When will that shit stop?"

"If Maggie were here, she'd scold you for your language. God, I miss her." Jesse covered her face. "Can you imagine what she and her family went through? Mr. Keegan was under suspicion, then released, then Timmy drowns."

"Or was kidnapped." Joe's low voice echoed what Jesse didn't want to imagine. "And killed, since his ghost is appearing to you."

"Oh dear, not another ghost." Susan took Jesse's hand.

"I told you they'd start coming to you." Marty poured wine into Jesse's glass.

Jesse sagged into her chair, the lasagna a leaden glob in her stomach.

"So why didn't they investigate Timmy's disappearance in light of all these abductions? Especially if his father was suspected?" Jim asked.

She nodded at him. "They did. But neither any of the boys nor the kidnapper were ever found. And the Keegans were convinced Timmy had drowned. Except Mrs. Keegan, who believes he was kidnapped and now lives happily ever after with some other family. It's her coping mechanism. Maggie told me that Mr. Williamson had seen Timmy playing on the dock. Courtney said he loved sitting in the rowboat, and when she awoke, the boat was gone. They figured he loosened the lines and the boat slipped out onto the lake with him in it. They found the boat, but they never found Timmy."

"So, in addition to the agony of Mr. Keegan's being taken in for questioning, they now had to deal with Timmy's apparent death." Joe said, tapping his fingers on the table.

"Yes." She blew out a puff of air, as if expelling the horror of what she'd discovered.

Joe rubbed her back.

"Timmy needs to tell me something, and it might be about the abductions." She took a sip of wine. "That Becker neighbor is pretty rude. And scary. Maggie's brother won't go near his cottage. Never has." Holding the stem of her wineglass, she rotated it, gently sloshing the red liquid. "But the kidnappings stopped and he's still around."

"What happened to the other man? What was his name? Cordell?" Jim asked.

"Yeah. Cordell Jefferson. I don't know. He probably left town after the way they treated him."

"I wouldn't blame him." Joe picked at the label on his beer bottle.

"True. But when did he leave and when did the abductions stop?" Jesse stopped turning her glass.

———

MAGGIE SCOOPED the last of the potato salad out of the bowl and spooned it onto a waiting man's plate.

"Thank you, Sister." He tipped his hat.

"You're most welcome." She'd been forcing smiles all day. Not that she didn't care for the people who came, because she cared very much about them. But the soup kitchen was especially busy today. It always picked up in the summer when farm workers came to harvest crops, especially the grapes that grew in abundance in the Finger Lakes region. For some reason, today had been non-stop. Probably because it was Sunday and they could have at least part of the day off.

"Just coffee for me, please."

Her head snapped up at the familiar baritone.

"Hey, Maggie. Can you take a break?" Marty's crooked smile melted her heart.

She checked the crowd. The line was much shorter, and two other sisters had just arrived to spell her and the others who had been there since seven that morning. "Sure." She caught the eye of one of the sisters and held up her spoon. The nun grinned and came over. Maggie relinquished the spoon and her apron, poured a cup of coffee into a Styrofoam cup, and handed it to Marty.

Walking into the sunlight was delightful after a morning of scooping salad and washing dishes. She inhaled air that smelled of summer warmth and honeysuckle.

"I—I mean, we all missed you at Jesse's dinner Thursday night."

She nodded.

They strolled past the workers who watched their children run around and squeal with glee. Musky-scented wisteria dripping with purple blossoms beckoned them to stroll along a path that led toward the lake. A cardinal trilled its song from a tree ahead of them.

She was grateful for the modified habit she was now allowed to wear. A stiff, thin, white linen band above her forehead held a small veil that covered her head and fell to her shoulders. Her skirt was mid-calf instead of floor length, and her shoes were pumps rather than the old-fashioned style with laces. The cotton-blend fabric was a vast improvement from the nylon material of her old habit. She was beginning to feel modern, maybe even feminine.

"Jesse misses you. A lot." He walked with his hands in his pockets.

"I miss her, too."

"She wonders why you haven't returned her calls."

She studied the path. "I've just finished teaching summer school. I had to give exams and calculate grades. I've been really busy." Her excuse sounded lame even to herself. What else could she say? *I knew you would be at Jesse's, and I don't have the strength to put up a good front right now?*

Not only that, she was afraid of what she might say to Jesse. She had been supportive when Jesse was dealing with the ghosts of Helen Cavanaugh and the Seneca woman, but even those two stretched her belief system. At one time, she had been right there with Dad's opinion about evil spirits before Jesse's ghostly encounters. But Timmy was different. He was her precious little brother. Thinking of him as a ghost haunting their cottage made her extremely uncomfortable. Now Timmy was what she had once thought of as an evil spirit. She had to work through this so she didn't say any more hurtful things to Jesse.

"Maybe you could just give her a call."

She stopped and faced him.

"Why?"

"Why give her a call? She's your best friend."

"No. Why are you coming here to intervene for her?"

"Because I care about you—and her. I think you're both miserable, and you need to kiss and make up. Well, not really kiss; I meant that as a saying, you know. If *we* had a fight, I would want to —" His face was as red as the trilling cardinal.

The image of them kissing for any reason made her dizzy. "I need to get back." She turned along the path they'd been walking.

"No, wait, Maggie. I didn't mean anything by that. *Ay yi yi,* sometimes I say the completely wrong thing." He reached for her arm.

Just that contact sent a thrill through her. She should turn back now. He'd said his piece, now she should leave him. But the pull was too strong. She wanted nothing more than to stay beside him for whatever time she could have. Her mind wrestled with the proverbial devil on one shoulder, angel on the other. She looked at his hand on her arm, then up at him.

"Please stay." His gaze was clear, and honest, and hopeful.

She nodded, and they continued along the path.

They reached a low bluff above the lake with a narrow path down to the water.

"You game?" Marty asked.

She stuck out one foot, showing off her shoe. "Sturdy and low-heeled. Let's give it a try."

He held out his hand. She took it, grateful for the support as she followed him down the short path. At the bottom, a light breeze blew across the water, welcoming them to the shore.

"Now pebbles are another issue altogether," she laughed.

They found a patch of soft grass and sat. The breeze blew her veil around her face, and she pushed it back. Even though she stared ahead at the water, his gaze burned her like a beacon. Pleasant warmth spread through her. For this moment, she didn't care. She yielded to the joy his presence brought, to her vibrancy when she was with him. She craved his touch.

Her veil billowed again, and this time he brushed it back. His hand lingered on her cheek, his fingers tracing the curve of her chin. Reaching up, she took his hand and held it for a moment. A blissful moment. Then she gently pushed it away.

"Maggie...."

"I need to go back now." Desire was rising too quickly. She didn't want to go back. She wanted to stay here with him in this secluded cove. She wanted to lie in his arms. How could this be? She had dedicated her life to God. She wasn't supposed to feel like this. Yet, here she was, feeling like this.

"One reason I keep coming to you about Jesse is because I just want to be with you. That's the real reason."

She nodded. "I know."

He took her hand again. "Maybe you should stay mad at her so I can keep coming back to plead her case."

Despite her inner turmoil, she chuckled. "You are a hoot,

Marty." *That's it. Keep it light.* When she looked at him, the passion in his eyes stunned her. And beckoned. He reached out to stroke her face again.

She stood and dusted off her skirt. "I need to get back."

He stood and offered his hand. "Let me help you back up the path."

"No, thanks, I don't need your help. I think it's best if I make it on my own."

She turned and clambered up using exposed tree roots as footholds. She slipped a couple of times, almost falling to her knee once. Seagulls mocked her from the shore, and they were right.

She may not have needed him, but she wanted him.

Chapter Thirteen

"I think you need to let this go." Joe fanned a newspaper across the grill until flames danced in the charcoal, sending a smoky-scented promise of delicious food to come.

Jesse inhaled, deeply savoring the blessing of a summer Sunday afternoon. "How can I? I can't control Timmy's appearances. Like it or not, I have to see this through. My hope is that it will bring not only Timmy but the entire family some peace. They still don't know how he died. Mrs. Keegan thinks he's still alive, living with some benign Ozzie and Harriet family." She unfolded a webbed, aluminum lawn chair and set it beside a small, metal table. Grabbing another, she unfolded it, too, setting it on the other side. Then she plopped down and placed her beer on the table. "Besides, Timmy must need my help or he wouldn't keep showing up."

Joe took a swig of his Genesee beer. He wiped the sweat off his forehead and backed away from the grill. "Has he shown up again? Since you've been back?"

"No."

"Then maybe all he needed was for you to connect with Courtney. Kind of hand him off to her, you know what I mean?"

"I don't think it works like that." She tapped her index finger on the arm of her chair. "Wouldn't it be great if it did? Just introduce a pesky ghost to someone else with the 'gift.'" Again, she inhaled the smoky smell of the charcoal but exhaled the sweet possibility of relief. No, Timmy was hers to deal with, and she worried that being away from the cottage interfered with his ability to connect with her. He'd been present here just the one night... the night the train whistle woke her.

"I need to go back to the cottage." She took a deep pull from her longneck bottle.

Joe latched the grill cover on the hook at its side and turned to her.

"How are you going to manage that? Mr. Keegan kicked you out—for good, if I recall. And Maggie isn't speaking to you."

"I have to figure out some way."

The phone rang, and she almost tripped over her chair as she jumped up to answer it. Running into the hall, she prayed it would be Maggie, as she had done with every phone call since their fight.

"Hello?"

"Hi, Jesse. It's Susan. We'd talked about riding to your shower together next Sunday. Will that still work for you?"

The shower. Oh, my God, with all that had been going on, she'd totally forgotten about her wedding shower. How could a person forget about her own wedding shower? Well, for one thing, she was dreading it. The last thing she wanted was a big bash *a la* Wyndham wealth. She'd be the center of attention, and more than a hundred people she barely knew—some she'd never laid eyes on before—would be curiously watching her like she was a monkey in the zoo. Once, she'd seen an ape get tired of all those onlookers, so he scooped up some of his own poop and lobbed it at them. She shook her head. No, that wouldn't work. Eloping. Now, that would work. She glanced through the open kitchen door to where Joe was grilling on the patio.

"Are you there, dear?" Susan asked.

"Yes, I'm here. I was just conjuring various coping mechanisms for this shindig."

Susan chuckled. "Now, you don't want to disappoint Ben. He's so fond of you."

"I suppose. He has been very kind since we discovered our family bond."

"I'll be right beside you, and so will Maggie."

Her heart sank.

"I wonder if Maggie will even show up."

"Oh dear, you two haven't spoken yet?"

"No." She wiped her hand across her forehead. "Buuuut, this shower could be the perfect reason to call her again."

"Sounds like a good idea. We'll talk later this week to finalize plans for Sunday."

"You can be my getaway driver."

Susan laughed. "Not what I had in mind. You'll get through this, Jesse. You've survived worse. Bye."

When she returned to the backyard, the burgers were sizzling on the grill and Joe was sprawled in a lawn chair.

"Maggie?"

"No, your mom. She wanted to check on our plan to drive to my bridal shower together."

Joe grinned at her. "You forgot about it, didn't you?"

She shrugged. "Yes. I admit it."

"Maybe you just blocked it from your mind. A Freudian slip or something."

"Could be. But, as I said to your mom, it's a good excuse to call Maggie again." Just making that plan lifted her spirits. "Surely, she'll be at the shower." Her gaze flicked to him.

Joe took her hand and pulled her to his lap. Brushing back her wayward curls, he kissed her cheek and nuzzled into her neck. "She'll be there," he whispered against her skin.

The aluminum chair squeaked in protest against their weight.

"We're going to collapse here." She slipped an arm behind him and kissed his forehead.

Joe gently pushed her off. "And the burgers are going to burn." He stood and lifted the dome cover off the grill. The crisp, savory aroma of perfectly done beef wafted to them.

"I smell food!" Marty's voice preceded him around the corner of the house.

"Plenty here. Pull up a seat." Joe slid a spatula under the first burger and flipped it onto a plate.

Jesse retrieved three fresh, cold beers from the ancient refrigerator in her kitchen and another paper plate and plastic silverware. "You okay, Marty? You look a little flushed."

Like a thermometer, scarlet started at his neck and rose into his face. "I just saw Maggie."

"Man, you've got it bad."

"How is she?"

Joe and Jesse threw their responses at him simultaneously.

He looked at Joe. "Yes, I do." He turned to Jesse. "I don't know."

"So, tell us what happened."

Marty related their encounter. "I never even talked to her about her father. How sorry I am that the department treated him like that. That guy must hate me—I represent all the shit they put him through. Who knows, maybe that's why Maggie won't give me the time of day."

"Maggie may not even know about her father being brought in for questioning. That family has never discussed anything concerning Timmy's disappearance. She won't give you the time of day because she's all mixed up inside with her feelings for you." Jesse took his hand. "This is so difficult for her. More difficult than we could ever imagine."

Marty nodded. "I know. I don't mean to hurt her or put her through all this. It's just that, well, I look for excuses to visit her. That's probably wrong." He glanced at them. "I need to leave her alone."

His face reminded Jesse of a lost spaniel puppy. She wanted to pat his head and assure him everything would be okay. But everything would not be okay. This was a recipe for heartache no matter how you looked at it. "She took vows. She dedicated her life to God, and for her, that means *only* God. Not a handsome, if goofy, Italian guy."

He snorted a laugh.

"Look, this is a real crisis of conscience for Maggie. And, frankly, I don't know what to tell you: 'Stay away and forget her' or 'Go for it and give it all you've got.'" She patted his hand. "Wish I had some sage advice for you."

"I'd say leave her alone." Joe's voice was low and soft. "If she's struggling like Jesse says, your coming around just makes it harder for her."

"You're right. I feel like I'm a magnet and she's the North Pole or something." He leaned his elbows on his knees and dropped his head into his hands.

Joe rubbed his shoulder. "I know exactly what you mean." He smiled at Jesse, then sobered. "This really stinks. I feel for you, man."

Marty sat like that for a minute then straightened. "I'm going to pull the abduction file and look through it. I want to read the report on Maggie's dad and figure out what he went through. I'm on night shift this Wednesday, so it'll be real quiet at the station. Jesse, I know you wanted to see the files to help figure out Timmy's disappearance. If you happened to come by, and I happened to have a file open on my desk... well, I can't help what you look at."

Jesse gave him a quick hug. "Thanks, Marty."

Joe was quiet.

Marty looked at him. "What?"

Joe shrugged. "Why? Why do you want to see that file? To help Jesse with her case? Or to get closer to Maggie? I think you need to figure that out."

"*Mannaggia*! I just want to know, that's all. I just want Maggie to feel better about me. For her dad to feel better about me. I don't know." He scrubbed his hands through his hair, creating the impression of a black palm tree growing out of his head.

She smoothed it down. "Doesn't matter." She shot Joe a look. "I think I might have to stop by the station Wednesday night."

Muted voices and quiet phones greeted Jesse upon entering the police station, about half the decibels of a daytime visit. A couple of cops chatted at a desk in the corner, one edging toward the door as they spoke, obviously on his way out at the end of his shift. They glanced at Jesse, waved, then resumed their conversation. She found Marty bent over a file on his desk, resting his head in his hands.

"Hey, Marty." She sat in the chair alongside the desk.

Startled, he looked up, his frown of concentration shifting to a half smile. "Hey, Jesse." He scanned the room, noting his two colleagues who were finishing up their conversation. As the off-duty cop made his last point, he pushed open the exit door. With a final wave, he disappeared.

The second cop nodded to Marty. "You got the phones for a little while? I'm going down to archives to file these." He held up a stack of folders, each jammed with paper.

"Got it, Dave" Marty called back. After Dave was out of sight, he turned to her. "It looked bad, really bad, for Maggie's dad at first." He turned the folder toward her and indicated an article from the *Finger Lakes Times* near the top of the file. "Somebody added this to the file."

She gasped. A newspaper photo of Mr. Keegan ten years earlier, outside the sheriff's office. He had more hair, his face was thinner, but he stared back at her with wide, fear-filled eyes. His mouth arced in a downward curve. Above the photo, the headline read, "Local Man Questioned in Kidnapping." The story detailed how the missing boy's parents had observed Mr. Keegan driving past their rented cottage several times the morning he disappeared.

"My God, how they must have suffered," she whispered. Her stomach turned over, and she shivered.

"Yeah, and this was on the front page." He indicated a penciled notation at the top of the clipping indicating page and the date: FLT, Page 1, July 21, 1953. He shuffled through the notes. "They did a complete background check on him, investigating to see if he was a pedophile." Marty grimaced. He held up a small newspaper clipping. "Unfortunately, three days later, his exoneration was buried on page three." There was no photo with this news brief in the Police Blotter section—it simply said, "William Keegan was cleared of suspicion in connection with the kidnapping of a boy who was vacationing with his family on Seneca Lake."

She rubbed her hands along her thighs. Just reading about this incident spiked her anxiety levels. How had the Keegan family dealt with it?

"How was he cleared? Do you know?"

"*Mannaggia!*" He shuffled through the papers again and fished out an incident report form. He held it up. "In this, written on day three, the day Mr. Keegan was exonerated, a witness confirmed that Mr. Keegan was fishing with him at their favorite weekly fishing spot. Mr. Keegan had forgotten his tackle box and drove back to his cottage to retrieve it. That means he drove by the rental property this family was staying in three times between seven and seven thirty that evening. The family said the boy was last seen playing in the yard around eight."

"Mr. Keegan would have been on the lake at that time."

He nodded. "And other fishermen confirmed seeing him out there. So, my question is, why did it take three days to check his alibi? No wonder he growled when I said I was a cop with Seneca Corners P.D."

"Who were the other suspects?" She lifted the next paper in the file.

"Well, besides Maggie's father, there were the two men you mentioned, Bruce Becker and Cordell Jefferson." He stood and peered over her shoulder at the file. "Oh yeah, some kid who drove an ice cream truck and another guy—a renter who was here the whole summer." He snorted. "That guy never came back to rent here again. The ice cream kid was cleared. He was some star high school athlete. Clean cut, nice kid."

She looked at him. "If the renter never returned and the kidnapper was never found, wouldn't he be a prime candidate?"

He lifted another sheet from the folder. "Police in Rochester kept a close eye on him for quite a while once he'd returned home. He was a model citizen, always had been. I'm surprised he didn't sue us or something."

She sank back in her seat. An ugly doubt wiggled like a worm in her stomach. "Marty, do you think Timmy was abducted like the other boys?"

He swiped the top of his head forward and backward as if to sweep away a cobweb. His hair stood straight up, and had it been blue, he'd look like a troll doll. But the somber look in his eye dispelled any sense of humor as he spoke. "Yes. I think he was. It all adds up. His body was never found, no witnesses. Just like the other three kids."

"But what about the drifting boat?"

"Yeah, that's a puzzle."

They sat in silence, reviewing the reports in the folder.

"If Timmy was kidnapped, the Keegans will be devastated. That just makes it all the more tragic." She rubbed her temples. Why did Timmy have to visit her? Was she going to be the messenger who delivered the awful news about his real circumstances? *Don't do this to me, Timmy.* She rubbed her arms as if that could erase Timmy from her life.

But he needed peace, and she was the only one who could bring it to him.

"If Timmy reveals he was abused, tortured, and killed, I destroy Mrs. Keegan. I bring more suffering to the whole family. And how does Maggie remain in my life when every time she looks at me she sees the image of Timmy's horrible death? Marty, your grandmother was wrong. This is not a gift. It's a curse."

Chapter Fourteen

The curving driveway leading to Wyndham Manor had never seemed so long as it did this afternoon. Jesse stared out her window. The ancient oaks lining either side loomed over the drive like storybook ogres. To the west, storm clouds hovered, dragging the sky down in leaden gloom, and her mood matched it. Ten phone messages Maggie never returned. *Great, how will I explain that my maid of honor just couldn't make it to my bridal shower today?* She twitched her lips to the side. *God, I'm turning into a teenager with all this weepy crap lately. But, next to Joe, Maggie is the most important person in my life.*

"Don't you think so?" Susan asked.

"What? I'm sorry Susan, I was lost in thought."

"It's okay. You've been lost in thought for most of the drive over here."

She nodded. "I'm not much company today."

She frowned at the green lawn, a velvet carpet sweeping up to the precisely manicured topiaries and flowering bushes that hugged the manor walls. Wyndham wealth on display, right down to a single blade of grass. Not that Ben and Monica flaunted their riches. In fact, they were known for their generosity, board members of many area foundations.

She appreciated their kindness, but with all the disruptions swirling around her, the last place she wanted to be right now was here with one hundred people she didn't know. The only person she wanted to be with today probably wouldn't show up.

Susan pulled her red Mercury Cougar up to the waiting valet, who opened Susan's door and tipped his hat. He spotted Jesse. "Afternoon, Miss Graham."

"Hello, Paul. How's your new baby?"

He grinned. "Growing like a weed! I have a picture."

"Show me!" She leaned in to look at the ready photo. "Blue eyes, just like his daddy's."

"That's right!" His chest puffed out, his face pink with pleasure.

Turning toward the inevitable, she studied the manor, resplendent with thick walls of red Medina limestone and beveled glass windows. As if asserting its consequence, the house thrust turrets toward the sky at each corner. Stone steps broadened out from the massive oak door crowned by a Tiffany window, its fleur-de-lis motif lustrous in the subdued daylight.

On cue, the stately door eased open as they approached, a tall, man in his late fifties in a crisp black-and-white butler's uniform standing erect beside the entrance, like a penguin. She wished she were in Antarctica. He bowed slightly.

"Good day, Miss Graham. Mrs. Riley."

"Hello, Gerald. How are you today?" She usually told a corny—sometimes slightly off-color—joke, delighting in pulling Gerald's chain in an effort to shake his stuffy demeanor. Though he'd always *tsk*ed and frowned, she'd come to believe he enjoyed the game. Today, she didn't have it in her.

He threw her a startled look. "Very well, thank you, Miss Graham."

In the foyer, shadows played off the intricately carved, high oak wainscoting wrapping the walls. Muted daylight streamed through the stained-glass windows with fleur-de-lis patterns identical to the one above the entry door. Though she was as tall as the suit of armor stationed at the foot of the grand staircase, she always felt Lilliputian in this foyer. She straightened to her full height and threw back her shoulders. She would give this gig her best shot. Tequila would work well.

Their heels clicked along the white marble floor, sounding like a ticking time bomb. Needing to focus on something, she visually traced the black and gray veins spreading across the white marble like spider webs. She paused at a twelve-foot gilt mirror to check her hair. Today she had combed it up and back into a beehive, a task impeded by stubborn Irish curls. Half a can of hairspray later and she had been satisfied it might hold through a couple of hours. Emerald drop earrings sparkled against her porcelain skin.

But when they entered the opulent living room and all heads turned to see her, it was all she could do not to turn and run. Susan's hand rested on her back. Was it in solidarity or to prevent her from fleeing?

Scanning the sea of faces—she wouldn't have recognized anyone if she'd tried—she pasted on what she hoped was a convincing smile and accepted an air kiss from Uncle Ben's wife, Monica Wyndham.

"Hello, darling. I'm thrilled to have your bridal shower here." Slender and elegant, Monica stood just a few inches shorter than Jesse. To say she wore a ponytail would be too pedestrian for her perfectly swept-back blonde hair, gathered in a sparkling clip whose glitter matched her five-carat diamond earrings.

Jesse patted her own hair, already escaping in disobedient spirals around her face. "You are so generous to do this for me. For us, Joe and me. You remember Joe's mother, Susan Riley?"

Monica held out her hand, and more diamonds sparkled in the lamplight that chased away the day's gloom. Jesse wondered how she could lift her thin hand with the weight of gold and diamonds her fingers and wrist held.

"Yes, of course. Welcome, Mrs. Riley."

"Please, call me Susan."

"Susan, I'm Monica." Monica turned to Jesse. "Soon we'll be calling you Mrs. Riley."

Jesse simply smiled. This was probably not the time to mention that she did not intend to change her name.

"I had hoped to hold this out in our garden; the flowers are so brilliant this time of year," Monica looked ruefully at the sky. "But I'm afraid the grand ballroom will have to do." She wandered off to the patio to usher in the brave guests who had gathered there despite the threatening storm. Most of them were smokers desperate to light up, damn the storm.

Jesse leaned toward Susan and whispered, "I hate it when we have to settle for the grand ballroom."

Susan stifled a laugh.

Monica returned to her side, taking Jesse's hand to loop her arm through her own. "Didn't Sister Angelina come with you?"

Monica may as well have punched her in the gut. She recovered, tucking a loose tendril back into place. "Well, I don't believe... that is, I don't know..."

Susan jabbed her in the side.

Surprised, she opened her mouth to ask what that was for, but Maggie's voice floated from behind her.

"Sorry I'm late, Jesse, Mrs. Wyndham. Hi, Susan."

She swung around to face her. "Mags, you're here."

"Of course, I'm here, Jess." Her slumping shoulders belied the strength of her voice.

Jesse wanted to grab her and pull her into a bear hug. She wanted all the guests to go away so the two of them could sit down and talk. She wanted anything but to be surrounded by strangers in that moment.

Susan turned to Monica. "Where is the grand ballroom? I'd love to see it."

Jesse caught her eye and mouthed, "Thank you."

Susan winked then followed Monica down a long hall.

She turned to Maggie, but before she could say anything, they were surrounded by guests who greeted them and swept them to the ballroom.

Monica stood at the door, Susan beside her. She grabbed Jesse and Maggie as they entered and stationed them in line.

Oh, my God, not a receiving line. Jesse bit her lip. Maggie gave a half smile and took her place beside her. Her mind exploded with questions. *Why didn't you return my calls? How are you doing? What can I do to apologize? What do I even need to apologize for?*

After an eternity of meeting one hundred guests, one at a time, Monica led her to a table on a dais at the front of the room. Sipping a glass of Riesling faster than was wise, Jesse absorbed her surroundings in the ballroom. White linen-covered chairs with large mauve bows tied at the back. Tall vases filled with roses, calla lilies, cosmos, and hellebores in muted pinks and mauves sat in the middle of tables draped with white linen tablecloths. Crystal glassware and delicate china place settings with platinum trim sat before each guest, pale rose damask napkins folded like fleur-de-lis held with a silver napkin ring resting on each plate. She gaped at the beautiful sight, almost light-headed, floating, like she was in a Cinderella movie. And she was Cinderella... during-the-ball Cinderella, not her usual before-the-ball self.

Maggie grasped her hand and, turning, Jesse caught her gentle smile. Things were okay between them. She was so reassured, a guffaw, half laugh, half sob, escaped from deep in her gut. Guests seated near the dais shot puzzled looks her way. She frowned and coughed mightily into her hand, then tapped the base of her throat and mouthed, "Sorry." She sipped her water as they offered sympathetic looks and returned to their conversation.

"Very classy," Maggie whispered out the side of her mouth.

Jesse squeezed her hand. When she was nine, she'd had the chickenpox; in fact, the doctor had said it was one of the worst cases he'd ever seen. She'd wriggled and squirmed trying to follow his orders not to scratch the sores. The itching was unbearable, and she'd rub her arms and legs against her bedsheets, dying for relief. That same drive infused her now. She scratched at the nape of her neck. Couldn't these people just enjoy a lovely luncheon while she and Maggie escaped to the kitchen to talk? She had so many questions. She so needed to spend a quiet afternoon with her best friend.

In a fog of impatience, she regarded the faces that glanced up and smiled then bent to whisper to a neighbor. Now that she had time to consider them, she recognized many she had met at previous Wyndham parties.

A long table stood in the corner, laden with elegantly wrapped gifts with silvery bows and satiny ribbons. *Oh, God. Do I have to open all of those today?*

As if choreographed, waiters dressed in crisp, white shirts and pressed-pleated black trousers appeared carrying trays of food. She was served first. The savory scent of vichyssoise cooled her itch to flee, and she sipped her Riesling while she waited for others to be served. Finally, Monica nodded to her, and she realized the guests were waiting for her to begin. *Forget Cinderella, I'm the damn queen.* With each spoonful, she settled into a calmer frame of mind, soothed by the delicious luncheon and Maggie's soft voice beside her.

JESSE GROANED INWARDLY as Monica announced a bridal shower game.

"We're going to play 'Ask the Bride.' Interspersed with Jesse opening the gifts, I will read off questions for her that you wrote down during lunch. That way, those of you who don't know her well yet can learn more about her."

Jesse lifted her lips in what she hoped was a smile while her stomach clenched in a knot. *What the hell are they going to ask me?*

Most of the questions were simple: How did she and Joe meet? How did he propose? What did she do for a living? What flowers would she carry? Where would they honeymoon? How many bridesmaids and what color would they wear?

"Maggie here, some of you know her as Sister Angelina from Saint Bartholomew's Academy for Girls, is my maid of honor. Since she is a Sister of St. Joseph, she will be wearing her habit, so I guess my colors will be black and white."

Stillness fell over the group, like when a grandmother blurts out something quite inappropriate and no one wants to scold her. One hundred pairs of eyes stared at her as each woman tried to process this. She could tell the minute it registered because the woman would blink, lean into her neighbor with a slight crease between her brows, and whisper something while they both looked at her.

Maggie stared at her hands. She took one of them in her own. "Maggie and I have been best friends since ninth grade. I can't imagine having anyone else stand beside me on the most important day of my life."

Maggie beamed at her and they hugged.

When she looked out at the women, their expressions had changed. Now a soft understanding took the place of judgment and disbelief. Spontaneous applause broke out and the room returned to its former gaiety.

The next question startled her.

"Tell us about your ghosts." Monica read the slip of paper before its meaning registered. "Oh, my." She fluttered her hands. "Perhaps we should limit our questions to bridal topics."

A chorus went up.

"No!"

"We'd love to hear about that!"

"Oooh, that sounds mysterious."

To her credit, Monica looked at Jesse to gauge her willingness to answer.

She nodded. "That's fine, Monica. We can digress for a moment." She gave a brief summary of her first two ghostly encounters, noting the range of reactions from disbelief to entranced.

One woman raised her hand. "Didn't the ghosts help you solve mysteries? One was a cold case, wasn't it?"

"Yes. That's true."

"So, is there another ghost now? Is there a spirit visiting you these days? And is there another cold case to solve?"

Maggie stiffened beside her. How to handle this question? From the determined look on her face, this woman would persist until she had something to chew on. How not to mention Timmy?

"There is an old case that's caught my attention. Apparently, some young boys were abducted around here maybe fifteen years ago."

A woman toward the back gasped. Her face drained of color, and she rose, sat back down, then pushed her hands against the table and pulled herself up. "My son."

The room fell silent.

"I'm so sorry." Jesse's voice was soft. How could she have been so stupid? Of course, someone here could have been affected by this.

"Do something." The woman began to approach. "Please, if you can do something. I need to know what happened to my little boy." The woman had reached the dais, her clasped hands raised in supplication. "I just need to know what happened to my Michael."

Monica stepped down from the dais and put her arm around the woman's shoulder. "I'm not sure there's anything Jesse can do, Ethel."

Ethel looked back at her. "Please."

Once Ethel was seated, Monica motioned to the head waiter, who disappeared through a swinging door only to reappear in a moment followed by a parade of waiters with trays carrying various selections of wine.

"Let's continue with the gifts, shall we?" Monica's smile did not reach her eyes when she glanced at Jesse.

"I FEEL like my face is going to break. I have never smiled this long in my life." Jesse rubbed her cheeks. She sat between Susan and Maggie on a settee that had replaced their luncheon table.

Susan patted her shoulder. "You were gracious and pleasant. A perfect bride-to-be."

"You handled the role beautifully, Jess." Maggie gave her a sideways hug.

The table that had been laden with festively wrapped gifts now cowered beneath the exposed contents of small appliances, china, silver, linens, and several sets of scandalously gossamer lingerie.

"You've received such lovely gifts," Susan said as they rose and strolled over to the table.

"Where are we going to put all this stuff?" Jesse gestured to the treasures.

Maggie picked up a particularly revealing black teddy and shook it so the fringe danced in sexy waves. "I wonder which Joe will prefer, this black number or the scarlet set with garters?"

Jesse grabbed the teddy and returned it to the box while her friends laughed. She looked sternly at Susan. "You should not even be aware that I have these."

"Oh, please. I hope my son isn't marrying a prude." She held her stomach and tried to stop laughing.

Scowling, Jesse turned on Maggie. "You're no help, Sister Angelina. You're not even supposed to know this stuff exists."

Susan and Maggie burst into renewed laughter, holding on to each other for support.

"Geez, you two have your underwear displayed for one hundred strangers to gawk at and imagine you wearing it and see how you like it."

"I'll be right back. I have to find the restroom, quickly." Susan said, still laughing as she hurried to the door.

"Oh, Jess, you are hysterical. You're the least prudish person I've ever known, but if you had seen the look on your face when you opened these..." Maggie wiped at her eyes.

"You, of all people, should be defending me here—" She

stopped and held up the black teddy. "Oh, my God." Laughter bubbled up. "You are so right, Mags. This stuff is hysterical. I hope they don't think I'm waiting for my wedding night to use these."

Maggie attempted a sober face, shaking her finger. "Now, Jesse, I must draw the line. Until you have celebrated the sacrament of matrimony..."

"Too late, Sister Angelina."

"I figured. Now, how do we fit all this into your Volkswagen?"

At that moment, Gerald entered, followed by two waiters.

"We will see that these items are delivered to your home, Miss Graham."

"Thank you, Gerald. What do you think of this little number?" She held the black teddy against her body.

Gerald coughed and averted his gaze, looking toward the ceiling. "I'm glad to see you're feeling better, Miss Graham."

Chapter Fifteen

꿏

E very surface in the living room, including the floor, was covered in shiny, new bridal shower gifts. Jesse sank onto the sofa. *Where the heck am I going to put all this?* How ironic that the song playing on the radio was The 5th Dimension's "Wedding Bell Blues."

She decided to pull a Scarlett O'Hara and "worry about it tomorrow." Grabbing the mail, she headed to the kitchen for a cup of tea. As the kettle heated, she sifted through the envelopes, sorting the bills from the advertisements for gutter cleaning and driveway paving. One envelope had no return address, and her name and address were scrawled in block letters. She jumped as the teakettle let out a shrill whistle.

Leaping up, she turned off the burner and poured boiling water over the teabag. Her hands shook, and her body was off-balance, shaky. Some of the water spilled on the counter, and she wiped it up. The letter lay on the table, stark white against the dark oak. A sudden urge to grip her letter opener came over her—an avoidance mechanism or protection? *You're just being silly. It's probably an RSVP to the wedding reception and they lost the envelope we enclosed.* She retrieved the opener from her secretary in the living room.

When she returned to the kitchen, Creedence Clearwater Revival was belting out "Bad Moon Rising." She stared at her name spelled in jagged printing. Was the radio eavesdropping on her life?

Sitting at the table, she tapped the letter with the opener. She wrapped her hands around the mug of hot tea. Maybe she should throw out the junk mail and organize the bills before she opened this. She always liked saving personal mail to the end so she could enjoy it. With her cup of tea.

But the envelope called to her. She picked it up and slashed into the flap, slicing it with the letter opener. One sheet of plain lined paper was folded inside. The message was clear: *Leave the past behind and mind your own business.*

JOE DIDN'T TOUCH the paper still lying on the table, but after he read the message, he drew Jesse into his arms. She melted into him, savoring his strength. He kissed the top of her head. "Did you call Marty?"

She nodded.

"Any idea who might have sent it?"

She shook her head. "None."

"You figure it's about the abductions?"

"Yeah."

"Aside from our friends and family, who else even knew you were interested in that case?"

"About one hundred of Monica Wyndham's closest friends."

He pulled back to look at her, his eyebrows raised. "How?"

As he led her by the hand to the sofa in the living room, she described the shower game questions they asked her and Ethel's plea.

"Why did you even say anything about it?"

"The original question was about ghosts—was I seeing any new ghosts now? I didn't want to talk about Timmy because it upsets Maggie so much. Plus, well, I just don't talk about ghosts if I can help it. So, I was trying to avoid the question, and that's what came out of my mouth."

"Do you think one of the women was involved in the disappearances?"

"Who knows? But with one hundred women in the community talking about the weirdo who sees ghosts that help her solve mysteries, anyone who was involved would probably hear about it."

He drew her into his arms again. "You're not a weirdo, Just Jesse."

"Thanks." She kissed him, his loving words wrapping her in a warm cocoon. "But I'm right. If people are talking about my interest in the case... it's like that gossip game we used to play at slumber parties. Who knows how garbled the message has gotten as the information passes from one person to another?"

"One thing's for certain. You've rattled somebody's cage. Any chance you'll let it go?" He rubbed her arm and kissed her forehead.

"I don't know. I guess I would if I could."

"What's stopping you?"

"Timmy. Ghosts appear when they need my help. I'm not sure what Timmy needs, but until I find out, he will keep appearing to me."

"Has he appeared to you lately?"

She thought for a moment. "No. That's why I have to return to the Keegans' cottage. I think he will show up if I'm there."

"Or, you could let it go."

How easy would that be? Just walk away. It wasn't her problem. Timmy had been dead for fifteen years. Yes, and Helen had been dead for twenty-five. The Seneca woman for hundreds. Yet each wandered in misery unable to find peace until she helped them. No, she couldn't abandon him. If not for Timmy then for Maggie and her family. They had been living in hell since his death. Especially Courtney.

"I can't, Joe. Not only does Timmy need peace, so does the whole Keegan family." Her insides jumbled, like clothes in a dryer tumbling over each other. But she had to admit that, despite the danger the previous ghosts had brought, she'd enjoyed the hunt. Uncovering clues as to who was responsible or how to right a wrong brought her satisfaction. *Maybe I should have been a cop instead of an English teacher.* She twitched her mouth to the side.

"Whoever wrote that note feels threatened. You need to be careful." Joe eased her up to face him.

She needed to pursue this, and Joe needed to be free from worry. Tilting her head, she smiled and ran lazy circles along his forearm.

His mouth hitched up in a half grin. "I know that look, Just Jesse. Don't try to deter me with seduction. I'm serious here."

"So am I." Smiling at him, she ran one finger along his lips.

He pulled it away, no longer smiling. "Focus. I don't want to visit you in the hospital again," he choked, "or worse. You've taken too many chances already. Whoever abducted those boys is dangerous. The boys were never found, so we can assume they're dead. He hasn't been discovered in fifteen years, and he's not going to sit by while you play detective."

She sat back and folded her arms. "I know. Don't think I haven't had this conversation with myself already." Like a butterfly, her mind flitted from one thought to the next as she stared at the floor. "Maybe this letter isn't from the actual kidnapper. Maybe he's long gone and a family member wrote it—like a mother or sister—who knew, or at least suspected him. Besides, I just want to find out about Timmy, and the Keegans don't think he's connected to this case at all."

"Well, unless you publish your plan in the *Seneca Corners Sentinel*, this guy or his family member is not going to know that. They think you're digging up new information about the case." He took her hand. "I worry about you. Sometimes you're impulsive and take risks without thinking about the consequences."

She opened her mouth to protest.

He pressed his index finger to her lips. "You do, and you know you do."

She slumped back against the sofa and crossed her arms. "Yeah. I guess you're right."

"Promise me you'll be careful."

She raised her right hand pointing her index and middle finger up. "Girl Scouts' honor."

He leaned toward her, brushing his lips against hers. "What can I say to get that look back in your eyes, Just Jesse?"

She smiled and peeked at him from the corner of her eye. "I have something to show you, Joe. It's a shower gift, but I think we can make use of it now."

AFTER ENJOYING THE BLACK TEDDY, Joe and Jesse lounged on the back porch sipping their beers, listening to The Young Rascals sing "Groovin." The evening sun dipped lower in the sky, shooting rosy stripes across the clouds.

She savored the pervasive serenity, listening to crickets chirping lazily in the July twilight and watching a doe and two yearlings creep through the woods on the edge of the property. A cool breeze rustled the leaves and tamped down the humidity of the day. She stretched languidly, then rested her elbows on her knees as she studied a caterpillar crossing her foot.

"Maybe I should move in with you now." Joe drew a lazy circle across her back.

"Mmmm. As much as I'd love that, Sister Therese would be scandalized."

"C'mon, it's 1969. Couples are moving in together more and more these days. It's not that unusual anymore."

"As long as you don't teach at St. Bartholomew Academy for Girls." Jesse looked over her shoulder at him. "I do have to be a good role model for the teens I teach."

He grinned at her. "Like you were this afternoon?"

She swatted his arm. "Shh. The girls must never know."

"Know what?" Marty appeared around the corner of the house.

"Are you up to something illegal? I'll have to take you both in, but I can't promise a cell for two."

Joe laughed. "Exactly what we were discussing."

"A cell for two?" Marty's eyebrows shot up.

"Not a cell. I'll get you a beer while Joe explains."

When she entered the kitchen, the letter immediately caught her eye. She called out the back door, "Maybe you need to come in and get your own beer, Marty."

He and Joe came through the screen door, letting it slap closed behind them. Marty spied the letter and leaned over it.

"So this is it." He inspected the paper then carefully studied the envelope. "Obviously, you've touched it. Have you, Joe?"

"No."

"I left it on the table after I saw what it said." She scowled at the note; too bad it hadn't disappeared while they'd been sitting outside enjoying the sunset. She rubbed her arms against a sudden chill.

"Since you've already touched it, why don't you refold it and put it in the envelope? Then put it in one of those fancy new plastic bags so I can take it to the station and have it checked for fingerprints."

She gingerly folded the letter, tucked it into the envelope, and slid it into a plastic bag Joe held out.

"You've done it again, Nancy Drew. You've kicked another hornet's nest. I like your style." Marty winked at her.

"Man, don't make light of this. Jesse could be in danger." Joe frowned and crossed his arms.

Marty shrugged. "You're right. *Bella*, you need to be careful. But if you find out anything..."

"Marty!" Joe leaned into his face.

"Okay, okay." He held up his hands. "What I'm wondering is how in the world this guy found out about your interest in this case." He took the beer Jesse offered.

"Let's sit outside. This will take a while."

The sun had set, leaving an inky, indigo sky. An owl's hoot from a nearby tree echoed above the leaves rustling in the night breeze. Each carrying a fresh beer, they resumed their seats on the aluminum lawn chairs.

Marty nodded and muttered "Uh huh, uh huh" as she once again described the shower game. His head snapped up when she mentioned Maggie's name, and he wiped his hand across his mouth, attempting to hide his smile.

Marty swallowed the last of his beer. "Bottom line is, this guy is still out there. He could start abducting kids again. Besides, he needs to pay for his crimes."

"Not at the cost of Jesse's safety." Joe's words held a warning.

"But it might not even be the kidnapper." She reiterated her theory of a family member.

Marty stared at the ground for a moment. "I don't think so. If the guy disappeared or moved away, why stir the pot? A family member would just lie low and see where this went. This is the act of someone who's spooked. I think it's our guy."

"So, if all I'm doing is trying to help Timmy, who they assumed drowned and wasn't abducted, I shouldn't be in danger at all. Right?"

"Wrong," Joe said.

"Right," Marty said in unison.

Joe glared at Marty. "Man, she is in danger if this guy even thinks for a moment she's going to dig something up on him."

Marty looked away. "Okay. But I'd sure like to catch the bastard." He rubbed the back of his neck. "I'm not convinced Timmy drowned."

"You think he was abducted." Her stomach lurched at the thought.

Marty nodded.

"Maggie and her family have been suffering for years. Discovering this would kill them."

Joe took her hand. "And it would kill me if anything happened to you."

Marty's glance flicked between them and settled on her. "I want to find this guy."

His unspoken words hung in the darkness: and you can help.

She squeezed Joe's hand. "I'll be all right." She tried to hide the quaver in her voice.

Chapter Sixteen

❧❧

Maggie adjusted the rearview mirror for the third time as she drove to Jesse's house. They hadn't had an opportunity to talk during the shower, and she had so much to tell Jesse. She fidgeted with the radio; "The Age of Aquarius" was a bit too buoyant for her today, so she switched it off and drove in the sounds of silence.

As she turned down Jesse's street and drove the quarter mile to the end where the Cavanaugh house stood, she passed a parked car. There was nothing noticeable about the tan sedan until the driver lunged away and turned his face from his window as she passed. Watching in the rearview mirror as he slowly made a U-turn and exited the street, she shook off the tingle of apprehension that zigzagged down the back of her neck.

It's just a car. But she was certain the driver did not want to be seen. A tryst with a neighbor?

Jesse threw open the front door and beamed at her. "Mags, it's so good to see you." She hugged her.

"You, too, Jess." She squeezed her friend close, but the usual ease and comfort of their greeting was not the same. Hurt, confusion, and anger wedged between them.

"We have so much to catch up on." Jesse pulled her into the kitchen where the table was set for lunch. "Beer?"

"No, thanks. Too early for me. Iced tea would be great."

While Jesse got condiments from the refrigerator, Maggie sat. The cheery room with its yellow walls, ancient appliances, and white Cape Cod curtains had always been a refuge for her, a gathering place for friends and Jesse's newfound family.

And Marty.

Somehow, the kitchen seemed different in his absence, bigger and hollow. She glanced toward the back door. He was known to appear at all hours... perhaps even this afternoon. She squelched the two-edged jolt of hope and fear that shot through her.

"Ham or turkey?" Jesse opened the two white deli wrappers and exposed the lunch offerings. A third one held sliced Muenster cheese, Maggie's favorite.

Though she was far from hungry, she constructed a hearty ham and cheese sandwich with mayonnaise and mustard. She speared a dill pickle and scooped macaroni salad on her plate. Then she folded her hands in her lap and stared at her plate.

"Oops, sorry, I forgot about saying grace," Jesse managed around the bite of food in her mouth.

She stirred. "Oh, yeah, grace. Bless us, O Lord, and these thy gifts that we are about to receive, from thy bounty through Christ, our Lord, amen." Even the rote blessing took effort, and she sank back in her seat.

Jesse set her sandwich on the plate. "Mags, I don't know how I hurt you, but I know I did. I'm so sorry. What can I do to make it up to you?" She held her hands out in a hopeless gesture. "I would sleep overnight in a mouse-infested basement if that would heal our friendship. You know I love you like you're my own sister— hell, more than sister-love based on families I've seen. Please, I want to make us okay again."

Maggie wiped her eyes and nodded. That was all she could manage at that moment. They sat in silence as the kitchen clock ticked away the pain. She inhaled and gathered her strength.

"I..." Her voice cracked and the word came out like a squeak. They laughed, a quick, self-conscious laugh.

"Now you sound like I did in the hospital after they rescued me from the Seneca woman in the cave." Jesse grinned.

Nodding, she smiled through her tears. "I do. Jess, there's been so much lately. Too many conflicts, too much confusion and pain." She rubbed her temples.

"But you've always come to me before. We've always shared what we were dealing with—good or bad." Jesse's voice dropped. "You never even returned my calls."

"I knew you had invited me to dinner, but I just couldn't come." She glanced at the chair beside her again. "I never saw the other messages until after the shower. I'd gone to the Mother House in Rochester for a while to pray and discern what I need to do. I went directly to Wyndham Manor from there."

Jesse's face transformed from pain-filled ashen to rosy excitement. "So, you weren't avoiding me? You don't hate me?"

"No, not at all." She grabbed Jesse's hand and squeezed it. "But I needed to be away from you for a while."

Jesse's face fell.

"Timmy..." She bit her lower lip. "Hearing you talk about him brought back all the grief of losing him. I didn't want to hear it. I didn't want to know." She took a tissue from the box Jesse grabbed off the counter. "I'm so afraid of what you'll find out. That he was one of the abducted boys who was probably abused then killed."

Her head throbbed and her throat ached as she finally gave voice to her deepest fear. Unable to hold her sorrow back any longer, she gave in, the sobs wracking her body. Jesse held her as she cried. Finally, in an agonized, soft voice she murmured, "I want to believe he drowned."

"I'm so sorry. I never meant to bring this suffering to you and your family." Jesse slumped down on her chair. "God, I'm an ass." She shook her head. Setting her elbows on the table, she rested her head in her hands. "I'm so sorry."

"I know."

Silence fell again.

"But there's no evidence that Timmy was taken by the kidnapper," Jesse finally said.

Her heart ached. "There's more to it. My father was under suspicion as the kidnapper for some time. When Timmy disappeared, the police wouldn't leave him alone."

"I know. He was exonerated though, right?"

"Eventually. They came by the cottage with a search warrant, and after that they cruised by at all hours of the day and night slowly, so we'd see them. It went beyond surveillance to harassment."

"Marty was right."

Her heart beat faster at the sound of his name, and she glanced at the door, afraid now that he might enter at any moment. "What do you mean?"

"He said your father's reaction to him seemed unusually antagonistic. He's a Seneca Corners police officer, and if that's how your father was treated by them, well, Marty brings back all that pain."

Maggie nodded. "I guess that would make sense. But I think Dad also dislikes Marty because Marty so obviously likes me."

The kitchen clocked filled the silence again.

"And you like him. Maybe love." Jesse's voice was gentle.

She nodded. Taking a deep breath, she forced the words out. "Yes, I do." Saying the words made it real. She clenched her fists, resisting the urge to throw the glass of iced tea across the room. How good the sound of shattering glass would sound right now. And the ice cubes smashing on the floor, bouncing and sliding until they exhausted their energy. Exhausted. Like her.

"Oh, Mags."

"This is tearing me apart, Jess." She buried her face in her hands. "Why is God doing this to me?"

"I don't think God 'does things to us.' I think stuff happens and then God, I don't know, sits around and laughs at us while we try to figure it out." Jesse snorted.

Maggie looked at her. "You're right, though I disagree with the laughing at us part. This is all so foreign to me, these emotions— like a tsunami explodes over me and carries me for miles against my will every time he's around. I'm like a silly sixteen-year-old girl again only without this experience for practice back when I was sixteen." Smiling, she reached for Jesse's hand. "Now I know how you feel when Joe's around. It's wonderful." Her smile faded. "But for me, it's terrible."

"Have you talked to another sister about this?"

"I have an appointment with Sister Therese this week. I don't even know how to begin. Plus, with Timmy showing up right at this moment, I'm overwhelmed." She covered her face again. "I don't know what I feel, or what to do, or worst of all," she looked at Jesse, "who I am anymore."

WAITING for Sister Therese to return from St. Bart's monthly board meeting was agony. Maggie flipped through the spring issue of the Sisters of St. Joseph quarterly magazine, not seeing the smiling faces of faculty in black-and-white habits and girls in requisite uniforms of boxy, gray wool blazers and pleated, plaid skirts. The magazine's efforts at convincing parents that St. Bart's was the only place on earth to send their daughters were lost on her.

She'd rehearsed what she planned to say many times, but now her thoughts buzzed like someone stuck a beehive on her head. *Well, Sister Therese, buzz, buzz, buzz. And not only that, but buzz, buzz, buzz.*

She had taken vows of chastity. There was no place within those vows for a dalliance with an Italian cop no matter how attractive he was. Would Sister Therese actually say, "Shit or get off the pot?" She giggled at the thought, then instantly sobered.

It was a binary choice. Remain a sister and reject any close relationship with Marty—for it was becoming unbearable for her to be near him and not succumb to his attraction—or leave religious life and pursue a relationship that could turn out well... or not. There was no "give it a try and see what happens." This was an all-or-nothing choice.

Voices echoed in the outer hall, and she spotted Sister Therese striding into the office. Standing to greet her, she smoothed her skirt and adjusted her veil.

"Good afternoon, Angelina. Thank you for being so patient." Sister Therese nodded for her to be seated as she sat behind her own desk. Her inspection darted from Maggie's face to her posture to her hands, clasped tightly on the desk. "How was your retreat at the Mother House?"

"Fine. Good." She squirmed under the nun's scrutiny. She had never gotten anything by her principal. Today would not be different.

Sister Therese studied her for a moment then rose. "It's a lovely day. I suggest we enjoy God's great gift of creation rather than sit in a stuffy, old office."

She followed her principal out to the grounds of St. Bartholomew. While she appreciated the glory of the summer day, she was anxious to just get this conversation over with. As they walked, girls' voices floated across the lacrosse field. Many students resided at St. Bart's throughout the year, depending on their parents' travel commitments. The lacrosse team was at full capacity and deep in athletic ability.

Meandering along the path in silence, her nervousness increased. Sweat pooled under her arms and dripped along her sides. Was this a method to psych her out? Did Sister Therese guess her reason for this meeting? Walking in the sunshine was not her principal's usual *modus operandi*. Perhaps Sister Therese was waiting for her to open the conversation. Where were all those thoughts she had rehearsed? A flock of birds rose and soared to the east, flying away like all her glib words.

Reaching the ridge above Seneca Lake, they sat on a wrought iron bench. The leaf-like scrollwork jabbed into her back. She shifted, and the bronze leaf now poked into her left shoulder blade. Sitting forward, she inhaled the cool air that drifted across the water and disturbed the tall sea grass several feet below them. She had to say something, the silence was unbearable.

"I had a particular reason for attending the week-long silent retreat at our Mother House." The tremble in her voice betrayed her.

Sister Therese nodded, gazing out at the gentle waves. "Setting an intention for a time of prayer is wise."

Ugh. That sounded so good, so saintly. She was far from saintly.

"My intention was discernment for a situation that has arisen in my life."

Sister nodded again but didn't speak.

It was as if a snake were coiled within her and Sister watched as she struggled to pull it out from her gut. It was torture. But so was the divided soul she was living with. *Just spill your guts and get it over with.*

"I've fallen in love."

Sister nodded again. Just that. She didn't jump up and scream. She didn't recoil in disgust. She just nodded. Calm. Peaceful. Everything Maggie wasn't in that moment.

"I prayed for those feelings to go away."

Now Sister Therese jerked her head to look at her. "Whyever did you do that?"

She sprang forward. "Because I took vows. I'm a sister..."

"Of St. Joseph. Yes, I know, dear. You are also a woman. And Officer D'Amato is a very attractive man. And clearly in love with you. Has been for a while now."

Buzzing filled her head as though hundreds more bees had taken up residence and were vying for the queen's attention. She tried to grasp one thought—any that would make sense of what she'd just heard.

"You know who I'm in love with?" She blurted out her first congruent thought.

Sister Therese's voice was filled with gentle humor. "Of course, dear. Perhaps you are the last to know."

There was nothing she could do to conceal her mortification.

Even so, she wiped at her cheeks as if that would erase the burning in her face. She shook her head and studied the lake, the beach, the grass below her feet—anything that would ground her. *Everyone* knew.

"But why did you say I shouldn't pray those feelings away?"

"Number one, because you never could. Love isn't something you can return at Woolworth's because it doesn't fit. Number two, because loving someone and being loved in return is a gift—the greatest gift. Why would you want to reject a gift? Number three, because sometimes we are given challenges that are like a crucible. We're tested to our limit so we know without a doubt that the path we've chosen is our authentic path. If nothing ever challenges us, how do we know for sure?"

"I must admit, I'm relieved."

Sister Therese shook her head, though a twinkle remained in her eyes. "Oh, don't be relieved, Sister Angelina. The struggle has just begun. I'm pleased to know that your first step was prayer, though perhaps misguided. Rather than pray for these feelings to go away, you may want to pray for discernment. What is God calling you to here? How will your trial in the crucible determine the next step on your journey? I assume you came to no conclusion while you were praying away your love for Officer D'Amato?"

Maggie slumped back against the bench. "You're correct. I have come to no decision."

"You are not the first sister to fall in love, though you may feel like you're the only woman who has ever suffered through this. However it happened, God called you to religious life, a unique gift few people can live up to. There was never any promise it would be an easy path, but it is a holy one. Your gentle spirit and deep faith are an inspiration to many, and you bring many gifts to our community. Keep in mind the vows you took and how extraordinary this calling is."

"Yes, Sister. I will."

"I will pray for you. And for Officer D'Amato. Both of you are dealing with the deepest of emotion. Given the difficulty you had 'coming clean' with me, as they say, I suspect no matter where this leads you, you will suffer incredible loss as well as incredible joy. But you will know. You will be certain, and while happiness may suffer at times, joy will be yours."

The lake blurred through stinging tears. Sun sparkled off the water in starry bursts as she digested Sister's words.

Chapter Seventeen

The cloying humidity plastered damp curls to Jesse's forehead as she left her Beetle, crossing Main Street toward Woolworth's lunch counter. No one moved quickly as the clammy air enveloped them in a treacly cloud. Nods were all that were exchanged between her and the people she passed; words would have cost hoarded energy. When she opened Woolworth's door, a blast of air-conditioned heaven smacked her.

Courtney had already arrived and was seated on the metal stool with its red vinyl padded seat. She concentrated on sipping a milkshake through a red-and-white striped straw. Seeing Jesse approach in the mirror, she pivoted, not relinquishing the straw and cool drink.

Jesse took the stool beside her, welcoming the coolness of the vinyl cushion against her legs. "Hi, Courtney. Thanks for meeting me today."

"Not a problem. I'm teaching a summer course at Hobart, so lunch worked out." She nodded her thanks as the waitress placed her BLT in front of her. "What's up?"

Jesse surveyed the diner for an empty booth, but all were occupied. She had no choice but to discuss her idea here. Low voices would be required. She eyed Courtney's chocolate milkshake but ordered a Cobb salad and an iced tea. Her wedding dress popped into her mind with every dietary decision lately. She was sure a milkshake wouldn't make the cut.

"So, you're teaching nearby?"

Courtney mumbled through a bite of sandwich, "Yes."

"Where are you staying?"

She played with the straw. "I'm staying at the cottage."

Her news drove a thrum of excitement through Jesse. "You're kidding."

"It's so like me to do that." Sarcasm dripped in Courtney's voice.

Her mind raced. "Are you staying there alone?"

Courtney studied her. She took a long sip of her milkshake. "So, is Sister Perfection asking you to check up on me now?"

"No. No, nothing like that. I need a favor."

Now Courtney frowned, leaning away from her as if she'd just offered her a dead rat. "What do you want from me?"

"I want to stay at the cottage with you."

With a slurping sound, Courtney sipped the last of her shake. "You want to see Timmy again." Her voice was flat.

"Yes."

Courtney chased the last remnants of milkshake bubbles around the bottom of the glass with the straw. Voices near them ebbed and flowed; normalcy reigned at Woolworth's.

"Well, I don't." She pushed her glass away.

"So Timmy doesn't show up if I'm not there?"

"I didn't say that." Courtney looked straight ahead at the mirror behind the counter.

"If he's showing up anyway, what difference does it make if I stay?"

Courtney shrugged.

"I think I can help Timmy to rest peacefully. He wouldn't show up any more." Jesse caught her gaze in the mirror's reflection.

Hope flitted across Courtney's face before she resumed a disinterested demeanor.

"Okay. Fine. No skin off my nose."

"Thanks, Courtney. And, uh, no one else needs to know I'm staying there."

Courtney eyed her. "So you and Sister Angelina are still not talking?"

"We're back in touch. I'll tell her, but your father might not like the idea."

"Got it."

Jesse resisted the urge to hug Courtney. She gripped her iced tea glass, afraid she would shatter it with her excitement.

Her plan was coming together. So far, so good.

Chapter Eighteen

A two-ton weight had been lifted off Maggie's shoulders. Not that life was carefree and rainbows, but neither was it black clouds and sin any longer. Just meeting with Sister Therese had assuaged the guilt she'd felt at harboring her secret feelings. Well, maybe not so secret since even Sister Therese had already recognized them.

She picked up another folder and started sifting through it, culling outdated lesson plans and organizing those she would use again.

"Mags, it's July—play time. What are you doing in your classroom?" Jesse leaned on the doorframe, arms crossed over a manila folder.

"Which begs the question, what are you doing here, Miss Graham?"

"Touché." Jesse held up the folder bursting with papers. "With the wedding and honeymoon in late August, I want to solidify my first unit's lesson plans."

"Once again refuting the myth that teachers get the summer off." She laughed. She hadn't laughed in quite a while.

Jesse cocked her head. "You look good, Mags. Better than you have in a while."

"Got a minute?"

Jesse nodded and sat on the student desk in front of her.

"Let me tell you about my talk with Sister Therese."

As she related the conversation, more tension released from her shoulders and neck as if a leaden boa had been draped over her and now lifted and floated away. Jesse hung on every word. A smile hitched the corner of her mouth and was a full-blown grin by the end.

"How do you feel about all that, Mags?" Jesse asked.

"Relieved. Still confused. No longer damned to hell." She closed the folder on her desk. "Like I'm still between Scylla and Charybdis." Resting an elbow on the folder, she plunked her chin on her hand.

"I love it when math teachers cite ancient literature." Jesse grinned even broader.

She tapped the desk. "I still have a lot of thinking to do. Discerning. Praying."

"Discern over dinner at my house tonight."

Maggie shot her a suspicious glance.

"Just you and me."

"I know what outcome you're rooting for here, Jess. But life isn't a fairy tale. Despite my feelings for Marty, I take my vows very seriously. They've been the scaffolding of my life for ten years. That's not something I can just walk away from."

Jesse turned serious. "I know, Mags. Bottom line, I want you to be happy."

"Thanks. I need your support right now. I can't open up to you if I think you'll try to push me in one direction."

"From now on, my support will be whatever you need. I will have to pray for discernment, too. Oh, God, did I just say I would pray?" Jesse scrunched her nose.

"Yes, and you said it in a most devout way."

IT WAS JUST like old times again. Dinner had been simple: grilled chicken, baked potatoes, and salad. She wanted to give Maggie her full attention rather than waste time fussing over a meal. After cleaning the dishes, they sat side by side on the sofa, reviewing the wedding planner. Jesse refilled their wineglasses and they toasted the fact that she had survived the Wyndham bridal shower.

"You still have to decide on your flowers, Jess." Maggie sipped her wine. "The florist has been waiting patiently."

"I know. I just want whatever is blossoming at that time. Nothing fancy."

"What color? I'll be in basic black, so I won't clash with anything." Maggie laughed.

"I've told you, you could stand up there naked and I wouldn't care. I just want you beside me." She took her hand. "It means the world to me."

Maggie hugged her. "Well, I don't think standing up there naked would be a good idea, but I have to admit, wearing a pretty dress is quite appealing. I haven't worn anything but black and white for ten years now."

"Are you sure you have to wear your habit? Couldn't you dress up once for your best-friend-almost-a-sister's wedding?"

Maggie shrugged, picking at an invisible piece of lint on her shorts.

Oh no, I didn't want to spoil this perfect evening—though I might later. What is it, Mags?"

"A black habit or a pretty dress? My vows or my heart? It's just not that easy."

"What are you going to do?"

Maggie bit her lip and looked toward the kitchen window. She swallowed twice, her slender throat moving each time, and placed a hand on the table, tapping her index finger. When she turned to Jesse, her eyes glistened.

"I have to give each option fair consideration. According to

Sister Therese, I can't pray my feelings for Marty away, nor should I. If I was willing to spend a week on a silent retreat trying to do that, I suppose I have to give equal time to being with him." She turned to face Jesse. "How do I do that? It's not like I can date him."

"No, but you can spend time with him and talk to him about what you're going through. Honesty is the best policy. Ugh, I'm so bad at this. You're a much better counselor than I am."

At least her ineptness brought a smile to Maggie's face.

"Just talking to you helps, Jess. All this emotion swirling in my brain has me crazy. Talking eases the confusion and helps me see things from different angles. I know that part of my discernment is spending time with Marty, but..." A rosy blush infused her face as she turned her wineglass in circles. Finally, she set it down on the coffee table. "When I'm with him, I don't feel like it's a fair fight."

"God vs. Marty isn't a fair fight because of Marty? That's saying a lot right there." She set her glass beside Maggie's.

"When I'm with him, I don't want to leave him. I want to be as close to him as I can be." Maggie shook her head. "Is that wrong?"

"*I* know it isn't. Sister Therese left that door open. Well, ajar. Now Maggie has to tell you it isn't." *What would it be like if I couldn't be with Joe? I can't imagine that pain.* Her throat tightened at the thought, and she swallowed against the ache it caused. *God, I just want to make this all right for her.* She reached out and took her hand. "You need to see him. There is no way to figure this out if you keep him as a fantasy. I love Marty, but 'familiarity breeds contempt' as they say. Maybe as you know him better, you'll discover this was a crush." *Which will crush Marty.*

They sat in comfortable silence for a while. Maggie needed time to think.

"Probably no beautiful dress for me. Basic black for your wedding." She smiled ruefully.

"Well, black is elegant and classy. Besides, no matter what you wear, you're beautiful. What's next on our agenda?"

"Just your decision on the flowers—oh, and how many tiers you'll need on the wedding cake."

"I've delegated that responsibility to Monica. She and Ben are so excited about having the reception, and I know she wants to help. I don't know how to divide the number of tiers into more than one hundred wedding guests. Why didn't we just elope?"

Maggie laughed. "I'm a math teacher. I could figure it out! But I'd rather be your sidekick, doing your bidding and adjusting your train."

She moaned. "I forgot about the train." Suddenly the image of her bridal gown was replaced with the image of the train engine running in Timmy's room. She had to bring up the subject.

Maggie refilled their glasses, pouring hers only half full. "I need to get going soon. I think we've got all the details caught up." She shot her a stern look. "Except the flowers."

"There's something I need to tell you." Jesse drained her glass.

Maggie's head snapped up. "I know that tone, Graham. What's going on?"

"It's about Timmy." She had to win Maggie over. Without Maggie's approval, she would not follow through with her plan.

Maggie slumped back against the sofa. "I knew we'd have to come back to this."

"Hear me out, please. Remember how Helen needed me to hear her message? And so did the Seneca woman?"

"Mmm hmm." Maggie dragged her response out.

"I think Timmy needs me to hear his message."

"What if I don't want to hear his message?"

"Your family is still grieving after all these years. You've all been dancing around it. You have no answers about Timmy. There is no healing until you know the truth. Please, Mags, please let me help Timmy. It might help all of you—especially Courtney. The guilt is killing her."

Maggie nodded. "Yes, Courtney's unhappiness surrounds her like a shroud. No matter how hard I try, she rejects any overture I make to be kind."

"Timmy has been appearing to her since his disappearance," she said softly.

Maggie's hand flew to her heart. "My God."

"Courtney thought it was Satan. She thought it was punishment. When she discovered that I'd experienced Timmy's presence, too, it gave her hope."

Maggie's eyebrows shot up. "She talked to you about this? When?"

"She came to my house right after your dad kicked me out. That's when she explained her encounters with Timmy. For the last fifteen years, she's been trying to ignore him, but she's known he's been there all along."

"Poor Courtney."

"And poor Timmy. If he's still appearing in the cottage, he hasn't found peace yet. Mags, there's something he wants us to know. Especially Courtney."

Maggie sighed. "My heart breaks when I think of him—and it's worse knowing he's not at peace."

"Your whole family is devastated by this; even Sean is affected, though he was too young to remember." Maggie seemed able to at least discuss Timmy, so she pressed on. "I met with Courtney again. She's staying at the cottage. She doesn't like being there alone." She let this sink in. Baby steps were the key to getting Maggie's approval for the plan.

Maggie frowned. "That's got to be difficult for her." Then her frown dissolved into a smirk. "But I see you have a solution."

Jesse hitched one leg underneath herself and tucked into the corner of the sofa. "As a matter of fact, I do."

Chapter Nineteen

❧❦❧

Buoyant was probably too optimistic. Dread was probably too pessimistic. Jesse's emotional state fell somewhere between the two. The conversation with Maggie the night before had been difficult, but she was now free to implement her plan and stay at the cottage.

Joe had signed on even though he wasn't thrilled with her idea. Maybe she wasn't either, and that's where the dread came in. After she checked all the lights and windows in her house, she hefted her suitcase and headed out to Bert, her Volkswagen Beetle. Halfway there, she stopped dead in her tracks.

All four tires had been slashed.

What the hell? Who would do this? Fear coursed through her body like hot lava. The sense of being watched crept over her; she glanced toward the woods beside her property. Walking back to the house, she set her suitcase on the porch and unlocked the front door. The door that, last night, had stood between her and whoever had assaulted Bert. Somehow, the lock seemed flimsy today.

With shaking hands, she dialed Joe's work phone. The receptionist said he was out on a site and wouldn't be back until afternoon.

"Please, I have to talk to him. Someone slashed—" Her voice trembled and she couldn't breathe. The thought of someone so violent just yards away from her door was a gut punch. She slid into the chair beside the hall table.

"Jesse? Are you all right?"

She nodded.

"Jesse?"

"I can't believe someone would do this to me."

"I'll get in touch with Joe right away."

The line went dead.

She hung up the phone and rested her elbows on the hall table, dropping her head in her hands. *Things were going so well. All my ducks were in a row.* Her shaking intensified. Once again someone was threatening her. *I can't catch a break.* She stared at the table until the spine of the phone book caught her eye.

"Damn it, nobody is going to get in my way." She picked up the phone and dialed.

THE FRONT DOOR flew open and Joe exploded into the hall. "Jesse! Jesse! Are you here?"

She ran in from the kitchen. "Yes, hi, Joe."

He looked around, panic etched in his face. "What happened? Your message—you said something about being slashed." He grabbed her into a bear hug. Then he pulled her out to arm's length and scrutinized her up and down.

"My tires, Joe. My tires were slashed." With a bewildered look, he glanced out the front window. "Where's your car?"

"At the tire store. I had road service tow it."

"Oh my God. I was so scared." He held her so close the frantic beating of his heart pulsed against her ear. Stroking her back, he kissed her forehead and drew her in tighter. "I was so scared," he repeated.

"I was pretty shaken when I called. I guess I garbled the message."

"All that matters is that you're okay." He pulled away, his face dark. "You're in danger again. How does this keep happening?"

A hot flame of anger flared in her chest. *It's not my fault. Geez, I don't call up lunatics and say, "Hey, come on over and try to kill me.* She took a deep breath before she answered. "I don't ask for this, Joe. I never set out to make people mad at me. What do you want me to do?"

"Leave things alone. Stop dredging up old secrets. These damn ghosts always lead you into danger." He scrubbed his hands through his thick, coppery hair. A scowl replaced the fear. "Can't you just let them be?"

"I don't go looking for them, remember? They chase me down and plop themselves smack dab in the middle of my life." He was being unfair, and right now she needed his support. "These people need help, and for some reason, I can help them."

"At what cost? Your life? You've told me that Timmy's presence is scarier than the Seneca woman's ghost because you totally lose control of your senses." His voice rose. "Jesse, do I lose you to the bidding of one of these... these ghosts? They're dead! Who cares? Their life is over and done. Can't you let them rest in peace?"

Her voice dropped to a whisper. "But that's the thing. They can't rest in peace until someone on this side helps them. Look at Maggie's family—they've been living in hell. Courtney is so full of anger and grief, she has shut the family out. Maggie entered the convent as a sacrificial lamb at her father's bidding, and now may sacrifice her own happiness out of guilt. That whole family is screwed up because they've never found answers. Geez, Joe, they don't know—have never known—what happened to their little boy."

"My God, Jesse! Can't they find their own answers? Didn't you say Courtney sees Timmy's ghost? Let her find out what he wants."

He paced through the living room like a lion in too small a cage. "Keep it in their family. Keep you out of danger."

"It's not that easy." She tracked his path, back and forth, back and forth. "That's why I have to continue with my plan."

He halted, staring at her. "You're really going through with this?"

"Look, whoever is after me knows where I live. Wouldn't I be safer at the Keegans' cottage?"

He resumed his pacing, slapping his hand against his thigh, weighing her words. Finally, his voice thick, he said, "So, the choice is a maniac who may want to kill you to silence you or a ghost who, as you said, 'turns you into a babbling child.'" He glared at her. "It doesn't matter what I think. You're going to do this anyway."

She stared back at him. He had always been so supportive, but he'd taken all he could. She choked back more angry words and a sick feeling gripped her. She could lose him. *Stop this insanity and do as he asks*, her brain said.

"I don't know how much longer I can watch you take risks like this." He shoved past her and slammed the door behind him.

Chapter Twenty

❧❧❧

Maggie had been kissed before—in high school. At the ninth-grade dance, David Bentley went in for a quick smooch, like a duck jabbing at a fish in the water. Her braces scraped the inside of her lips, reducing any romantic intention David had planned.

Kevin Marvin's attempt was much more sophisticated, though his lips locked on hers and then never moved. She could almost hear him thinking, "What do I do next?"

Kip Stansky was the first to use his tongue, and he drooled into her mouth. At the senior prom, Charlie Vieau's hand kept slipping down her back to rest on her behind. She didn't sense it was a purposeful move, more a careless lack of attention, as she was sure he was thinking of the next day's track meet.

None of this was the reason she opted for a life of chastity.

The reason was intangible. She hadn't heard God's voice say, "Margaret Keegan, enter the convent. Reject sex and live your life in devotion to me." Still, she had believed religious life was her calling. Something within her, something she couldn't see or touch or even name in her imagination drove her forward as she discerned and then accepted her vocation. Of course, the conversation with Dad had sealed the deal.

Now she stood before this man who permeated her being, who seemed present to her all day—all night, in her waking and her dreaming. She stared at his shirt, unable to move, to speak.

"Maggie."

Marty's voice, a deep timbre, carried her name on his breath, directly from his heart.

She closed her eyes. She ached—for what? For him to hold her? To run away, back to the convent where she belonged? Could she live out her life within those walls now? Her life had been so full, so complete. She loved the routine of morning prayer, teaching, vespers, compline. Her wonderful community of dedicated women full of faith, living out their spirituality in social justice and service to children's education.

Perhaps she should resent him for disrupting her peace. *My life had been fine until you came along.* But what would her life be if he'd never come along?

Jesse was right; she had to face her attraction, give this love the chance it deserved. Sister Therese's words floated to her mind: "... because loving someone and being loved in return is a gift—the greatest gift. Why would you want to reject a gift?"

The lake had settled to gentle waves that lapped the shore and washed over their feet. Birdsong filled the trees behind them as robins and cardinals beckoned mates to the nest. Somewhere upwind, a campfire blazed on the beach, wrapping its smoky wood smell around them. All of nature wrapped them in a cocoon, pulling them closer together until this moment where she stood before him, relishing the caress of her name on his lips.

"Marty." She hadn't realized she'd spoken his name. Like fire blazing through tinder, heat spread through her body.

His gaze locked on hers. He drew closer, squeezing her hand, wrapping his other arm around her and pulling her near. His head bent to hers, watching her, their gaze never breaking.

Oh, my God. This is so wrong.

His breath ghosted across her face, soft and sweet. Her knees trembled. Could she even remain standing? His face drew nearer, and she closed her eyes as his lips brushed hers. Soft, velvet. The flame within her was now hot lava flowing from her belly to her fingertips and toes. She tried to remain standing, but she had no doubt—he was holding her up.

Oh, my God. This is so right.

She received his kiss like a sacrament. Her arms slid up along his broad shoulders, wending their way around his neck. Time stopped, and all that mattered was him. His lips parted, tentatively, as if requesting. She responded, inviting him, tasting him. A moan escaped, low in her throat. He pulled her closer.

She pulled away.

"I can't, Marty." Her heart pounded a litany of *stop, go, stop, go, stop, go.*

He backed away. "I'm sorry, Maggie. I thought..." He held out his hands, contritely.

"I know." Her voice was a rasp. "I'm sorry. I didn't mean to..." She folded her arms as she tried to regain her composure. Staring at the ground, she dug her toe into the pebbles.

"Maggie."

At the sound of his voice, she whimpered, then shook her head. *What is wrong with me? Get control.* Her life as a nun had been so calm, so predictable, so comfortable. Now, she was on a Tilt-a-Whirl spiraling into infinity. Her heart ached. Oh, how it ached.

"I need to go home. To the convent." As if he didn't know where she lived. As if confirming it for herself. She glanced at him. His brows creased down in disappointment. He reached out but dropped his hand before he touched her.

"Okay." His voice was resigned. "Maggie, I—"

"No. Please, Marty, no."

He bit his lip then nodded.

Images swirled in her mind. Of Dad's face lit by a bonfire, his eyes pleading with her. Of his voice calling her Sister Angelina. Of her mother's pride when she stood beside her, introducing her as

Sister Angelina. Of Sister Therese's look of disappointment should Maggie tell her she was leaving the convent. She pressed her fingers against her temples, all her certainty collapsing into one single awareness. Was her angst centered on not disappointing people? Vocations weren't based on what others expected. What about disappointing Marty?

"When I'm at the convent, it all seems so clear. When I'm with you, this," she caressed his face, "all seems so clear."

He stepped closer, but she held her hands against his chest.

"So many thoughts are racing through my mind right now." Maggie reached out and touched his hand. "If I leave the convent, there's no going back. The life I've known is over. My calling, my vocation, what does it all mean?" She shook her head, trying to clear it, trying to find some definitive answer. "It's too much right now. I need to go. Good night."

As she walked away, his voice followed, soft and low. "Yes, it's too much."

Chapter Twenty-One

✿❀✿

Jesse wrangled her suitcase out of the trunk of her VW Beetle. "Sorry you've been through so much today, Bert. I promise to keep you safer." She patted the hood after she closed it and winked at the front windows of her car. "I know I'm crazy to talk to you all the time, but we've been through so much together."

She traced the deep tread of one of the brand-new tires. Since she hadn't been able to pick up Bert until just before closing and still needed to grab some fast food for dinner, she arrived at the Keegans' cottage an hour later than she'd planned. Based on the darkness of the windows, she guessed Courtney was still at work.

To the west, lightning morphed the deep indigo to lavender and back again. Thunder rolled across the lake echoing off the water. Jesse hustled to get inside.

The Keegans kept a key hidden above the doorframe to the shed. Stretching, she couldn't quite reach the top of the door trim. She had to jump up and down as she ran her hand along the molding until her hand connected with the key. *Maybe I should keep it with me while I'm staying here. Or have a copy made. I'll ask Courtney's permission.* After unlocking the cottage door, she resumed her jumping to return the key to its hiding spot. Just as she landed her last jump, she stumbled as someone barked at her.

"What the hell are you doing?" His voice was a growl, like a dog before it attacks.

Her heart hammered until she thought it would burst through her chest. Turning, she was face to face with a man in dark clothes, his face in shadow. But she recognized Mr. Becker, the next-door neighbor who'd creeped out Sean all these years. Who creeped her out right now.

He glanced at her Beetle then back at her. "Hmmph." His dark eyes squinted, ink spots in his face, studying her intensely. "The Keegans aren't home." He looked at the dark cottage while he stated the obvious.

"I know. I'm staying here—with Courtney." *Make it clear I'm not here alone.*

"She's not here." Walking over to the garage, he peeked in the windows then looked at the cottage. "Maybe she's out."

Show no fear. "She's expecting me." Jesse fought to keep her voice steady.

"Hmmph." He glanced at Bert again then back at her. He turned and slowly walked back to his cottage.

Jesse shook as she pulled a box of curriculum materials out of the trunk. Hurrying to the back door, the box shifted and two notebooks fell to the ground, the three-ring binders clacking open, papers splayed out on the lawn. Damn. She wanted to get inside and lock the door as quickly as possible.

She set the box on the floor just inside and quickly picked up the wayward papers and notebooks. Jamming them into her arms, she hastened inside, slammed the door, and locked it. She leaned against the door for a minute, taking deep breaths.

The familiar scent of lemon wax mixed with the charred scent from the wood stove soothed her. Lightning flashed again, shooting eerie shadows against the wall. Flipping the light switch, she squinted in the fluorescent light from the overhead fixture. As she moved through the cottage, she turned on lamps, softening the light to a warm glow in the living room.

Just as she turned toward the stairs, her heart stopped. Sprawled on the floor in front of her bedroom, Courtney lay motionless, her lips blue.

"Courtney, oh my God, Courtney!"

Jesse placed two fingers against her throat. Thank God! She'd only had basic first aid, but she remembered something about checking pupils. When she gently lifted one lid, Courtney blinked. Jesse jumped back.

"Shit! Get the hell offa me!"

"Geez, Courtney, I thought you were dead!" She squatted back on her heels. "What happened?" She examined her room. An empty gin bottle was tipped over on the nightstand. "Oh no."

Courtney covered her face and moaned. "I need a drink." Her speech was slurred, and her head dropped as she dozed off.

Thunder growled, louder and closer than before.

"Courtney, stay with me. I'm going to call an ambulance, but you've got to stay awake."

"No. I wanna sleep. I jus' wanna sleep." Her eyes rolled back, her head lolling to the side. She softly snored.

Advice from a Red Cross film popped into her mind, and she rolled Courtney to her side.

"Damn it, leave me alone!" Curling into a fetal position, the girl started coughing, then vomited. "Jesus." She wiped her mouth.

Jesse moved Courtney's head back from the mess.

"'m fine. Feel much better—" She vomited again.

"Oh, honey, you're a mess. Let's get you into the bathroom."

Courtney flopped like a rag doll as Jesse helped her to the bathroom and eased her down to the floor beside the toilet. Grabbing a towel off the rack, she cleaned up the vomit, keeping one eye on Courtney the whole time.

"You need to go to the hospital." Jesse rinsed the towel in the toilet, flushed, and rinsed it again.

"No. I'm not goin' anywhere." Courtney's head swayed, the

motion causing her to vomit again. This time she almost made the toilet.

Thunder crashed above them as lightning strobed at the windows.

Jesse wiped up the floor and resumed rinsing out the towel.

Courtney propped her elbows on her knees and dropped her head into her hands. "I'm such a freakin' loser. I never get anything right."

Jesse sat beside her, placing an arm around her shoulder. "You're not a loser."

Courtney's head bobbled as she looked at her. "I got my little brother killed. That's pretty awful.

Jesse brushed back strands of hair that stuck to Courtney's face. Snatching a clean washcloth hanging on the towel rack, she wet it with warm water and gently patted Courtney's face. What could she say? As she'd told Maggie, she was no counselor. Her heart ached for Courtney, but she couldn't think of one wise word to say to help her.

"You didn't get Timmy killed. Whatever happened that day was not your fault."

"Then why is he haunting me? Why won't he leave me alone? I can't take this anymore." An agonized cry gushed from her, her body shuddering.

Jesse wrapped her arms around her. After a while Courtney's anguish quieted and she lay with her head against Jesse's shoulder. At first, Jesse thought she was sleeping, but then she spoke, her words clearer, softer.

"I just wanna sleep."

"I know." She patted Courtney's back. "You need to be checked. I'm going to call an ambulance."

Courtney bolted upright. "No! She skidded away from Jesse and curled up in the corner. "I thought I could trust you."

"I'm concerned about you." She reached out, but Courtney slapped away her hand.

"You know what they'll do to me, right? They'll call the fuzz and put me in detox."

"Courtney..."

"So, you think I'm bonkers, too? 'Cause I'm pretty convinced I am. Geez, my damn brother's ghost won't leave me alone."

"That's why I'm here. We're going to deal with Timmy's ghost together. I won't leave you, I promise."

Courtney eyed her suspiciously. "Why?"

"Why what?"

"Why do you want to help me? Nobody else seems to care. Not even my parents." She snorted and looked away.

"I think your parents are suffering as much as you are."

"They sure hide it well. Life's great with them. Especially their saintly daughter—the *other* daughter, I mean." Her head snapped up. "You can't tell her. Please, promise me you won't tell Maggie about this."

Jesse's head swam. How could she keep this secret from Maggie? But she understood where Courtney was coming from. She raised one hand, crossing her heart with the other. "I promise."

Courtney sank back and sighed. "Thanks."

"On one condition."

Opening one eye, Courtney sneered. "Of course."

"You let me call Susan Riley to come and check you over. She's a nurse."

After a moment, Courtney nodded slowly. "All right. I'll agree to have Susan check me over."

Jesse helped Courtney to her bed, placing the wastebasket beside it. "If needed, aim well."

Courtney actually gave her a half smile.

She dialed Joe's home, praying he wouldn't answer. Right now, things between them needed resolution, and this wasn't the time. Fortunately, Susan answered on the second ring.

"Hi, Susan, it's me."

"Hi, Jesse. Joe's—"

"No," Jesse interrupted her quickly. "I need to talk to you." She explained Courtney's current condition.

"Goodness. We'll be right over." The line went dead.

We'll be right over? Great. Joe was coming with her.

It was going to be a long night.

Chapter Twenty-Two

Susan left the door to Courtney's bedroom open. "Wow. You'll need to stay with her tonight. Keep her propped up against the pillows." She put her bag on the kitchen counter and poured a cup of coffee. "Poor thing. She's really a mess."

Jesse nodded. "Okay." She sat in a chair opposite the sofa where Joe sat. Their conversation had been limited to the events of the day and the evening. How could it still be the same day Bert's tires were slashed? That seemed like ages ago. Neither had broached the subject of their argument that afternoon. She wasn't sure she had the strength tonight.

"You've told me a bit about her, but fill me in more if you can." Susan sat beside Joe on the sofa.

Jesse related the story of Timmy's disappearance, Courtney's overwhelming guilt about it, and Timmy's appearances to both of them.

"I wonder if Timmy appearing to me is what pushed her to this." Jesse got up to refill their coffee cups. Joe didn't make eye contact as he reached for his cup. Surely, they could heal the hurt from their last conversation.

"Whatever it was, she was desperate." Susan drained her coffee. "She needs rest and liquids—water is best. No more alcohol, no caffeine for a day or so."

They stood, and she hugged Jesse.

"You've had a tough day, sweetie."

She nodded, her throat tightening with emotion. Susan was the antithesis of Jesse's own cold, uncaring mother, or rather, the woman she had thought was her mother. Susan was the mother everyone deserved.

She turned to Joe. How to say goodnight to him? Nothing was resolved. "Thanks for coming, too, Joe."

"I was planning to stay." He nodded toward Courtney's bedroom. "In case you need help in the night."

"Thanks, Joe." A whisper was all she could manage. His meaning was clear.

Susan raised an eyebrow. "Well, I'll leave you two to hold down the fort. Call if you need me." She picked up her bag, placed her cup in the sink, and closed the door behind her.

Jesse stared at the cup, white against the stainless steel. Once again, she'd made a mess of things.

JESSE AWOKE WITH A JOLT, not sure where she was, but Courtney's pale face against the pillows helped orient her. A blue and cream lighthouse nightlight glowed softly above the baseboard, casting shadows against the far wall. Her back ached from being curled up in the easy chair she and Joe had dragged into the room. Stretching, she yawned and tucked herself against the cushions.

From above, the sound that had awakened her echoed.

A train whistle.

No. She wanted nothing to do with ghosts tonight.

The engine click-clacked as it circled the tracks. What if Courtney also heard it? She had to go to Timmy before he woke Courtney.

And Joe. He was asleep in her room upstairs. She tossed back the afghan that covered her and slipped out of the room.

The usual icy cold greeted her when she entered Timmy's room. Mesmerized, she watched the train circle the tracks, gaping at the small circle of light that punched shadows against the walls as it chugged along. She pulled her attention away from the train, her dizzy head thrumming.

Where was Timmy?

In the corner of the murky room, a glimmer flickered. A shape faded in and out, four feet tall and slender.

Jesse rubbed her arms against the chill of the room. "Timmy?"

The glow flickered like a spent candle.

How could she learn what he needed? She peered around the dark room, searching for something that could link them the way the infant's bracelet had linked her student to the Seneca woman.

Along his dresser, tin soldiers marched in front of a teddy bear propped against the mirror. She caught her reflection—tousled hair, a wrinkled blouse, a frown. She stared at her expression, and then she studied the teddy bear who wore a blue-and-white striped train engineer's cap.

Why are you mad? Don't you want to play?

The words echoed to her as if from down a long tunnel. Across the room, the glimmer ebbed and grew, flickering in and out. Like a mirage on a country road, her self-awareness shimmered just out of reach. A giggle bubbled up as she lifted the teddy bear and hugged it.

"Yes, let's play." Her voice was high and musical, and she could not control it. She watched from inside her mind, as if an observer, unable to take control of the child she had become. On some visceral level, she panicked.

Can Courtney play with us?

"She's sleeping."

No, she's not. She never sleeps.

Her adult consciousness was slipping away. *Hold on. Hold on.* She couldn't.

Plopping down on the floor, she danced the teddy bear in the center of the train track, making it jump each time the train circled around. She giggled again.

"Jesse?" Joe's voice was quiet.

"Aww." Jesse pouted when the train stopped and the light turned off. Annoyed, she turned around. "We're playing."

"Holy shit." His voice held fear.

"What's going on?" Courtney stood behind him. "Jesus."

Courtney's here! I miss you, Courtney. Come and play with me.

"Hey!" Jesse cried as Joe scooped her up in his arms.

"My God, you're freezing." He carried her into her room and tucked her under the covers. "Are you all right?" He rubbed her hands between his.

Dazed and dizzy, she surveyed the room. "What happened?"

"I don't know what the hell was going on in there," Joe said, his face a thundercloud.

Courtney whispered. "You were playing. With Timmy."

Chapter Twenty-Three

Neither spoke.

Rain pattered against the cottage window as pallid sunlight gave up the attempt to shine through. A dismal day, matching Jesse's exhausted mood.

Joe stared at her from across the kitchen table, and she didn't know how to read him. She propped her elbows on the table and balanced her head in her hands. The incessant ticking of the cat clock drove her nuts. She wanted to grab its swinging tail and hurl it into tomorrow. *I'm a freaking mess.*

Finally, she looked up at him, unsure what to expect.

"What the hell happened last night?" He sat back and folded his arms.

"You mean with Courtney?"

Leaning forward, he pounded the table, rattling their cups against the saucers. "You know exactly what I mean. When you were in that room with... whatever." His brows slashed down, and his lips pulled taut.

"Shh. You'll wake Courtney."

"I don't give a damn if I wake the dead." He snorted. "Geez. I guess they're already awake."

"Joe, stop—" She'd never seen him this angry.

"Me, stop? I don't think I've done anything I need to stop. You, on the other hand, could you stop? Would you for one minute consider staying safe? You were out of your mind last night. It was as if you were five years old. My God, Jesse. What if you can't snap out of that? Don't you see the danger here?" His voice rose.

Courtney's door opened, and she held her hand over her eyes against the thin morning light. "Geez, you two. Can you have your lover's quarrel somewhere else?"

Jesse scowled at Joe.

He ran his hand across his mouth and looked out the window.

"Sorry, Courtney," Jesse said.

"I'm going in to work." Joe stood, almost knocking over his chair.

"It's Sunday," Jesse whispered.

He glanced at her, hesitated, and left.

Jesse crossed her arms and rocked against the ache that gripped her.

"And I thought *my* little incident was the highlight last night," Courtney smirked as she poured coffee into an oversized mug and sat at the table.

She would not rise to the bait. The depth of Courtney's pain was evident in her binge the previous night. The events surrounding Timmy's death had to be revealed so healing could begin. For Courtney. For the whole Keegan family.

"How are you feeling this morning, Courtney?" Jesse reached for her hand, but she pulled it away.

"Like I got hit by a Mack truck." She rubbed her forehead. "Look, I'm sorry you had to clean up after me and everything. But I'm not— Forget it."

"You're not sorry about getting drunk." Jesse tried to keep her voice gentle.

Courtney glared at her. "No. I'm not." She hugged herself, hunching her shoulders. "You saw him last night. I can't deal with this anymore. And it's not just here. I can't escape him. You can leave and he'll never bother you. He's always with me."

"He's followed me, too," Jesse said.

Courtney's mouth dropped open. "What?"

"He's made his presence known to me at my house."

"No shit." Courtney stared at her.

"Does he speak to you?"

Courtney grasped her coffee mug, turning it around and around. "What do you mean? He's a freaking ghost."

"Do you hear his voice? In your head?" She needed to know exactly what Courtney had been experiencing with Timmy.

Courtney stood. "Just because I got hammered... I'm not a freaking psycho! You're all itching to have me committed, aren't you? That way this damn family can be done with me." She turned and stormed off toward her room.

"Because I heard him last night." She kept her voice steady.

Courtney froze at her bedroom door. She turned slowly. "What did you say?" Her voice squeaked.

"Last night. I could hear Timmy." *And so could you.*

Courtney collapsed down the wall and buried her head in her hands. She cried until she crumpled to the floor.

"I'm not crazy." Her words sounded muffled between her fingers.

"Only as crazy as I am." Jesse bundled her in her arms.

LIKE A CENSER AT EVENING PRAYER, the air offered that "all's right with the world" crispness after the morning rain. But all was not right with Jesse's world, and any sense of that would be a brief interlude. Heavy gray clouds thickened in the sky to the west, promising another round of thunder and lightning. Even the seagulls swooped and soared in frantic anticipation of the coming storm.

Jesse had convinced Courtney to take a walk with her. They

strolled in silence as waves churned along the shore, creating a slippery track across the slick stones. They had made it to the marsh and were returning to the cottage when the wind gusted, and they had to lean forward to keep their balance. A stronger gust snatched the scarf Jesse wore to confine her curls and hurled it into the marshy reeds. Strands of hair whipped around her face, one stinging her eye before she brushed it away.

In unspoken agreement, they broke into a run toward the cottage a hundred yards down the beach. Hearing a voice, Jesse slowed her pace and spotted Mr. Williamson waving his arms at them.

"Jesse! Courtney!"

She grabbed Courtney's arm and pointed to him. Together they changed direction and sprinted up the steps leading from the beach to the Williamsons' cottage.

Tall grasses on either side of the steps whipped their legs. Courtney slipped on some grass flattened on the steps. Catching herself, she regained her balance and led the way to the porch where Mr. Williamson stood beckoning them into the screened-in porch.

"What's... wrong... Mr. Williamson?" Jesse gulped air.

"Myra's out of her medicine. I didn't realize she took her last pill before bed last night. I have to run to town." He glanced at the door to the living room, then back at them, nervously. "I normally don't leave her, but she's so agitated. She's afraid of storms, you see." He took off his railroad engineer's cap, wiped his thin hair back, and looked over at the bedroom door. "She's sleeping right now and probably won't wake up until I get back. But I can't leave her alone."

"We'd be happy to stay with her." She glanced at Courtney. "At least I can if you want to get back to the cottage, Courtney."

"So, you'll trust me on my own?" Courtney raised an accusing eyebrow.

She had to admit, the thought had crossed her mind this morning that leaving Courtney alone might be dangerous. But the gin was gone, and all that was left at the cottage was one lonely Genny Cream Ale. Besides, she suspected Courtney's actions might have been a desperate cry for help. She had thought Jesse would arrive by supper, in plenty of time to help her. She ignored Courtney's jab.

"We'll both stay. No problem." Courtney smiled at Mr. Williamson.

He ushered them into the quiet cottage. By now the sky had darkened to a deep charcoal. Except for the front windows that faced the porch and lake, all the curtains were drawn, and a single lamp beside the recliner emitted a comforting, soft yellow glow. Their bedroom door was closed, but a guestroom was open, revealing a handmade quilt covering the bed.

A quilting frame stood in one corner of the living room, and embroidered samplers covered the walls. Crocheted afghans and pillows spilled over the sofa and side chair. While Mrs. Williamson was no longer seen outside, she'd certainly made her presence known within the cottage.

"You can work this puzzle if you'd like. Myra would never notice." He led them to the dining room table, one end of it covered with jigsaw pieces all turned face up, and the frame of the puzzle completed. He stroked the frame. "She likes doing the edges first. Won't touch the inside til the edge is all done." He looked wistfully at the closed door.

He put on his horn-rimmed glasses. "Thank you, girls. I won't be gone long. Already called in the refill, so I just have to pick it up." He glanced at the door. "She won't wake up til I'm back." Yet, he didn't move.

"Would you like me to go pick up the prescription?" Jesse asked.

He pondered this for a moment. "Can't. I have to sign for it."

"She'll be fine, Mr. Williamson. Go ahead, we'll stay here." Jesse took his arm and walked him to the back door.

"Coffee's on. Help yourself." One more look back and he was out the door.

Shortly after he left, the windows shook with the fury of the wind. Lightning zigzagged into the lake, and a clap of thunder shook the cottage.

"Uh oh," Courtney whispered.

They both looked at the bedroom door as it slowly opened. Mrs. Williamson's eyes were round with terror. She stopped at the sight of the two girls standing over the puzzle. Shaking, she surveyed the cottage. "Harold? Where's Harold?" Her voice rose with panic.

"He's at the pharmacy picking up your prescription, Mrs. Williamson." Courtney kept her voice as soothing as possible. "He'll be back in a few minutes. This is Maggie's friend, Jesse Graham."

Lightning flashed, and Mrs. Williamson jumped, her hand flying to her heart.

Courtney placed an arm around her shoulders. "Why don't you come do the puzzle with us?"

Mrs. Williamson shuffled over to the table and studied Courtney. A soft smile spread over her face. "Hello, dear. How nice of you to come by. Are you looking for the little boy?"

Jesse gasped and caught Courtney's gray face as she grabbed the back of the dining room chair.

"What little boy?" Jesse asked.

Mrs. Williamson's hands fluttered at her. "Oh, you know who I mean, dear. The little railroad engineer." One hand floated to her mouth, tapping her lips. "Now, what was his name? Oh, yes, of course. Timmy."

The silence in the room was more deafening than the thunder outside.

Mrs. Williamson looked around the cottage. "Now, where did Timmy go?"

Courtney sank into the chair, trembling like an autumn leaf about to give up its last. Her wide brown eyes were dark against her pale skin.

Mrs. Williamson patted her back. "Now, don't worry dear—

we'll find him. When you came over last time he was out in the garden with Mr. Williamson and me. You go back to your sunbathing, dear, and I'll send him home in time for lunch."

Courtney gaped at the woman. "I came over before?"

Mrs. Williamson gave her a confused smile. "Why, yes, dear. You checked on him a couple of times earlier. Don't tell me your memory is getting as bad as mine."

A sharp crack sounded in front of the cottage as lightning strobed through the front windows. In the flash, Jesse saw a slender branch fall near the steps to the beach. Mrs. Williamson grabbed Courtney's hand.

"It wasn't storming when you came over earlier," she whimpered.

Courtney stood and gently eased Mrs. Williamson into the seat next to hers. Sitting back down, she held the woman's hand. "The storm will pass. You're safe with us."

"But the boy is out there." Mrs. Williamson's hands fluttered again, indicating the back door.

Jesse's gut wrenched.

"Timmy's not out in the storm. Do you know where he is?" Courtney asked.

The back door flew open and Mr. Williamson rushed in, slamming the storm out.

"Thank you girls for—" He halted when he spotted his wife. "Myra?" His question held fear as well as confusion. He hurried to her. "Are you all right, dear?" His voice was tender.

Myra caressed her husband's face. "Yes, dear, I'm fine. Courtney and..." She frowned at Jesse. "I'm sorry, you never told me your name."

Courtney and Jesse glanced at each other, then back at Myra.

"I'm Jesse Graham, Mrs. Williamson."

Mrs. Williamson raised one thin hand and softly tapped her thigh. "Oh, of course you are. Maggie's friend. Sorry, I get so confused these days. Has Maggie decided to enter the convent? You know her father really wants to give her to God." She bestowed a look of adoration on her husband. "Of course, if she does, she'll never have a wonderful man to take care of her like my Harold." Her smile was radiant.

Jesse shifted from one foot to the other, chilled by Mrs. Williamson's assessment of Maggie's calling, unease growing in her gut with each passing minute. It was evident how far Mrs. Williamson's health had deteriorated.

Courtney still held the woman's hand, and now pressed it. "You were telling us where Timmy is."

Mr. Williamson dropped the package he carried. "What?" he shouted.

Thunder clapped again as lightning lit the sky, and Mrs. Williamson shrank back. Which had scared her, the clap of thunder outside or the thunder in Mr. Williamson's voice?

With trembling hands, Mr. Williamson retrieved the paper bag, shaking it a few times to get the brown, plastic bottle out. "Here, Myra, you're way overdue for your medication."

She waved him away. "I'm feeling fine, dear. Why don't you put on the teakettle for us girls?" She winked conspiratorially at them.

According to Mr. Williamson, she avoided people and was afraid to leave the cottage. Yet Jesse believed that, if not for the storm, Mrs. Williamson might want to stroll the beach with the two of them.

"Your wife mentioned that Timmy had been out in the garden with you... that day." Jesse said.

He glanced at Myra. "She gets confused. Yes, he was, but he must have left us to go sit in the rowboat." He shook his head slowly. "So sad what happened to him."

"What do you mean?" Jesse asked.

He went to the kitchen to pour a glass of water. Over the noise of the running faucet, he talked back over his shoulder. "You know, floating out on the lake and drowning." Returning to his wife, he set the glass in front of her and opened the bottle. His hands still shook a bit as he tapped one pill onto the table. Recapping the bottle, he said, "We shouldn't even be talking about this. I know how it upsets you, Courtney."

Courtney sat up straight, her face composed. "That's all right. I'm very interested in what Mrs. Williamson was saying about me checking on Timmy a few times."

He looked at his wife, frowning. "Did she? I guess I didn't know that."

"Yes, the boy was out back with us, wearing his railroad engineer cap, just like yours." Myra smiled up at his cap, then told Courtney, "Timmy loved being in the garden with Harold. That boy helped him dig the holes to put in the railroad crossing sign and the signal light."

Her speech was beginning to slur, and her glassy gaze drifted as she tried to focus. She pulled her robe tighter, and withdrew her hand from Courtney's. She shrank toward her husband.

He glowered at Courtney. "Yes, we were out back with Timmy. That is, until he left. He must have gone down to your dock. Past where you were sunbathing."

Courtney gasped and slammed back into her chair as if she'd been struck.

Jesse glared at Mr. Williamson. "That was unfair. It's clear from what your wife has said that Courtney was keeping an eye on Timmy."

"Until she fell asleep."

Jesse wanted to slap him. Didn't he see what his accusation was doing to Courtney? She pulled Courtney from the chair, turning to him before she opened the door. "That was a cruel thing to say."

But the look on his face wasn't cruel. His eyes drooped with despair. His hands lay on his wife's shoulders, while his own shoulders slumped like a man who'd been beaten.

Chapter Twenty-Four

✤

Maggie strode along the corridor to her classroom. This is what she loved. This is what she lived for. Her morning had started at five a.m. with Morning Prayer, then breakfast. She'd strolled in the garden as she said the rosary, relishing the birdsong and gentle morning breeze. Now she would work in her classroom.

A perfect day. A fulfilling day.

She touched her lips. No, she would not think about him.

Focusing on the sound of her sensible shoes on the polished marble floor, she counted each step. *One, two, three.* But the sound of Marty whispering her name floated behind each count.

Maggie, Maggie, Maggie.

"Maggie?" Sister John Mary, the only sister who called her by her given name instead of Sister Angelina, tugged at her elbow. "You're somewhere over the rainbow." Her laugh was husky and usually infectious.

"Oh, hi, Jam." In turn, Maggie originally had called her by her initials, J.M., but now she elided them into her nickname.

Jam had been rebellious all her life, growing up in a housing project in a rough downtown neighborhood in Rochester, New

York. She'd skipped school to travel south and join the Freedom Riders and march with Martin Luther King. When he was assassinated in April the previous year, Jam fell apart.

During her involvement in the marches, she met several sisters from the congregation who were also marching for civil rights. With their support, she returned to high school, graduated, and attended cosmetology school. Once she confided in Maggie that, while she struggled with the rigid structure of her religious vows, the dedication to social justice she found in the community beckoned her in. As she'd said, "I found my family, even if I look like the black sheep."

Now she smiled warmly at Maggie. "Hey, did I get the time wrong for your haircut this morning?"

Maggie slapped her forehead. "Oh dear. I completely lost track of that. Am I too late?"

"No, let's do it now."

They hurried off to Jam's room.

Leaning over the sink as she enjoyed the delicious scalp massage, Maggie drifted into a reverie. Just being cared for so gently by Jam lulled her into letting go of the tight rein she'd held on her emotions. Unbidden, tears flowed with the water that ran along her face and swirled down the drain. Jam squeezed out what water was left in Maggie's already short hair, then rubbed it vigorously with a soft terry towel.

Maggie's raw emotions bubbled to the surface. Her shoulders shook as the towel hung down, concealing her face.

"Sorry, was I too rough?" Jam knelt in front of her and raised one corner of the towel.

Maggie wiped her face. "No. Not at all. I'm just dealing with some tough problems right now."

"You know hairstylists observe the seal of confession, right? Before they bestow us with our shiny new shears, they force us to sign a document, 'Writ of Confidentiality.' In blood. Which we extract with our shiny new shears."

Maggie's shoulders shook with a mix of crying and laughing.

"Stop." She managed a grin. "Thanks." She sat in front of the bathroom mirror.

"It's cool." Jam tossed the towel on the counter and waved a pair of shears at the mirror. "My symbol of discretion."

"I can't really talk about it." Maggie's throat tightened.

"It's cool." Jam quietly worked, trimming her hair into its pixie cut. "My little bit of mutiny," she snickered, pulling out a can of styling spray.

"You rebel, you." Maggie wiped a last tear and smiled into the mirror. Jam watched her, so she quickly looked away.

"I don't have to be holding my shears of secrecy to be in accord with the writ. Anytime, Maggie."

The lump that had formed in her throat blocked her from speaking for a moment. She nodded. "Thanks, Jam." *Why am I so fragile?*

She could deal with difficult situations, she could deal with angry people, she could deal with disappointment. But dealing with indecision had always been her struggle. When it came to wrestling with choices, she was at the Olympic level. Weighing all her options, calculating ramifications, projecting outcomes played in each decision. But none had ever involved her heart. Love was a factor this math teacher wasn't familiar with.

She looked down at her hands. "I'm...I have feelings for someone. Deep feelings."

"Damn." Jam set down the spray can and leaned back against the counter. "Details, sister."

"Have you met Marty D'Amato?"

"Yeah, the Italian cop. At least it's mutual."

"Good God, you, too?"

"Anybody knows who's within ten feet of him when he's around you. You, however, have been quite sly."

"Good. So, I'm discerning right now."

Jam folded her arms, giving her a hard look. "Is this a fair fight?"

"What do you mean?"

"I know you too well, Maggie. You will give God more of a fighting chance than D'Amato."

Maggie pursed her lips. "That's what Jesse said."

"Jesse's wise. Look, you're one of the most spiritual, dedicated people I know. But life outside the convent can also be spiritual and dedicated. I know this for a fact. In addition to the Writ, I also carry a diploma from the College of Hard Knocks. My faith was what got me through some tough shit."

Maggie's stomach flip-flopped. *Life outside the convent. Was that because the convent had been so safe and secure for the last ten years?*

"Leaving presents so many challenges—big and small. For the last ten years, I haven't had to pick out a different outfit every day. I've had a secure job, a place to live, no bills to pay. I didn't even have to think about what to have for breakfast. What would life be like without that security? Can I make it on my own?" She wrapped her arms around her stomach.

Jam rubbed her shoulder. "I know it's scary out there. I've lived it, but I made it. And with a lot less going for me than you have." She picked up a comb, fluffing Maggie's hair as she styled it.

Maggie bit her lip. Scary was right. Another benefit to living such an insular life was its emotional protection. Insulating her from the sorrow underlying every visit with her parents. Insulating her from Courtney's abyss of guilt. Was it because leaving would go against her father's wishes? Was she being disloyal to her family? Was she being unfaithful to her vows? To God? What about life with Marty? Her heart soared at the thought of him. Perhaps that was a clue.

Jam spoke as if reading her mind. "Listen to your heart. Don't 'should' on yourself."

Maggie chortled.

"Seriously, lots of people 'should' on us from the time we're little kids. 'You should do this. You shouldn't do that.' You can't live someone else's vocation for them."

"Or be the sacrificial child to God."

"Amen, sister," Jam shouted. She picked up the styling spray, shook it, and sprayed a mist around Maggie's short hair. "You need to do something fun to take your mind off your troubles. Shopping is always a good antidote to a confused state of mind over possible life-changing events. Call Jesse and go shopping. By the way, what are you wearing as her maid of honor?"

"My habit, of course. At least it will be my modified—."

"What? Girl, you can't wear that! It's a wedding! You need a dress. Jesse can help you."

"I am a Sister of St. Joseph."

"Yeah, so what?

"So, I have to dress like one."

"Man, you are deep into this shi—" Jam frowned at her in the mirror. "Stuff. Go call Jesse. Go dress shopping. Try on a pretty dress. Think of it as practice for dating Marty. A habit or a pretty dress? Religious life or marriage? Holy Mary, that's a great metaphor."

Maggie smiled and patted her hand. "I'm not sure you're a good influence on me, Jam."

Jam nudged her. "Go. Now. Call Jesse."

Chapter Twenty-Five

When Joe walked through the door, Jesse jerked forward, dropping the book she was reading to the floor. She wanted to run to him, jump in his arms, and wrap her arms and legs around him. But Joe's green eyes were dark when he glanced at her then looked away. The energy she'd felt drained through her like a running faucet.

"Hi, Joe." She uncurled her legs, picked up her book, and rose from the corner of the sofa. Meeting him in the kitchen, she stood before him, searching his eyes. She caressed his face, and some of his anger melted away.

"It's not that easy," he said.

"I know." She pulled her hand away.

"Don't you get it? I am so afraid of losing you." His eyes glistened.

"I get it." She ached for him to hold her.

"You're putting a ghost ahead of me," he said, his voice raspy.

Her breath hitched. Is that what he thought?

"We're getting married in less than two weeks. Has that been on your mind at all?"

She flinched.

"I thought not."

"I'm sorry, Joe. This encounter with Timmy has thrown me for a loop."

"Will there always be a ghost? Some spirit who wedges between us?"

She recoiled, and anger flashed, burning her gut. "I don't call these spirits to me. They just show up. I didn't ask for this damn curse. I can't control them. What the hell do you want me to do?

"You can't control them, but you can control you—what you do, how your respond. God, Jesse, it's not the damn ghosts I object to. It's the danger they always put you in. Twice now I've almost lost you—you almost died." His voice broke. "I don't want that to happen again."

"Joe, it's just Timmy. I don't see any danger here. I just have to figure out how he died. Without that answer, he'll never rest and the Keegans will never find peace, either. And neither will I. That's the only way Timmy will leave me alone."

He looked at her, weighing her words. "Is this what our life will be? Ghosts appearing so you have to deal with other people's problems?"

The floor seemed to tilt; she grabbed the counter to steady herself. "I don't know, Joe. I don't have that answer. Maybe Timmy is the last one. But I can't promise that."

His eyes were dark with anger. And maybe fear.

The words stuck in her throat, and she had to force them out. "Do you want to call off the wedding?"

The look he shot her might as well have been a spear. He slammed out the door.

Oh my God. She sank to the floor.

SUNLIGHT HAD CHASED the last of the storm clouds but brought unbearable humidity. Jesse pulled at her blouse to loosen it from her skin, and she could feel her hair curling into spirals. The thought of food made her stomach lurch, but she knew Courtney needed to eat. She decided to grill her favorite—Zweigle's white hots—for dinner. She needed some comfort food tonight.

Courtney was already sitting at the kitchen table when Jesse carried in the plate with the hot dogs. She saw a bowl of potato chips and a plate of sliced tomatoes and dill pickles on the table.

"Thanks, Courtney."

Courtney just nodded.

She set the plate down and poured water in their glasses. She desperately wanted that last Genny Cream Ale, but after Courtney's binge the previous night, she knew better. Getting drunk sounded appealing to her tonight, and she felt more sympathetic toward Courtney than she had when she was cleaning up vomit.

Jesse had to take small bites and force them down, her throat ached with sobs she couldn't release. She was grateful for their silence, because eating was tough enough without having to make conversation. She started when Courtney spoke.

"All these years I've thought Timmy's disappearance was my fault. That I'd just forgotten about him." She dropped her head in her hands.

"But you did check on him, Courtney. You were keeping an eye on him." Jesse rested her bun-wrapped hot dog on the plate.

"Yes." Looking up, Courtney cocked her head. "If Timmy had come back to the boat, he would have come right by me. Even if I'd been asleep, he would have hugged me, or at least patted my hand. He definitely would have checked in with me, because he needed permission to sit in the boat."

"Mrs. Williamson confirmed that you were diligent. You kept checking on him." She rubbed her forehead. "Did you know Timmy was with them the day he disappeared?"

Courtney thought for a moment. "I guess I don't remember hearing that. But I was only twelve, so there was a lot my parents didn't tell me."

Jesse's mind whirled with conflicting thoughts. Mr. Williamson's tender care for his wife. His generous offer of taking them skiing around the lake. His affection for the Keegan family. His sickly wife. Mrs. Williamson's glassy eyes once he'd given her the medication. Then, his cruel remark, so out of character.

Her stomach flip-flopped.

Then Joe walked through the door, and her heart joined in the dance.

"Hey, Joe, the hots are still hot." Courtney got up to get another plate.

Jesse was grateful for Courtney's unusual kindness since she had no idea what to say in that moment. She smiled at him, but he glanced away.

"I'll eat after I shower. Thanks, Courtney." He nodded to them and went upstairs.

Courtney nodded then jumped up when the phone rang. "That's probably Mom checking on how the job's going. I trust you'll keep what happened last night confidential."

"I doubt your parents want me around to chat, but, yes, I'll keep it confidential."

Courtney grabbed the receiver from the harvest-gold phone hanging on the wall next to the back door.

"Jesse, it's Maggie." Courtney held out the phone, her face stony.

It will take her a long time to break old habits. Like her jealousy of her sister." She took the phone from Courtney. If only she could pour out her hurt and her heart to Maggie right now. But she had to hold it together for the time being. "Hey, Mags, what's up?"

"Apparently, I need to go shopping."

Jesse held the phone out and looked at it as if she could see Maggie at the other end. Placing the receiver against her ear again she asked, "Who is this, really?"

"I know. Jam has been on my case. So, do you have any free time tomorrow?"

Jesse eyed the stack of curriculum materials stacked precariously on one end of the kitchen table. A mountain of research she'd hoped to conquer during her quiet stay at the cottage. Her agenda for tomorrow was creating lesson plans for a new unit she'd be teaching in the fall. Plus, if she went shopping with Maggie, that would leave Courtney here alone. But Courtney seemed better. The visit with Mrs. Williamson surely had assuaged some of the guilt she'd carried for the last fifteen years. And Jesse missed Maggie. "What time should I pick you up?"

After settling the details for the shopping trip, Jesse returned to the table.

"He mostly says, 'I love you.'" Courtney concentrated on the apple she was slicing.

Jesse looked at her, then at the stairs. "Joe? I guess he does."

"No. Timmy. When I hear him. He mostly says, 'I love you, Courtney.'"

"ARE you going to wash the pattern off that plate?"

Courtney's voice jarred Jesse back to the present. "Oh, sorry. Here you go." She handed her the plate. All the while they worked, Jesse had one ear cocked for Joe's reappearance. *What should I say to him? Apologize? For what? Make him apologize? For what?* Somehow, they had to sort through this and get past the hurt.

She almost dropped the plate she was washing when she heard Joe's footsteps.

"What's wrong with you tonight?" Courtney grabbed the plate from her.

Jesse turned to Joe. "Hi."

He nodded.

"Ready to eat?"

He nodded again. "I'll get it myself."

Courtney looked from one to the other. "Okay. I'm going to run to the store for some beer."

Jesse opened her mouth to object.

"Beer, Jesse. Not gin." She grabbed her purse and left.

Jesse sat at the table across from Joe. Through the open porch window, she heard a motorboat speeding by. A crow scolding from the elm that shaded the cottage. Kids splashing in the water. Normal sounds for normal people. When had her life veered from normal?

"I can't believe you'd even question that." Joe's voice was low, his gaze on the table.

Jesse scrambled to understand. Question whether she was normal? How did he know what she was thinking? Surely being a ghost empath wasn't considered normal. "Joe, I know I'm not normal." The words flew out before she realized she'd said them. She slapped her hand across her mouth.

He squinted at her. "What?"

She jumped up. "Holy Mary, I see flipping ghosts." She paced to the living room and back to the table, flailing her arms. "I know I'm not normal. I can't help that I'm not normal." She pressed her eyes shut to stop the tears. She would not cry.

"I don't know what the hell you're talking about. That's not even what I meant. See, even when I want to talk about us, ghosts get in the way."

"What did you mean?" She collapsed into her chair.

He looked out at the lake and back at her. "I can't believe you'd question whether or not I want to go through with the wedding. How could you even think that?"

"Well, look at us. You think I care more about ghosts than I do about you. You couldn't be further from the truth. I love you, Joe. I love you so much that when I think about you, I feel like I'll explode with happiness. When I hear your voice, my heart beats like a crazy drum solo." Her voice shook. "I don't know how to show you how much I love you." She sniffled and wiped her nose with a paper napkin. "But sometimes I wonder how you can love me. I'm a stinking mess."

"So you question my love for you." His voice was flat.

"No, no I don't. I just...I don't know." She rubbed her forehead, trying to wipe away the ache that stabbed behind her eyes. *What can I say that won't be wrong?*

The sound of tires on gravel sounded from behind the cottage. Courtney was back.

"Look, tomorrow I have to leave for that conference in Rochester I told you about. I'll be gone for about three days. When I get back we can talk."

Jesse nodded. Maybe not saying anything was best right now.

Chapter Twenty-Six

J esse pulled down her sunglasses to peer over them. The bright sun was one reason she wore them, the other was to hide her eyes, red from crying and lack of sleep. Usually, when Maggie was out in public, she wore her habit. Today, she was dressed in what she called her "civvies": tan capris and a short-sleeved madras button-down blouse. A white silk kerchief covered her head and draped over her shoulders, and she wore large, dark sunglasses. She could have been cast as Audrey Hepburn in *Charade*.

"You're looking rather dour this morning," Maggie said.

"Joe and I had a fight. Our worst ever."

"Oh no, Jess. What about? I mean, it's none of my business, but if you want to talk about it."

How could she tell Maggie they were fighting over Timmy's ghost? "Just pre-wedding stress. It'll be fine."

At one time, they could talk about anything. Timmy's ghost was slowly destroying her dearest relationships. She fought down resentment of him and forced a cheerful expression. "Hey, let's go shop!"

She couldn't believe her luck at finding a parking space right on

Main St. She loved the challenge of parallel parking, and beamed at Maggie when she slid into the slot perfectly on the first try. "Groovy, right?"

"It's the little things, Graham."

As Jesse exited her Beetle, a woman in a flowered dress and sunhat ran along the sidewalk, waving. "Hello there, Jesse." Her voice was shrill, echoing along the street. A tall, sandy-haired man in his thirties tried to catch up with her. Though he was tall with broad shoulders, he juggled packages and bags that slowed him down.

She tried to place the woman. Ethel. From her shower. But what was her last name? Monica had never said, just Ethel. *Oh no. And this day had started out so fun.* "Hello, Ethel." She took the woman's offered hand.

"Have you had any luck with your investigation? Are you any closer to finding the monster who kidnapped my boy?" Though she still spoke loudly, the catch in her voice made the unresolved grief sharp.

The man caught up with her, finally corralling the packages in his muscular arms. "What's wrong, Aunt Ethel?"

"Oh, this is my nephew, Eddie Morgan. Eddie, this is Jesse Graham and—" She leaned forward peering into Maggie's face. "Is that you, Sister Angelina?"

Maggie smiled wanly. "Yes, hello. It's nice to see you again."

Ethel turned to her nephew. "Eddie, Jesse is reopening the kidnapping case of—" She caught her breath and, like a magician yanking a rabbit out of a hat, made a handkerchief appear from the bosom of her dress. She pressed it to her nose. "She's going to find the monster who kidnapped Michael."

Passing shoppers slowed, looking in their direction. A stout woman with thick glasses pulled her little boy closer. Her gaze already magnified by thick lenses, the bespectacled woman's eyes expanded until Jesse expected them to pop out and hang by springs like a trick pair.

"Aunt Ethel, we need to go." Eddie grabbed her arm and tried to move her along the sidewalk, but Ethel was like a boulder.

Jesse shifted from one foot to the other. The day was summer warm and sticky, already. She didn't need Ethel to ramp up the heat with her gossip. Hopefully, her deodorant would endure this incursion. She glanced at Maggie, who tugged her scarf forward as she studied the window of the hardware store through her dark sunglasses.

"How is your investigation coming along?" Ethel leaned into Jesse's face.

"Well, I've learned more about the case, but I haven't really discovered anything the police didn't already know." Jesse had barely had enough energy to get out of bed this morning, and if it hadn't been for Maggie's invitation, she might still be there with the covers over her head. She wished she were under those covers right now. How much more of this woman could she take?

But Ethel was just getting started. "I'm so glad you're digging into this. The cops just gave up on finding that monster. Just gave up!" Her voice rose in fury. "I know you had luck solving the Helen Cavanaugh cold case. And with the help of a ghost." She nodded at the small group that now surrounded them.

Could this get any worse?

Ethel was on a roll. "Yes, Jesse Graham sees ghosts."

Maggie studied the window. Eddie studied Jesse.

If "kidnapped" and "cops" caught their attention, "ghost" was like flypaper, and eavesdroppers were all sticking around to hear more. Murmurs and sidelong glances chugged through the group like Timmy's engine.

Jesse held up her hands. "I am not a police officer or a detective. My solving the Helen Cavanaugh mystery was pretty much a fluke. I'm not officially investigating anything."

"But a ghost is appearing to you, right? One of the little boys who was taken?" Ethel leaned in, her hands curved like claws as she reached toward Jesse.

"I need to go now." Jesse grabbed Maggie by the elbow and pulled her down the street.

With one mind, they slipped into the bookstore, the bell above the door chiming their presence. The cool interior air refreshed their bodies, and being surrounded by books would surely raise their spirits.

"Good God in heaven," Jesse gasped, leaning against the door.

"Are you all right, Jess? That was awful." Maggie slid her glasses down her nose.

Jesse glanced out the window before she abandoned the door.

"I'm okay. At least I will be once I erase my brain of that encounter. Coming into town is getting trickier these days."

"You know you'll replay this all day, right?" Maggie pushed her glasses back up her nose.

"All I need is a good book. I've been dying to buy Michael Crichton's latest, *The Andromeda Strain.* A world threatened by an unknown agent that threatens to destroy humanity. Kinda puts my woes in perspective."

"I'm looking for *The Long Loneliness* by Dorothy Day. I want to pick up a copy for the convent library." Maggie headed toward the spirituality and religion section.

Perusing the shelves for almost an hour settled Jesse's mind. After selecting an armload of books, she found Maggie reading a copy of *Jane Eyre.*

"Those Bronte sisters were quite the romantics." *Stop it, Graham.* If only she could eat her words. She'd promised not to try to influence—or make light of—Maggie's discernment.

Maggie shut the book and set it back on the shelf. "Let's check out."

"Sounds good to me. I think I bought half of Lakeside Book Shop's Agatha Christie section." As they headed to the register, Jesse checked the street. Ethel had disappeared, and only a man walking his dog and a woman with her ice-cream-eating six-year-old daughter were visible. "Looks like the coast is clear."

They purchased their books and headed outside.

"Let's put these books in your car and head to Shelby's across the street." Maggie nodded toward a department store.

Hefting the books to one side as she dug her keys out of her pocket, Jesse stopped. "Oh, no. On top of everything else, did I get a ticket?" After setting the books in the back seat, she tugged at the paper tucked beneath her windshield wiper.

"It doesn't look like a ticket. Maybe someone dinged your car and left a note." Maggie circled the car, examining it for dents.

"Crap. It's not a ticket." The scrap of napkin trembled as she read the scrawled message. "Go away." She inspected the sidewalk on both sides of the street, but the few pedestrians visible were strolling along, paying no attention to her. All the cars nearby were empty. No one even slouched down trying to hide.

Maggie stood beside her. "Oh, Jesse. Not another one."

"It's somebody involved in the abductions. I'm sure of it." Jesse crumpled the napkin.

"Wait! You need to take that to the police. It's evidence that someone is threatening you."

Jesse balled the note in her hand, ready to throw it in a nearby trashcan, but Maggie grabbed it.

"You need to face up to this, Jess. Somebody is threatened by the questions you've been asking. And Ethel's little display here didn't help."

"Well, I'm not going to stop asking questions." She looked at the note as Maggie smoothed it out. "And I'm not going away."

The police station was abuzz with phones ringing, cops interviewing witnesses, and cops leading suspects to the interrogation rooms. Along the wall, a menagerie of people waited. A man in a Rolling Stones T-shirt held a bag of ice over his left eye; another wearing all black slept with his head tilted against the wall, snores emanating from his slack-jawed mouth. A woman with hair teased into a dangerously tall beehive, rhinestone earrings dangling to her shoulders but missing several stones, a red tube top, black leather hot pants, and white go-go boots scowled at them as they walked past.

Jesse and Maggie approached the sergeant at the desk and waited while he finished a call. Jesse shifted from foot to foot.

Maggie kept her sunglasses on while she casually scanned the desks. Did she look relieved or disappointed?

The sergeant finally hung up the phone. "What can I help you ladies with today?"

"Is Marty D'Amato in?" Color rose in Maggie's face as she spoke.

"He's out on a call. Can I help?"

Maggie glanced at the people sitting on the bench along the wall. Speaking in a low tone, she held out the napkin by one corner. "Miss Graham got another threatening note."

"*Another* threatening note?" He took the corner she offered, holding it up to examine it. "Looks like a prank to me." He handed it back to Maggie.

This was all too much. Jesse pulled on Maggie's arm. "C'mon. He's right—it's probably some kid's prank." She wanted to get out of the station. She didn't want the note to be real. She was tired of being threatened. When would life be just ordinary? Do the laundry, write lesson plans, drink a Genny on the back porch. When would she get to be bored?

Maggie shook the note at him. "No! Look, Sergeant, you need to test this for fingerprints or whatever you do. This is the second note she's gotten."

He smirked at her. "Look, lady, you wanna file a complaint? I can give you a form."

"I don't want a form. I want you to take this threat seriously." Maggie's voice had risen, and she shook with anger.

"Settle down, lady."

Maggie leaned into the desk. Her voice dropped, her words staccato. "Don't you call me lady. Look, this is serious. Someone is threatening Miss Graham's life. Don't dismiss it like some prank." She practically growled at him.

"You tell him, sister," the beehive woman on the bench said.

Jesse chuckled. "Yes, she's a 'sister,' all right." She glanced at the sergeant. "Perhaps not a lady. You don't want to tick off this Irish girl."

"You both better settle down or I'll have you waiting right along with these miscreants," he bellowed. Other cops turned to see what the noise was about. One rested his hand on his revolver.

Maggie glared at the sergeant until he reluctantly reached over for a pad of paper. She stared him down until he wrote down what she dictated: "Marty, Jesse got another note." He glared back. "Ya' happy now?"

"Thank you, Sergeant." Maggie's words were slow and precise. She tucked the napkin into her pocket.

"We're leaving now. Come on, Mags." Jesse took her elbow and steered her toward the door.

"If you girls ever need a job, look me up down on Maple and Main. Ask for Peaches," the beehive woman said as they passed.

"Thank you, Peaches. I may need a job soon," Maggie said politely.

Jesse burst out laughing. She doubled over, her guffaws filling the hall.

The sleeping man stirred, looking at her through bloodshot eyes. He turned his head and peered in her direction as if that would clear his vision.

"You two get out now or I'll arrest you for disturbing the peace!" the sergeant yelled.

Jesse pushed Maggie through the front door and out into the street. As her laughter erupted, Jesse grabbed the light post to hold herself up. She wiped her tears as she gasped for air.

"Is that your career choice, Mags? A Sister of St. Joseph or a hooker?" She held her stomach while she shook with laughter.

Maggie looked back toward the police station door. "She was a prostitute?"

"Oh my God, Mags! You are such an innocent!"

"I didn't know we even had them in Seneca Corners."

"That's one of the things I love about you. The world is such a good place in your opinion." She looped her arm through Maggie's and headed down the street. "Let's go shop."

"On one condition."

"What's that?"

"You promise to give this note to Marty." She handed the napkin to Jesse.

Jesse withdrew her arm and stared at it. "Maybe the sergeant was right. Maybe it was a prank."

"Promise me."

"Why don't you give it to him?" Jesse waggled her eyebrows.

"This isn't funny."

"Okay. I promise. On my honor." Crossing her heart, she held up the Girl Scout salute. "Now, what do you want to shop for?"

"Dresses."

Chapter Twenty-Seven

❧❀❧

"Dresses? For whom?"

Maggie shrugged. Jam had made this sound so easy. So why was her stomach churning? "I just want to try on a dress. For fun."

Jesse's mouth dropped open. She snapped it shut. "Okay. I'm in. Let's go look at dresses." She rummaged through her purse. "Where should I put this damn note?" She finally tucked it away in an inside pocket.

Shelby's was crowded with vacationers from nearby cottages searching for summer sales. Most of them were milling around the shorts and swimwear departments. Smooth jazz from Rochester's native son Chuck Mangione serenaded them as she and Jesse made their way to the women's department where two clerks chatted while they organized new stock. The younger one who wore powder blue bell bottoms and a silk paisley top turned to them.

"May I help you?"

Maggie gawked at the array of choices. *Where do I even begin? Why am I even beginning?* She drew her lips in as if to keep a secret.

Jesse whispered, "You look a little dazed." She turned to the clerk. "My friend would like to try on some dresses. Size six. For a fancy party."

Maggie let out her breath.

"Sure, my name's Amber, and I'm happy to help you today. I know some styles that would look great on you." She smiled at Maggie.

Maggie stepped back. *I haven't worn clothes like this in over ten years.* Her heart raced.

Jesse put her arm around her shoulders and pushed her along as they followed Amber.

After looking through several racks, Amber selected five options. Maggie eliminated two: a silver lamé with a low neckline and an off-the-shoulder peasant-blouse style.

Her fingers slid along the silk fabric of a deep blue maxi with a white belt. *My God, it's heavenly. More heavenly than my habit.*

Stop!

Then she studied the lacy pattern of a burgundy cocktail dress with a cap sleeve and full-skirt. Finally, she held up a classic princess style shantung dress in rosy pink.

"Oh, my word." She eyed Jesse and Amber. "This requires a lot of work."

Jesse grinned. "But it's fun, right?"

Maggie smiled softly. "Yes, I guess so." She felt queasy.

Amber bundled her into a fitting room. "Do you need help?"

The clang of the hangers against the metal hook made Maggie jump. "No, no, I'm fine."

"Just call if you do. I'll be right outside.

"Do you want me to help you?" Jesse stood behind Amber.

Maggie needed to be alone. "Not yet. I'll let you know."

Instead of undressing, Maggie sat on the padded, velvet stool and looked at her reflection in the full-length mirror. Jam made this sound like it would be so much fun, but right now, she felt like vomiting. Was she being unfaithful to her vows to even do this? Why was she even here? But she knew why. She was trying on more than dresses.

"Mags? You need help?" Jesse called.

"No, I'm good." *Liar.*

Her fingers trembled as she tried to undo the top fabric-covered button of the navy-blue silk dress. The button kept slipping out of her grasp. She finally clutched it, but the buttonhole was too tight. She worked the button until her fingers stung. *Maybe this is a sign. Maybe I need to leave right now.* She gave it one more go, and magically, the button pushed through.

When she emerged in the dress, Jesse's mouth dropped.

"Holy Mary! You look gorgeous in that!"

Amber directed Maggie to a small platform before a full-length, three-way mirror. Her eyes were wide as she took in her own image.

Was it delight or fear?

"Turn around, Mags. Get the full effect," Jesse urged.

Maggie did a half-turn in each direction, nodded, and stepped down. She'd never had a panic attack, but she might be close now.

Amber led her through the curtain and, mercifully, undid the buttons along the back of the dress. Then she slipped out.

Maggie took a deep breath and stepped out of the blue silk and hung it back on the hanger.

The second dress, the burgundy lace number, had a zipper. *Just don't think. Just put it on.* She donned it easily and stepped out of the dressing room.

"Another winner. You look stunning," Jesse said.

Maggie nodded her thanks. This time, she did a full turn and checked herself from all angles. In the mirror, she caught Jesse's wink. Stepping down, she returned to the fitting room.

The third dress was the rosy pink shantung dress. Her skin glowed against the fabric. She turned around a couple of times and smiled into the mirror at Jesse. *I do look stunning. I feel stunning.* "I certainly feel much different than when I wear my..." she glanced at Amber "... uniform."

Jesse chuckled. "I'll bet you do."

Amber beamed at her. "Any one of these will look beautiful on you."

"Thank you for your help, Amber." Maggie stepped off the platform.

"Which dress can I wrap up for you? Or would you like to try on some others?"

Maggie backed up a step. "I need to think about it. I'm not sure right now."

"I can hold them for you for three days. That should give you time to decide." Amber took the two from the hook in the fitting room. "Just hand that one out when you've taken it off."

"You don't have to—" Maggie began.

Amber waved her hand. "It's no problem at all."

"No, but I'm not going—" Maggie said.

Amber clucked. "You are so sweet. Really, it's no extra work for me." And she walked away toward the service counter.

Maggie grabbed Jesse's arm and pulled her close. "I'm not going to buy any of these," she hissed.

"Don't worry. People come in and try things on all the time without ever intending to buy them," Jesse said, carefully studying the skirt of a green cocktail dress.

"I just wanted to try..." She held her arms out like a beseeching penitent.

"Hey, it's cool. You gave her something to do besides count all the stock that just came in. Helping you was much more fun."

"It's not that." Maggie flopped on the small bench near a three-way mirror.

Jesse knelt in front of her. "Then what is it, Mags?"

"Jam thought this would be a good idea. She thinks I should wear something pretty, not my habit, to your wedding. She thought trying on dresses might be a rehearsal for..."

"Trying out a life with Marty," Jesse finished for her.

Maggie nodded and pressed her fingertips against her throbbing temples. "Making a life decision isn't as easy as buying a dress."

"FOOD HELPS EVERYTHING. Especially greasy food washed down with a cold beer." Jesse took a deep draught of her Genny Cream Ale.

Maggie laughed, then sobered. "Thanks, Jess." She had finally stopped shaking.

"For what? Gulping my beer?"

"You goof. For cheering me up. I've felt like a teenager lately. I don't get it. I've never been nearly as emotional as you."

"Me? I'm a stoic."

Maggie almost spit out her Orange Crush. "You're kidding, right?

"There they are! The two rabble-rousers who shook things up at the station today." Marty's voice rang across Tony's Restaurant as diners swiveled in their chairs to see who was in trouble.

Maggie sat up and brushed at imaginary crumbs on her blouse.

He sidled over to their booth, shaking the handcuffs hanging from his belt. "I shoulda' known you'd still be hanging around, bustin' up the town."

"Hi, Marty!" Jesse put her arms out to be cuffed.

Maggie slid over, and Marty grinned at her as he slipped in beside her.

"Hi, Maggie."

When he said her name, it was like a prayer.

Maggie smiled at him so wide she wondered if she looked like the Cheshire Cat. Try as she might, she couldn't stop herself. "Hi, Marty."

Jesse picked up her beer took a long swig. "Well, I'd better get going."

But Marty had already signaled the waitress and ordered another round. "Sit down, *bella*. I'm going to interrogate both of you. So, my sergeant said two dames came in to see me..."

"Dames!" Jesse growled, her fists clenched. "What a jerk."

"No argument from me. Anyway, he said you raised a ruckus."

"You should have seen Maggie put him in his place. It was great."

He beamed at Maggie, and she frowned. Her Irish was up again.

"He wouldn't listen to us." She pulled a face.

Jesse laughed. "Maggie, you look like a bulldog."

"I don't know why we're laughing. It isn't funny. Show him the note, Jess."

"Geez. Fine." She withdrew the note from her purse. Laying it on the table in front of Marty. "It was under my windshield wiper. I thought it was a ticket. Now I wish it had been."

Marty studied the note. "This napkin could be from a dozen restaurants along Main Street. Where were you parked?"

"Across from Shelby's."

"Not far from Woolworth's, but Greta's Kitchen is right there, too." He stared at the napkin as if it would give up its secrets. "Maggie's right. This isn't funny. Especially after this guy slashed your tires."

"At least you're staying at the cottage with Courtney for now," Maggie said.

Jesse squirmed and looked away, picturing Courtney vomiting her guts out.

"You're at the cottage? I didn't know. That means this guy also doesn't know you're there."

"True. That makes me feel safer," she said.

"Makes me feel better, too." Maggie smiled at her.

The waitress brought their drinks, and Marty paid her. After he returned his wallet to his back pocket, he casually draped his arm across the back of the booth behind Maggie.

"Okay, well, I'm heading back." Jesse started to rise, but Marty caught her hand. She slid back into the booth.

"*Bella*, why are you staying at the cottage?"

She looked at Maggie, asking for permission. Maggie nodded at her.

"I'm trying to connect with Timmy."

"Is that a good idea?" Marty scratched the five o'clock shadow along his jawline.

"Yes. Ghosts usually contact me because they need to remedy something from their life. Remember, like Helen? And the Seneca Woman? I think Timmy wants something resolved about his death."

Marty shifted and removed his arm from behind Maggie. Leaning his forearms on the table, he widened his eyes at Jesse. "Do you think that's a good idea?"

"Of course, why wouldn't I?" She sipped her beer.

He rolled his eyes back toward Maggie and raised his eyebrows.

"What, Marty? Just say it."

He lowered his voice. "What if what Timmy wants to tell you isn't... pleasant?"

Maggie crossed her arms and sank back against the red leather booth.

"I don't know what you mean," Jesse said.

He shifted in his seat and checked out the nearby diners.

Voices rose and fell in the natural rhythm of a crowded restaurant. A woman two tables over laughed, the man in the booth behind them argued with his wife. Kids at the next table squabbled over a Tonka truck while their mother tried to distract them with "Just one more bite."

"Maybe not knowing what happened is easier." He turned to Maggie and took her hand.

Her shoulders rose as she inhaled deeply, then puffed out her breath. "You mean if Timmy had been abducted."

He nodded and squeezed her hand.

Jesse leaned in. "But that never showed up in the report. There was absolutely no mention of his disappearance being connected to the kidnappings." She looked around and lowered her voice. "We combed through the file."

Marty took a generous swig of his beer. He set the bottle down and picked at the label. "I've been digging around in the archives." He glanced at Maggie again. "Mr. Keegan was on the city council at the time of the abductions. He'd just voted down an increase in hiring for the police force. That could be why they were so rough on him when they questioned him. Then, according to my source, to make it up to him, there was never any mention in the press of Timmy's disappearance being connected to the abductions."

"Oh no." Maggie buried her face in her hands.

Marty wrapped an arm around her, pulling her close. "I'm sorry." He kissed the top of her head.

Jesse was glad they were in the farthest corner of the restaurant. She studied the diners. No one was paying any attention to them. Maggie never liked to make a scene in public, except maybe with belligerent police sergeants. Being a Sister of St. Joseph, she took her role as an ambassador of the Church very seriously. At this moment, any onlooker wouldn't believe that, seeing her wrapped in the arms of one of Seneca Corners's finest.

"So, Timmy could have been kidnapped." Maggie wiped her eyes with a napkin.

Marty shrugged the shoulder she wasn't leaning against. "It's possible. But not for certain." He looked at Jesse with a puppy-dog look that shouted, "Help me out here."

"I think what Marty means is, if Timmy continues to appear to me, it may lead to answers we never wanted." Jesse raised her eyebrows at him, and he nodded.

Maggie sat up and reached for another napkin from the chrome holder. "The one comfort my family has taken all these years is that he drowned." She gave a wry laugh. "That's odd to say, but drowning was easier to deal with, you know?"

"I know, Mags." Jesse reached across the table for her hand.

Maggie sighed. "The truth shall set you free, right? No matter what happened to Timmy, I want to know. I want him to be at peace." She took the last sip of her Orange Crush. "I need to get back."

"I'll take you." His voice was as soft as a summer breeze.

Maggie nodded her thanks, and Marty looked at her with such tenderness, Jesse got teary-eyed.

"That will save you some backtracking, Jess," Maggie added quickly.

"You don't need to make excuses. I'd leave with him, too, if he looked at me like that. Call me tomorrow, okay?"

"Sure thing."

They slid out of the booth, and Maggie hugged her goodbye. Jesse wanted to say, "Don't do anything I wouldn't do," but that would have left endless possibilities.

Maggie stopped when they reached the front sidewalk. "Give Courtney my love."

"Yes, I will. Of course I will," she stammered.

Maggie frowned quizzically. "You okay?"

"Yes... I am." *Cool it Graham, a secret is a secret.* "'Night." She turned toward her car.

"Jess," Maggie called after her.

She turned back.

"Whatever Timmy tells you, it's best to know the truth."

Jesse nodded and walked to her car.

"The truth shall set you free," she whispered.

MAGGIE HELD herself stiffly in the passenger seat. If she relaxed, she would surely dissolve into a shuddering mass, judging by how her limbs tingled. Had it only been a few hours ago that she stood in front of the mirror at Shelby's and hardly recognized herself?

She looked at Marty's profile in the dashboard illumination. His scruffy whiskers, strong jawline, and Roman nose made her want to melt into him. What would it be like to have him in her life every day? To come home to him, to be there when he came home? To share a life, to share a bed? Perhaps to have—?

He glanced at her. "What are you looking at?" He laughed self-consciously.

She smiled and lowered her voice for her best Humphrey Bogart imitation. "I'm lookin' at you, kid."

He laughed. "No fair. I want to be lookin' at you."

"Okay," she whispered.

He swiveled his head to her, to the road, to her.

"What do you mean?"

"Maybe we could stop. For a few minutes."

He slowed down and pulled into a turnoff to a dirt road leading to someone's cottage. Shutting off the engine, he kept his hands on the steering wheel.

"Didn't you want to look at me?" She didn't recognize her own voice.

He turned and took her hand. "Every day of my life."

"I need to take this slowly. I'm not certain of anything. But I owe it to you to be open to possibilities."

"Okay. Slow it is."

"I don't know how to navigate these waters, Marty. I have one foot on the dock and one in the boat. A precarious position." She caressed the stubble along his chin. Although her mind urged, *stop*, her heart commanded *go*.

He leaned forward and kissed her, softly, tenderly.

She wanted more. Oh God, she wanted more. But, as she'd said, she needed to take this slowly. She sighed as he ran his hand along her arm and down her side. She laid her head on his shoulder, and he kissed the top of her head.

"This feels good, holding you, being with you." His husky voice broke the stillness.

"Yes." It was all she could offer for now.

He tipped her face up and covered her mouth with his. His lips moved slowly, enticing, inviting, but leaving the intensity up to her. Her lips parted, and he gently ran his tongue along her lips. She answered in kind. Finally, she pulled away, smiling softly.

"I'd better get you home."

His words startled her. *Home?* "Home is where the heart is, Marty. But you can take me back to the convent."

He grinned at her and started the engine. "First, I need to know one thing. Am I the dock or the boat?"

Chapter Twenty-Eight

❧❧❧

Jesse's heart sank as she pulled up to the cottage. Prickles stung the back of her neck and ran along her arms. She did not want another encounter with Mr. Becker. She scanned the yard but saw no movement, no one lurking. She studied the dark windows. *Please, Courtney, not again.* Her legs were leaden as she tried to turn and get out of the car. *For God's sake, hurry, Graham.*

The door was locked—just as it had been previously. She'd had a duplicate key made, and now she fumbled with her keychain looking for it. Grasping the key, she unlocked the door and swung it open. The full moon cast a silvery shadow across the kitchen counter and zigzagged to the floor.

"Courtney?" she called out. A soft buzzing hummed from the overhead light when she switched it on. She quickly locked the door. "Courtney?"

A note lay on the table. Jesse's pulse raced as she grabbed it. She glanced toward Courtney's room. Only darkness.

Jesse,

I'M OKAY, SO DON'T WORRY! I'm not going to get crazy drunk again. My roommate is visiting from San Francisco, so I'm staying with her tonight. I'm doing fine. See you tomorrow.

Courtney

She let out a long sigh and patted her chest to calm her heart. Dropping the note back on the table, she headed to the phone to call Joe. *Man, I miss him so much already. Even though we haven't sorted things out yet, I just need to hear his voice.* While she fished the number of his hotel out of her wallet, she hummed the Beach Boys' "Wouldn't It Be Nice." Wouldn't it be nice if only her wedding filled her mind? As she reached for the phone, it rang, the jangling loud in the empty, silent cottage.

Great minds think alike.

"Hi, Joe, I was just going to call you."

Silence.

"Joe? Are you there?"

She pressed her ear against the receiver as if it would help. "Hello? Joe? We must have a bad connection."

The silence on the other end was deafening. Exactly like those phone calls last summer. The ones that preceded being stalked and held at gunpoint, almost murdered, in her basement. She slammed the receiver down and backed away from the phone, as if that would distance her from the caller.

She checked the back door, ensuring the bolt lock had been thrown. Slapping her hand along the wall, she switched off the overhead light. Again, the glow of the moon cast eerie shadows across the countertop, the faucet reaching out like a black claw, the vase of daisies, a spidery web against the pearly Formica.

The jangling phone jarred the darkness. She jumped, stumbling against the stove, a burner knob carving into her hip. The clang was strident, and she clenched her teeth so hard, she bit the inside of her mouth.

She pressed the receiver to her ear. "Joe? Is that you?"

Silence. Then measured breathing.

She slammed the receiver down. Maybe it was Joe. Maybe it was a bad connection. Maybe she was imagining danger that didn't exist. But she had been here before, and her gut told her it was not Joe.

The phone rang again. Piercing. Insistent.

Fear erupted into anger, and she grabbed the receiver.

"Stop it! Whoever you are, stop bothering me!" Instead of the commanding voice she intended, her voice sounded shrill—and scared.

"Jess, are you all right?" The panic in Maggie's voice shot through the line.

"Oh my God, it's you." Jesse slid down the wall, gripping the receiver like a lifeline. She thumped to the floor on her butt and pulled her knees to her chin.

"What's going on? Is Courtney there with you?"

"No, she's staying in town tonight."

"Who did you think I was?"

"I just got two calls. I thought it was Joe. There was only silence. Like before, Maggie. Like last year when... Mags, it's freaking me out." Her voice shook as she spoke. Her whole body trembled.

"I'll call Marty. We'll be right there." The line went dead.

Jesse laid the receiver on the floor. If she didn't hang it up, he couldn't call her back. She remained curled up, her head resting on her knees. Whoever it was knew she was here. Probably followed her. Mr. Becker's face loomed in her mind. *Oh, my God.*

Beside her, the phone emitted a staccato *beep, beep, beep, beep* and she kicked her feet, scrambling to get away. Holding her hands over her ears, she could feel her heart pounding against her ribcage, a rhythm matching the insistent beep. The noise continued, but she didn't want to hang up the phone. Hanging up the phone would allow another call to come through.

The beeping was a jackhammer pounding into her brain. Was it getting louder? Faster? Even with her fingers jammed into her ears, it attacked. Her teeth ground against each other as cold terror surged along her neck and shoulders. She couldn't bear this constant beeping, even for a minute, so she replaced the receiver on the hook.

Easing up to her knees, she pulled back a corner of the curtain on the back door and peered into the dark yard. Not even a tree branch stirred in the still night. The moonlight that cast unnerving shadows inside magnified them ten times outside.

Was that someone by the tree? Did something move along the shed? Who was crouching beside her car?

Maggie would have to call Marty, he'd have to drive over to get her, and the cottage was twenty minutes away from the convent. It could be an hour or more before they arrived. If an assailant came to the cottage, Jesse was on her own.

I need to defend myself. Skimming the kitchen, she spotted the knife block tucked in the corner of the counter.

Mrs. Keegan took great pride in her expensive set of knives— "one in every size for every kind of job," she'd bragged. *Well, I'm going to need the biggest size tonight.*

She pulled out the butcher knife and stared at it. Would she really be able to use this against an assailant? She didn't know. Who knew she could shoot a man? But she had—in self-defense. If she'd protected herself once, she could do it again.

Who is after me? And why? Was this about the abductions? Or was this about Timmy? Or were they the same thing? She needed answers.

As if in answer, above her the train whistled in Timmy's room.

Chapter Twenty-Nine

E ach time her focus drifted from the back door to the stairs, she shook herself and resumed her stance.

After propping a kitchen chair against the door, she gripped the knife and stood, waiting. At first, she was frozen in place, but the engine whistle persisted, a siren song.

"Not now, Timmy," she whispered into the dark kitchen.

Above her, the train circled and circled in its spellbinding path. Hypnotic.

"Not now, Timmy," her voice was lighter, younger.

Come play with me. A whisper in her mind.

"Timmy," she protested in a singsong voice.

Where's Courtney? I want to play with Courtney. His voice quavered.

"Okay. I'll play with you." She dropped the knife on the counter and stomped to the stairs.

In Timmy's room, the train circled the track, its engine light a beacon in the dark.

"I'm here, Timmy. Where are you?" She rubbed her arms against the frigid air.

In the corner of the room, a soft glow wavered.

"Timmy?"

Where's my hat?

"I don't know." She sat cross-legged on the rug.

She has my hat.

"Who?"

Downstairs the resounding ring of the phone blasted through the dark. The glow disappeared as the room warmed.

Jesse shook her head, dazed. *What the hell?*

She unfolded herself and stood. *How is this happening?*

The phone continued to ring then stopped.

The knife! She'd left it on the counter.

She crept down the stairs, trying to remember where the creaks were. She surveyed the dark rooms, and, reassured she was still alone—except for Timmy—she grabbed the knife. She jumped when the phone rang again.

Without thinking, she picked it up and pressed it to her ear.

"Jesse? Are you there?"

"Oh my God, Joe!"

"I was worried when you didn't pick up a minute ago. Are you okay? I just wanted to check in. How did your shopping trip go?" His voice was warm and unconcerned.

Was it just today that she and Maggie had gone shopping? It seemed a lifetime ago.

"Joe, did you call earlier?"

"No, sorry. Our meetings just finished. Why?"

"Someone called. They didn't speak."

"What?" The warmth in his voice changed to alarm. "Who is there with you?"

"Right now, no one."

"My God. Call the police. It will take me two hours to drive back. I'll be there as fast as I can."

"No, Joe! Marty and Maggie—" But he had already hung up.

JESSE'S HEART skipped as a shadow moved across the curtain on the door. She backed into the living room, bumping into Mr. Keegan's recliner. Losing her balance, she fell into the leather chair, still gripping the knife.

A gloved hand punched through a windowpane and reached in, groping for the lock. Her heart reached a staccato beat. The intruder turned the lock and pushed against the door, but the chair she'd propped against it held. A muffled grunt sounded through the broken windowpane, and adrenaline shot through her as the man began slamming his weight against the stuck door, trying to burst through.

Running to the farthest bedroom, she crouched between the wall and the Keegans' double bed. The faint scent of Mrs. Keegan's lily of the valley perfume drifted to her as she tucked herself as far into the corner as possible. The flowery scent mocked her choice, churning her stomach. Why had she cornered herself here? Why hadn't she run out the front door through the porch? She could wake Mr. Williamson. He could call the police.

The intruder entered, each measured step punctuated by glass crunching into the linoleum. His labored breath preceded him as he crept forward into the cottage. He stopped in the hall just outside the bedroom, and she had the insane image of him sniffing the air like a wolf.

She clung to the butcher knife, holding it along her side.

The man was silent and still. Maybe he was playing with her, letting her fear ooze out until he could smell it and find her. Sweat rolled down her sides.

Her gaze darted to the window on the wall beside her. While it was big enough for her to fit through, by the time she opened it, removed the screen, and hoisted herself up, he'd have shot her twelve times. If shooting her was his intent. Maybe he would strangle her. Or stab her. She looked down at the knife. This might not have been a good idea.

He moved to the living room, and she let out the breath she'd been holding. Maybe he wouldn't find her here. Maybe she could still get away. A spark of hope lit within her...tempered by his foot-steps in the living room. She pictured him peering around the brown-and-white plaid sofa. Like hide and seek. Only this game was hide and die.

"Damn."

The whispered curse meant he stumbled into something. Prob-ably the end table beside Mr. Keegan's recliner.

Good. She leaned down to crawl under the bed. No room. Apparently, this was where Mrs. Keegan stored all her yarn and needles and pattern books, all the afghans she made and couldn't find takers for. Besides, if Jesse trapped herself under the bed, she wouldn't have a good angle to stab the intruder.

She eased back to her knees, doubled over to stay concealed. Not a good idea. Her legs cramped up, so she wouldn't be able to spring at him. That was her only hope—to spring at him and surprise him, then stab him in the gut.

Oh, God.

The bottom step creaked. She smiled. He didn't know the secret way to avoid the squeaks. *He's going upstairs. I can escape while he's up there.*

Cautiously, she crawled out from beside the bed. Reaching the door, she peeked into the living room. Empty. She stood, but a Charlie horse gripped her left leg and she almost collapsed. When she grabbed the doorframe, the door swung back and hit the wall with a *thump.*

Footfalls above her hurried back to the stairs. She willed her legs to move, and sprinted, half-hopping, toward the kitchen door.

The intruder ran down the stairs, closing in on her fast. She reached the door; he grabbed her ponytail and pulled her back-ward. A stinging burn ran through her scalp and along her neck. Instinctively, she reached back to fight him off, and in the process, the knife clattered to the floor.

He released her and dove for the knife, but she kicked it away. In the shadowy moonlight, his dark eyes glinted through the holes in the black ski mask as he spun back to her. She backed up, gasping as the handle to the refrigerator dug into her back. He lunged at her; she swung the freezer door open, hitting him in the face.

Staggering back, he clutched his eye.

She ran to the door, and was reaching for the knob when his arm snaked around her waist, tumbling with her to the floor. Broken glass pierced her forearm, stinging into her skin, as she slid along the linoleum. Wrestling away from him, she reached for the knife, only inches away, but his arm was longer. He grabbed it but in doing so lost his grip on her. She rolled toward the door just as it was thrust open.

"Ow!" she screeched as the corner of the door rammed her forehead.

"Jesse, are you okay?" Marty's voice boomed into the darkness.

"Yes, look out—he—has a knife."

Marty aimed his pistol, but the intruder was too fast. He bounded at Marty.

The sickening sound of a blade piercing flesh and muscle spewed into the dark. As Marty fell, the man pushed off him, and disappeared into the night.

Chapter Thirty

❦

That dark cottage was all wrong. If Jesse were safe, the lights would be on. Maggie wanted to follow Marty and see for herself that Jesse was all right. Waiting in the car was agony. She chewed her thumbnail as she watched him angle around the trees in the moonlight, using their shadows to escape detection. He approached the kitchen door, suddenly bursting through it.

She heard him yell Jesse's name then disappear into darkness. Her heart leapt to her throat and she clapped her hand over her mouth to muffle her scream. She wanted to call to him, but would that endanger him more?

Though it was just a few seconds, it seemed like an eternity before a masked figure exploded out the back door and melted into the shadows.

"Oh dear God. Please, God. Let them be okay."

She struggled to open the passenger door, but her fingers kept slipping on the metal knob. Finally, it released, and she sprang from the car and sprinted to the cottage.

Entering, she almost tripped over the figures on the floor. "Oh, no! No!" She flipped on the light. Her heart raced faster than her thoughts. *What happened? Is Marty dead? What should I do?* She couldn't breathe.

Jesse was pressing a kitchen towel into Marty's side.

"Quick, Maggie. Call the operator! Get an ambulance."

Taking a ragged breath, she stepped over them to reach the phone. Her fingers trembled so, she could hardly dial "o."

"Operator. Number please." The voice was clipped.

"Please, we need an ambulance. Please hurry!" The words tumbled out in a panicked jumble.

"Your address, please." The nasal tone could have been asking for a dinner order.

"Address... address, um, I don't remember." Numbers swirled in her head, but none made sense. Her gaze locked on Marty. "Jesse, is he...?"

"No. Here, come hold this. Press it as tightly as you can against his abdomen." Jesse grabbed the phone from her.

She dropped to her knees and gripped the towel, pushing it into Marty's side. Blood seeped through the fabric and stained her hands.

"Thirty-one sixty-two Lake Road. Seneca Corners. On Seneca Lake." She heard Jesse's voice through her haze. "A police officer has been stabbed; please hurry."

As Jesse returned the receiver to the hook, the operator intoned, "Thank you. I will call for an ambulance." The emotionless voice was followed by a *click*.

Maggie's arm trembled as she kept the pressure against Marty's wound. His eyes were glassy, and his focus strayed.

"Marty, I'm here." Her voice caught. He was still and pale as death.

His lifted his hand, but dropped it to the floor. *"Cara..."*

"Shh, shh, don't try to talk." She caressed his face with one bloodied hand as tears ran down her cheeks.

His eyes fluttered, he blinked, focusing on her. "I have... to tell... you."

"Shh, be still." Gently kissing his face, she whispered. "I love you, too."

Then his eyes rolled back, and he exhaled.

All the life drained out of her.

Chapter Thirty-One

T he constant *beep, beep, beep* signaled Marty's fight for his life. Maggie sat beside his bed, holding his hand, as she had done throughout the night. The muscles in her back were rigid, as if held in a vise that tightened with her every move. She'd turned off the overhead light, eliminating the constant buzz that had caused her head to throb, but the throbbing had taken up residence and refused to leave.

But she would not leave him.

Marty's parents had just left, taking her advice to get some rest now that he was stabilized. They promised to return and spell her around noon.

His mother's parting words were "Marty will be fine. Sister Angelina is guarding him."

Pasting on a gentle smile, she'd nodded. Inside, every nerve in her body screamed. *Don't put that responsibility on me! I am not God. I'm a woman.*

After the door closed behind his parents, she looked at Jesse.

"Why do people always want me to be the savior?" Her voice shook as it rose. "The sacrificial lamb? I'm not some talisman. My prayers are no better than anyone else's." She pounded her thigh, her voice raspy in an effort to keep it low. "Damn it! My prayers are as desperate as hers. My heart is as broken as hers. I'm not sitting here like Mother Mary watching over him. God, why do people expect so damn much from me! I'm only human, too."

Jesse put an arm around her shoulders. "I know you are."

She leaned her head against Jesse's shoulder. "I'm so scared. Look at him. He's fighting for his life. I don't have any bag of tricks. I don't have a special line to God." Sitting up, she pulled the sheet up on his chest and caressed his cheek.

"Talk to him, Mags. They say even when someone is unconscious, they can still hear you. He probably just heard you swear."

Maggie gasped out a chuckle. "Thanks, Jess." Then she frowned, taking in the lump above Jesse's left eye and the gauze covering the cuts along her arms, splotchy with bright orange Betadine solution. "You look like shit."

Jesse's eyebrows shot up in disbelief as she pointed to Marty. "You're going to shock him awake if you keep up that potty mouth."

"If that's what it takes." She turned back to Marty, her whole being pouring love and strength into him.

Joe walked in with two steaming cups of coffee. He handed one to Jesse and offered the other to Maggie.

Jesse stood. "I'm starving. Let's go get something to eat, Joe. What can we bring back for you, Mags?"

Maggie shook her head. "Thanks, but I'm not hungry."

Jesse lifted her chin, pointing it at Marty. "Go ahead and tell him to shape up and get the hell out of that bed." Her voice caught and tears welled in her eyes. "Please."

They left.

Maggie laid her head beside his on the pillow, her lips near his ear. "Marty, can you hear me?"

He lay still as death.

"I need you to come back to me. I need you in my life. I never knew..."

A nurse eased open the door and asked, "More coffee?"

Maggie didn't sit up or make any pretense of decorum. If the nurse knew she was Sister Angelina, so be it. She shook her head. "No, thank you." Through the large glass window, she watched the nurse return to the central nurses' station of the intensive care unit.

Her body burned with fatigue, tiny spasms ticking through her arms and legs. She yawned, and as she listened to his soft breathing, she dozed off.

The door opened again. "Really, I don't want any more coffee."

"Angelina?"

She sat up. "Hello, Sister Therese." She didn't let go of his hand.

"How is Marty? I've been told his wound is grave."

"They're watching him closely. He had emergency surgery to stop the bleeding as soon as they got him here, but he'd already lost a lot of blood." Words seemed hard to form.

"And you? How are you doing?"

She gave a small smile. "Pretty tired."

Sister Therese nodded. "I came over as soon as I learned about him, but I can't stay. I must get back for Lauds. We'll especially hold Marty in prayer."

Is it dawn already? Maggie looked toward the window. Soft gray light suffused the drawn blinds, tossing dancing dust motes through the air.

Sister Therese touched her shoulder. "It's good that you are here." Then she was gone.

Maggie rested her head next to Marty's again.

Where else would I be?

AMONG THE MANY odors Jesse hated in hospitals, the smell of institutionally prepared food rated right up there with unemptied bedpans. She wrinkled her nose at the combination of industrial dish soap and waffles.

"Thank you for coming." Jesse picked at her bagel. Her head throbbed where the door had slammed into it. Gingerly, she touched the spot, a large tender bump just above her left eye. Probably black and blue. Perfect for wedding photos.

"I got here as soon as I could," Joe said. He sipped his coffee and winced. "Hot."

She adjusted the gauze wrap covering her forearm. The doctor had given her a local anesthetic while he removed glass shards, but tiny stinging pinpricks foreshadowed the medication wearing off.

"It was agony not knowing if you were okay. Worst drive of my life." The muscles in his jaw twitched. "This is what I meant, Jesse. I was afraid I was losing you again."

She nodded, unable to get words past the lump in her throat.

"Sorry. That was unfair. You've been through hell tonight." He took her hand. "But we've got to work through this."

"I don't know what the answer is, Joe. I don't know what I'm supposed to do here."

"For now, just rest up."

Joe took a bite of his Danish then dropped it on his plate, tossing his napkin over it.

Two uniformed police officers got off the elevator, nodded at them, and headed to the coffee machine. Several more off-duty officers hovered upstairs near Marty's room, taking turns going in to check on him.

"Let's head back to the room and see how Marty's doing. When they stood, Joe brushed Jesse's hair back, stopping when she winced.

"Ow." She scrunched her shoulders up.

"Sorry. You okay?" he asked.

"The guy yanked me back by my ponytail. My scalp will sting for weeks."

He pulled her to him, ignoring the people glancing their way. "I'm so glad he didn't hurt you more." Gently, he kissed the top of her head. "Did you get a look at him?"

"No, he wore a ski mask." She pulled back, searching for a

clock. "What time is it, anyway? I have to go to the police station to follow up on the report I gave at the cottage."

"Almost six."

She looked at the light filtering through the windows. "Okay, that gives me a couple of hours."

"Do you remember anything about the guy? Any way you could identify him?"

"Well, he swore when he bumped into something, but he whispered, so hard to tell. He'll have a facial bruise or a black eye because I hit him with the freezer door."

She recognized Joe's 'trying to make sense of this" face.

"When I backed into the refrigerator, he came at me. I swung the door open. It was the only thing I could think to do."

He shook his head. "You're amazing."

The clatter of dishes and silverware increased as the breakfast crowd grew. Tables around them had gradually filled up with medical personnel hurrying through a bite during a break and with families, their faces drawn with various degrees of despair and determined hope.

Heading to the elevators, Jesse tugged on Joe's arm, pulling him to a stop.

"Joe, I know Marty is your best friend, but Maggie is close to falling apart."

"Yeeees..."

"She'll need to stay close by him, too."

He hitched one corner of his mouth into the half grin that always sent shivers through her body. "I know. As you would if it were me up there."

"Exactly. More so every day."

The elevator doors parted, and they moved aside to let a father and his toddler step out. The toddler wore a shirt that said, "Big brother." The father wore a face that said, "I need coffee."

"Congratulations," Jesse said.

Dazed, the man looked at her. "It's a girl." Then he made a beeline toward the coffee urns.

Chuckling, they entered the elevator, and Joe pushed the fourth-floor button. He took her hand. "We can't avoid the elephant in the room."

Uh oh. Jesse rubbed her forehead—not a headache but maybe a stall tactic. She wasn't sure she was ready yet.

He gently took her hand away from her face. "You can't go back to the cottage."

"I can't go home, either. Whoever this guy is, he seems to know where I am at all times."

"That's my point."

Jesse's head pounded. Now she did have a headache, and certainly not from lack of caffeine. How did it come to be that ghosts and danger followed her around these days? In the last year, she'd had three ghostly encounters and almost lost her life as many times. It's not like she invited it. *Hey, Fates, over here, the redhead. Need a little fun? Send me some ghosts and a couple of murderers. I'll run a tab til my luck runs out.*

But Joe was right. If this continued, her rosy future with him disappeared. No "happily ever after," not even "happily most of the time after." The intruder could have killed her.

She stumbled against Joe and not because the elevator stopped.

He bundled her in his arms just as the doors opened. With his arm around her shoulders, Joe led her to a quiet lounge at the end of the hall. In lieu of the harsh fluorescent overhead light, three lamps placed around the room lent a soft glow, inviting family members to a respite from their vigils.

Near the entrance, a mother sat on a padded vinyl bench the dull green color hospitals seem to think was soothing but reminded Jesse of fruit turning moldy. The woman stared at her little boy playing with a set of wooden blocks. Though she watched him, her focus fixed on a room down the hall. She didn't notice them enter.

They sat on a small matching sofa at the opposite end of the room. Jesse surrendered to Joe's arms. The trembling that had started on the elevator had not subsided, her shivering relentless.

She tightened her muscles commanding them to stop, but to no avail. Joe deepened his embrace.

"Do you need a blanket?" His lips were soft against her forehead.

"No." She closed her eyes.

They sat in silence until the child's wooden structure clattered as it tumbled to the linoleum floor. Jesse jumped, her eyes flying open.

"Timmy, shh." The mother had been startled out of her reverie, too. "I'm sorry." Her gaze dragged from her son to them, dazed at the realization of her surroundings.

Smiling, Joe held up a reassuring hand. "Don't worry. He's fine."

The mother sat back, and the boy resumed his construction.

"What should I do, Joe? Courtney can't stay there anymore, either. What if that guy comes back thinking I'm still there?" Jesse whispered.

Joe stroked her back. "Good point."

"And even if I go home, he'll track me down there. Plus, I haven't figured out what Timmy needs."

At the sound of his name, the boy looked up at her.

"I need a crane. And a 'struction helmet."

Startled, Jesse stared. His words nudged a memory. A construction helmet? Kids loved wearing hats that defined their playtime. Like construction helmets. And train engineer hats.

Joe smiled at the boy. "Your name is Timmy, too?"

Nodding, the boy shrank into his mother's legs. She seemed unaware that a conversation was occurring.

"Well, Timmy, you're doing a fine job of building there." Joe gave him a thumbs-up.

"Is your name Timmy, too?" He held onto his mother's leg, anchoring himself.

"No, I'm Joe."

"Is Timmy your kid?"

Joe laughed. "No, I don't have a kid yet." He glanced at Jesse and winked.

She barely followed their conversation. This Timmy—alive Timmy—was echoing ghost Timmy's question. *Where's my hat?* And then his statement. *She has my hat.*

She bolted up. "I have to return to the cottage. Timmy's ghost was about to reveal something important when the phone rang." A flush of certainty ran through her, a recognition of truth. "I have to go back."

Joe searched her face, worry combined with resignation.

"I'll get Helen's pistol from my house." The gun had saved her life once already.

He let out a long sigh, the sibilant *sssss* a release of any losing argument he might have offered. "I'll stay with you."

"Thanks, Joe."

Chapter Thirty-Two

Maggie swam, pushing the water back with steady strokes, struggling against the current, straining toward the light above. The water was dark, swirling around her in a frenetic eddy, pulling her back into the blackness. Unable to breathe, unable to reach the surface, her chest about to explode, she battled panic. She jerked her arm back, and woke with a gasp. Heart pounding, head groggy, she surveyed the room to gain her bearings.

Beep, beep, beep.

Marty.

Inching her head off the pillow, she looked at him.

And he looked right back at her.

"Marty!" She grasped his hand.

A weak attempt at a smile curved inside the plastic oxygen mask covering his nose and mouth. The effort cost him, and he closed his eyes.

She stroked his brow. Should she speak or let him sleep?

But he wasn't sleeping. His was studying her. The usual sparkle wasn't there, but the fight for life was.

She squeezed his hand, and he responded with a faint tug.

"Good morning, Marty."

He slowly turned his face toward the window. A short nod acknowledged her greeting.

Leaning forward, she kissed his cheek.

He gave her a drowsy wink.

A doctor strode in garbed in white and efficiency, carrying the requisite patient chart.

"How is Officer D'Amato this morning?" His strident voice slammed against the soft glow of early morning in the room.

Should she state the obvious, or was the doctor actually addressing the sleeping Marty? It seemed rhetorical, so she remained silent as he checked Marty's vital signs.

A nurse bustled in with a new IV bottle, and carefully removed the elastic that held the oxygen mask to Marty's face, leaving slight impressions like two dusty paths along his cheeks. She held his wrist, timing his respiration, then nodded at the doctor. She removed the oxygen apparatus and headed into the bathroom to emerge with a wet washcloth and towel, and proceeded to gently wash Marty's face, arms, and hands.

He stirred and moaned.

Maggie followed some of the doctor's comments, noting encouraging numbers in his vital signs. He was stable; he would live.

"He's come through surgery fine, and so far, there is no indication of infection," the doctor said. "His vitals look good, though it will take some time for him to recover from the loss of so much blood. We're going to cut back on the morphine he's receiving and see how he manages the pain. Sound good?"

She nodded. "Yes, I guess so."

He nodded, and she suspected had she said, "Absolutely not!" he would have done what he wanted anyway. *Oh well, he's the expert.* He hurried on to the next patient.

The nurse adjusted the IV flow to lessen the morphine going into Marty's system.

She smiled at Maggie. "He should gradually regain consciousness. We'll see how he does with the pain, and if need be, we can increase it again." She gathered the old IV bottle and the oxygen apparatus and slipped out of the room.

Maggie rose and arched her back, lifting her arms and stretching out her spine. Flexing her wrists and elbows, she walked to the window. Cars lined up to enter the parking structure, medical personnel hustled through the revolving front door, and an ambulance wailed its way to the emergency entrance. Suffering was daily life here.

She returned to her seat and once again laid her head on the pillow beside his. She focused on the gentle sound of his breathing, allowing it to flow over her, lulling her back to sleep. Her eyes flew open at the whisper.

"*Cara mia.*"

FOR JESSE, walking into ICU was like stepping into another world. Dim lights along the corridor encouraged whispers, and nurses spoke in hushed voices, noting instructions on charts. Doctors entered and exited patient rooms, sometimes giving instructions to eager interns. The symphony of machines sang the tune of the edge of life. In some rooms, soft crying drifted into the hall, in others, silence.

She fought the urge to get back on the elevator and go to a café or a movie. The quiet atmosphere in the intensive care unit overwhelmed her, creating an unbidden urge to suddenly yell out some insane word like "lettuce" or "tractor." The sort of feeling she'd had when she'd stood looking at Niagara Falls, battling the sensation that she would unintentionally pitch herself over the side.

Perhaps the urge stemmed from a hidden desire to escape the fear.

She and Joe hurried past the nurses' station to Marty's room. Pushing open the door, she gasped at Maggie's tears. Her stomach dropped like a roller coaster ride.

"Oh, my God, Maggie—is Marty okay?" She rushed to the bedside and looked down into Marty's sleepy, but extremely happy, eyes. A croaky laugh bubbled up as relief surged through her. "Geez. You two scared the crap out of me." She grinned at him. *"Buongiorno, Marty."*

"Bella." His whisper grated against his dry throat, and Maggie held the straw from his water glass up to his mouth.

Joe patted his arm. "Man, it's good to see you alive and almost kicking."

Marty reached for his hand. "Thanks, Joe."

Maggie updated them on the doctor's visit. "Marty's been more awake since they lowered the morphine." Despite her disheveled appearance, she glowed as if she were Queen of the May.

Jesse hugged her. "I think it was my powerful prayers."

Maggie swatted her arm. "You goof."

The nurse came in with fresh water and a small paper cup. "Time for your morning meds, Officer D'Amato." She looked at the others. "And for attention to some personal care issues."

Jesse noticed the full plastic bag hanging beside the lower frame of the bed. "Okay, we'll book it." She checked her watch. "I've got to stop by the police station and give them a description I don't have."

Marty stirred in the bed. "A couple inches shorter than me." His voice rasped, and he struggled to speak. "Soft arms."

Jesse scrunched her face at him. "Soft arms? Are you tripping now? What drugs are you on?"

"Only legal ones," the nurse said, imposing herself between them and the bed. She waved her hand to push them out. "Shoo. Out you go. You, too, Sister Angelina."

Maggie's mouth dropped open. Then she looked at Marty and smiled. "I'll just be outside."

Jesse studied Marty. "Soft arms?"

He nodded and then began to snore.

"LET ME GET THIS STRAIGHT. You didn't get a look at this guy at all? You just heard him swear once?" Officer Dave Sanders didn't look up from the form he was filling in. Running his fingers through his blonde hair, he skimmed the dearth of information he'd entered. "Do you remember anything else? Anything at all? Any limp? Tattoo? Odor?" His clear blue eyes met hers, encouraging and a bit desperate. This report wasn't going to advance his career. He studied the page as if a significant detail would suddenly blossom on one of the empty lines.

Jesse had been through this kind of interview before, and this discussion was nothing compared to when Detective Holden arrested her on suspicion of murder. She shivered at the memory. Joe took her hand. Now, she truly wanted to help. Heck, anything to nail this guy and get him behind bars.

"Sorry. It was dark, and the only contact we had was when he jerked my ponytail and pulled me to the floor. He had a good grip." Her voice raised, hopefully. "Oh, and I walloped his face with the freezer door."

Joe stifled a chuckle.

Officer Sanders stopped reading the report and stared at her with a mixture of confusion and disbelief. "The freezer door?"

"Yes. When he trapped me in the kitchen and leapt toward me, I pulled open the freezer door and he ran into it. You need to look for someone with a black eye or a bruise on his face."

"It's six hours after the bars closed. We'd have a lot of suspects."

"Well, I don't think you can discount it."

He slipped the report in a manila folder and closed it, dismissing her. "Thanks for your time, Jesse."

Joe smiled and squeezed her hand. "Give it a minute. Breathe. Relax. Something might come to you."

Her mind scrambled for any detail she might have forgotten. *Damn. This guy is still out there.*

She sat forward. "He had soft arms." She looked at Joe. "Remember? Marty said he had soft arms."

"Marty did say he had soft arms." Joe nodded at Officer Sanders who frowned and gave Jesse the side-eye.

"Marty is under the influence right now. And what are we supposed to do, go out and grope the arms of every male over five-foot-seven?"

"You could if they have a black eye."

He stood. "Let us know if you remember anything that might help us."

Her hopes sank.

When they reached the sidewalk, Joe paused by her Beetle. "I have a meeting with the building inspector in half an hour. Let me stop by his office and cancel it. I'll take you home so you can get some sleep."

"No, I'm okay. I'll drop you off and head back to the hospital."

"Are you sure?"

She nodded.

"Why don't we stop by the diner for breakfast? I can walk to his office from there."

Jesse glanced at the sky. "Well, you'd better take an umbrella."

"A few raindrops won't kill me." He winced. "Hurt me." He winced again. "Bother me."

She laughed, and some tension melted away.

Jesse didn't believe she could put away a full farmer's breakfast, but hunger had finally returned. As they rose to leave, she searched the booth for her purse.

"Oh crap. When we followed the ambulance to the hospital, I totally forgot to grab my purse. I've been driving without my license. I'll have to run out to the cottage and get it." A chill skittered along her arms.

"I'll come with you."

"No. You'll be late for your appointment. I'll be fine." She kept her voice steady. She didn't want Joe to sense her discomfort. That would add fuel to his argument about danger in her life. "I'll run in, grab my purse, and head to the hospital."

He frowned, unconvinced.

"It's daylight. That guy isn't going to return in broad daylight. Plus, the cops may still be out there finishing up their investigation now that it's light outside."

He twitched his lips to the side. "You're probably right. Just run in and out, promise?"

She crossed her heart and held up her right hand. "Promise."

He gave her a quick kiss, and headed toward city hall.

She hated having to return to the cottage. Her thoughts returned to the previous night, and she broke out in a sweat. The sound of the intruder's soft curse, of dark eyes peering through the ski mask, of him grabbing her in the dark raced through her mind. She grabbed the steering wheel to steady her shaking hands. *Please let the cops still be there.*

Her mind was so preoccupied as she pulled out from the curb, she almost hit the tan Chevy in front of her angling to pull out, too. "Sorry!" she shouted, waving at the driver. He must not have noticed since he looked away toward the diner as she passed.

A light rain pattered against the windshield as she drove, and the rhythm of the wipers echoed her tumbling thoughts. What else of importance could she have told Officer Sanders? What was the intruder's hair color? His exact height? Age? Facial hair? She knew none of this. She wracked her brain but couldn't think of anything additional. The wipers echoed her frustration. *Swish. Swish. Damn. Swish. Swish. Damn.*

Traffic was heavier than usual with the influx of vacationers in the cottages along Seneca Lake. Naturally, she hit every light, though there weren't that many in this small town. As she turned onto the highway leading toward the lake, cars became fewer. Checking the rearview mirror, she noticed the Chevy behind her. *Glad I didn't ding you since you're heading my way.*

Listening to the Beach Boys crooning to a surfer girl, she turned down the dirt road leading to the cottage. She bumped along slowly, crossing the deep grooves along the railroad track carefully. The Chevy followed.

Cars that followed her made her nervous ever since one drove her off the road and nearly killed her the previous summer. The fact that this one was hanging behind now made her want to punch the accelerator and speed away. Of course, his Chevy could probably overtake Bert in a matter of seconds.

She gripped the wheel and leaned forward. Should she push Bert to his limit? She glanced in the rearview mirror again; was he going to rear-end her? Instead, the car drove past and continued down the road.

Exhaling, she drove to the cottage and parked. The yard was empty. The only sign of a police presence was the yellow and black tape forming a large X across the kitchen door. She grabbed her keys but didn't get out of the car. At the sight of the back door, she clutched her stomach to quash the wave of nausea that surged through her. She stared at the piece of wood secured into the place where the intruder had broken the pane. *Don't be silly. The guy isn't going to come back in the daylight.* She glanced at the Becker cottage. *Or is he already here? This might have been a huge mistake.*

You're being an ass. Just go inside and grab your purse.

She had to bend down and angle through the police tape to enter the cottage. Stepping into the kitchen, she rubbed her arms against chill bumps that arose. The thin daylight drifting through the windows did little to alleviate her fear. The sound of crunching glass and a whispered cuss echoed in her mind. She shook her head, pushing past the kitchen and heading up the stairs to her room.

She snatched her purse off the dresser and stopped. *I'll get some clothes and shower in Marty's hospital room. I'll take a lot of grief if I do, but I'm not sticking around here.* After grabbing capris, a blue top, underwear, and sandals, she headed for the stairs. The door to Timmy's room beckoned, but no train whistle sounded on the other side. She hurried past.

Ordinary noises greeted her back on the main floor. Waves along the shore, rain on the window, a car driving by. *Relax, Graham. No one is going to break in during broad daylight.* Her heart pounded as she rushed through the kitchen. She had to wrangle her way under the tape again, which slowed her down. *Damn, I'll be glad to get away from here.*

She inhaled the fresh air as she locked the cottage door. She'd made it safely through her foray into the cottage. The rain had intensified, and she'd have to sprint to her Beetle. Not that it mattered; her hair was springing like Medusa's snakes and her blouse was already damp.

Gripping her purse and change of clothes, she ran toward Bert. She skidded on the wet grass as the tan Chevy pulled up, blocking her path.

Jesse lost her footing. Her skid accelerated to a fall, and she twisted her ankle on her way down. Brain-freezing pain shot up her right leg. Her change of clothes fell into the mud, along with her purse.

"C'mon, bitch." The man beside her roughly grabbed one arm and pulled her up, forcing her to stand. She hobbled a step, favoring her injured leg. Thrusting a cool metal cylinder into her ribs, he slammed her against the car.

She opened her mouth to scream, but he slapped his hand over it, holding her tightly against his chest. With the other hand, he opened the driver's side door and shoved her in, pushing in after her. She scrambled to escape out the passenger door, but the handle had been removed.

She screamed, and he slapped her across the mouth.

"Shut up or I'll kill you right here."

Gunning the engine, he turned the car toward the highway, swooping in front of the Williamson cottage where Mr. Williamson was just emerging. He saw her. Dear God, she hoped he saw her. Her stomach turned over as she caught his eye.

He ducked inside. Maybe to call the police? *Please call the police.*

Chapter Thirty-Three

M aggie needed to walk.

Marty was sleeping peacefully, so she took advantage of his rest to head to the cafeteria. She wasn't hungry, but perhaps moving would alleviate the anxiety that skittered around in her chest like a mouse in a maze. She rubbed the worry lines creased along her forehead, her concern not only for Marty, but where was Jesse? Her interview at the police station shouldn't have lasted three hours.

She'd called the cottage and Jesse's house but got no answer at either place. Normally, Jesse would be right at her side during a crisis like this. *Where are you, Jess?* When she got on the elevator, her stomach dropped as the car did. *Maybe I should call Joe.*

The doors opened to the busy lunch crowd, trays lining up along the cafeteria food line like a hungry train. Passing the tray stack, she grabbed a cup and headed to the coffee station. The toasty aroma soothed her. *Maybe I'm just on edge because Marty has been so badly injured.*

But his injuries were a result of protecting Jesse. Whoever was after her was still out there. She left her coffee cup sitting on the counter, the aromatic steam floating into the air. The pit in her stomach told her Jesse was in trouble. She ran back to the elevator and watched as it stopped at every floor on the way down. She tapped her foot, but she wanted to scream.

When she called, Joe's voice echoed her panic.

"I thought she'd be back with you by now. I'll stop by her house —she could be mowing the lawn or doing something outside and not hear the phone." He was trying to convince himself as much as he was her. "If she's not there, I'll head out to the cottage."

"Let me know as soon as you find her."

"Find who?" Courtney stood at the door to Marty's room. "Oh my God," she said, taking in Marty's colorless face. "What happened?"

Maggie's hand shook as she returned the receiver to the phone base. "Jesse. She had to go to the police station to report—"

"What the hell is going on? I ran into Dave Sanders, and he said Jesse was in to give a report about an assault." She gaped at Marty. "Did Marty...?"

"Lord, no. We went to the cottage to help her. The intruder stabbed Marty." The muscles along her shoulders constricted, pulling her shoulders forward as his brush with death hit home again. "I don't know where she is right now. The guy got away. She was supposed to be here hours ago." Unable to hide her exhaustion and fear any longer, she broke down, her teeth chattering as she trembled.

Courtney wrapped her in her arms. "Shh. It's okay. I'll run out to the cottage and check on her. Jesse will be okay."

Maggie wasn't sure about that. But she was sure her sister had never been so tender.

Chapter Thirty-Four

Maggie fought down panic as Joe and Courtney described what they found at the cottage.

"Joe was trying to pick the lock when I got there," Courtney said.

"Her car is still there, her purse and some clothes were on the ground nearby." Joe scrubbed his hands over his face. "The police have dusted for fingerprints, in her car, in the cottage."

"I shouldn't have stayed in town." Courtney's voice caught. "I should have gone home. Then she wouldn't have been alone and maybe Marty wouldn't have almost gotten killed." She sniffled into a tissue pressed against her nose.

Marty raised his hand from the bed. His voice was weak, but his eyes were more alert than earlier that morning. "Don't think like that, Courtney. That guy would have overpowered both of you. You can't blame yourself."

"The police are canvassing the neighborhood to see if anyone saw anything unusual." Joe sat with his arms on his knees, hands together. He stared at the floor. "I feel so helpless. I want to be out there."

Maggie rubbed his shoulders. "I know you do, Joe. But where would you begin?"

Just then Officer Dave Sanders entered, his face obscured by a large bouquet of fresh flowers. He peered around them. "Hey, man, these are from all the guys." He looked around the room, tried to give them to Marty, realized that wouldn't work and aimed them toward the nightstand, where there was also no space.

"Here, let me take them." Courtney brightened. She left to see to a vase, and Dave watched her until she disappeared down the hall.

Maggie had never seen her sister light up like that before. She studied Dave, who continued to look down the hall. Courtney and Dave. His face was glowing.

Quite a contrast to the despair in Joe's face. The last time he'd looked like that, Jesse lay in the hospital bed, close to death from injuries resulting in a run-in with the last ghost.

"You took one in the side, huh?" Dave asked.

Marty nodded. "So they tell me. Any news on Jesse?"

Joe's ears perked up, and he looked hopefully at Dave.

"Yeah. The next-door neighbor said she left in a tan car with some guy."

Maggie's heart sank. To her knowledge, Jesse didn't know anyone who drove a tan car.

Joe leapt to his feet. "Let's go! Let's go look for the guy."

Dave held his hands up to settle him down. "We've got cars patrolling the area, searching for cars matching that description. But, geez, do you know how many tan Chevy sedans there are out there?"

"My God! Why are we standing here talking about this?" Joe paced a small area in the cramped room. "I've got to go look. I've got to do something." Again, he scrubbed his hands over his face.

"We're on it, Joe."

"Looks to me like you're just standing here, Dave." Joe thrust his face into Dave's.

Maggie put a hand on his chest. "The police have this, Joe. Let them do their job."

Dave eased away from him. "It's okay. I'd be frustrated, too, if it was my girl."

Just then Courtney entered with an aluminum water pitcher. Dave looked away quickly, and then scratched his jawline. "Funny thing is, when we first questioned that neighbor, he said he didn't see a thing. Not till his wife reminded him that he'd mentioned seeing Jesse looking scared out a car window."

"Shit." Joe slammed his hand against the wall. "Why the hell would he lie at first?" He looked at Courtney. "You know, Jesse told me he acted weird when you two stayed with Mrs. Williamson."

"Yeah, not weird, but kind of mean. He's usually so nice." Courtney stared at the window. "But I think he was just distracted because Mrs. Williamson woke up while he was gone. He wasn't expecting her to be visiting with us. It's so sweet how he takes such tender care of her."

"C'mon. I'll take you in my patrol car." Dave swatted Joe's shoulder. "Maybe we can jog his memory about this guy a little more."

Maggie shot him a look of gratitude. Waiting for news of Jesse had taken its toll on Joe. He had to do something.

"Get him." The weakness in Marty's voice couldn't mask its intensity. "Not for what he did to me. For what he might do to Jesse."

Chapter Thirty-Five

❧

J esse leaned forward to rub her throbbing ankle. Her abductor grabbed her by the hair and yanked her back up in the seat.

"Ow! Geez, why do you keep pulling my hair?"

He shot her a quizzical look. "Just stay put. No funny moves."

Watching his speed and constantly scanning his mirrors, he had driven away from town, past most of the side roads that led to cottages. Now, he turned down a dirt road with a scattering of older cottages. Beside a gravel road that veered closer to the lake was a weather-beaten sign that had once announced Beachside Retreat, but the "B" was missing and someone had scratched out half of Retreat so it said "eachside teat." On a normal day, Jesse would have found that hysterical. But today, it might be the last thing she ever read.

The road turned away from the lake, and a two-track headed into the woods. The jarring ride along the rutted road turned Jesse's headache into a throbbing cacophony of pain. Her stomach gurgled with a threatening bout of nausea. \

Think, Graham. Think.

Where do I know this guy from? I know I've seen him before. I need to be able to describe him to the police. Sandy-colored hair, about six feet, no distinguishing marks or tattoos. Clear gray eyes.

She was surprised he hadn't blindfolded her, but—her body tingled as adrenaline exploded through her like an electrical charge—he didn't need to blindfold her. She was never going to escape. At least not alive.

She had to get out of this car.

Sneaking glimpses at her captor, she waited for him to look in the side-view mirror, then, mustering all her strength, she thrust her full weight against the door. She gasped as a sharp pain stabbed through her shoulder.

He sneered. "You think you're getting away from me? No chance, little bitch." He grabbed her around the neck and forced her to look at him. "It isn't going to happen." He flipped her head away and a crack sounded in her neck. His arms were strong. She glanced at the sinewy muscles that bulged against his T-shirt. There was nothing soft about them.

She shook her head in confusion, aggravating the headache. She prodded fingers into the back of her neck to stem the insistent pounding. Something wasn't making sense.

"How did you find me at the cottage?"

"You wanna talk? Okay, we can talk for a while. My name's Ed, what's yours? Oh, yeah. Jesse Graham, nosiest broad in the world." He laughed again, a taunting snicker.

"You're Ethel's nephew Eddie. You were there when she cornered me on the street."

"So what if I am? So I was there. Maybe I was around more often then you know." He smirked at her.

She repeated her question. "How did you find me at the cottage?"

"I followed you, dummy. Right after you almost dented my bumper."

"That was today. I mean last night. Did you follow me to the cottage last night, too?"

His glance slid toward her. "What the hell are you talking about?"

"You broke in last night. You tried to attack me." She swallowed the bile that surged up, burning her throat. He had no bruise on his face. His arms were strong and solid. "Oh my God, it wasn't you."

He hooted, a loud guffaw that rang around the car. "You mean I got competition? Shit, if I'd known that, I woulda planned a contest. 'Who could kill the bitch first?'" He slapped his knee and burst out laughing again.

Was he distracted enough to attack? What would she use? She studied the dashboard. Nothing of any use. If she bent to get her sandal, he'd probably kill her on the spot. But maybe that would be a better way to go than whatever he had planned.

The road wound farther into the woods, tree branches slapping at the windows. Each slap underscoring how removed she was from any help. Every so often, she glimpsed the lake a short distance off through the trees, but the area was too marshy for cottages. A fork in the road held a sign with a grotesque imitation of Smokey the Bear puffing on a cigar and pointing to the right. "Brian's Beer Camp one mile" was carved into the wood.

Ed took the left fork. "Who else did you piss off?" He grinned, his eyes steely gray.

The man peering out through a ski mask... even in the dark she could see the dark eyes—not gray—that had threatened her. And this guy was at least as tall as Marty.

"It wasn't you."

"No, it wasn't me. Looks like I'm doing somebody a big favor."

Her mind spun, but she had to focus on surviving. *Think, Graham. Think.*

What was his weakness? She glanced at his arms again. Certainly not physical weakness. She doubted reason or a plea to his humanity would set her free. If he wanted to get rid of her, he must be connected to the abductions.

She guessed he was in his mid-thirties. He would have been in his twenties back then. That had to be the reason. And Ethel's little encounter yesterday must have panicked him.

"You kidnapped those young boys. Fifteen years ago." She kept her voice steady.

He glanced at her. "What makes you say that?"

"Why else would you kidnap me? People have been talking about my interest in the case."

"What about your other attacker? It was probably him who killed those boys."

"He used a knife. You used a gun." It was a wild guess, but he had a gun now, so she went with it.

"I didn't shoot them—" Realizing what he'd said, he glared at her. "I didn't take those boys. Your midnight friend did."

"I don't think so. He's not as muscular as you are. They could have gotten away from him. I did."

He unconsciously flexed his upper arm muscles in response to her comment. "I guess you'll never know."

Egomaniac. "Whoever he was, he was as smart as he was strong, because he was never caught."

He smirked and straightened in his seat.

"I guess it couldn't have been you then."

The sharp slap across her face jolted her back against the head-rest, her teeth snapping in a loud *clack.*

"Shut it, bitch," he shouted.

Reaching up, she touched her swelling lip, feeling the warm blood dripping down her chin. She reached toward the glove box. He grabbed her hand, wrenching her wrist.

"Don't open that." This shout louder than the last.

"I was looking for a tissue or a napkin. You split my lip, and I'll bleed all over your car."

"Use your damn shirt or something. I'm not Suzy Homemaker. Geez."

Tucking her head toward her arm, she pressed the short sleeve of her shirt against her mouth. A red stain seeped into the fabric.

Precious time was passing, the distance from help growing by the minute.

Finally, he pulled up to what she assumed was a hunting cabin. To say it was rustic would be a compliment. The old wood had weathered to gray, though patches of what might have been dark green showed through in a few spots. Uneven sheets covered the grimy windows, the fabric's stripes faded and dirty. The chimney had been tossing bricks on the roof for years, and the middle of three steps to the porch was missing. Trees crowded the structure, offering little light and scant space for the car. Add to that the gloomy sky, and she could have been in a Hitchcock movie.

I can't let him get me into that house.

He expertly backed into a clearing beside the cabin. Obviously, he'd spent a good deal of time here. Was this where he'd taken the boys? She imagined their terror. And their end. Her thoughts overwhelmed her, and she fought for control. Fear would paralyze her, and she was very close to that threshold. She had to think clearly.

Ed got out of the car, and she almost reminded him to take the keys out of the ignition. But given the dense woods, there was no danger of car theft out in this wilderness.

Then she remembered she still had her own keys in her pocket.

As he walked around to her side of the car, she tried to pull her keys out, but he moved too quickly. She stuffed them back into her pocket just before he opened the door.

"Get out."

She turned, planting both feet on the muddy earth to ground herself. This was her moment to make her move. But he turned toward the house. *No! That was my best chance to catch him off guard.*

Thunder growled, echoing off the lake in the distance.

"I wouldn't try to run, bitch. Besides the storm coming, there are wolves and bobcats out there." He nodded toward the woods.

"Is this where you brought them? The boys?" She remained seated in the car.

Lightning flashed through the clouds.

His nostrils flared, his face stormier than the sky. She thought of a bull in the ring, and she waved the red flag again.

"It's isolated, no one could hear them screaming for help."

He took a step toward her. "Stop."

"Are they buried out here?"

He glanced toward the trees just east of the shack, then back to her.

"It wasn't me."

"You're strong enough." She didn't mention his intellect.

If he'd been a bull, he'd be digging in his hooves, kicking up dust, ready to charge. Maybe she'd pushed too hard.

He grabbed her, yanking her arm, pulling her out of the car, and slamming the door. Icy hot pain shot through her sprained ankle. She almost crumpled to the ground. Grabbing the side-view mirror, she doubled over.

"What the hell's wrong with you?" His voice ricocheted off the trees, intensified by the pre-storm hollowness of the air.

She stayed bent over, gripping the mirror. "My ankle. I sprained it when you attacked me."

"I didn't attack you, damn it!" He leaned over her to grab her arm again.

As the thunder rolled, she heard something else, a high-pitched tune, a descant above the thunder's bass notes.

All the live long day…

Chapter Thirty-Six

J esse searched the trees to the east but saw only leaves, turned upward to receive the promised rain. *Where are you, Timmy? Are you buried there with the other boys?* If he'd been abducted by this monster, Maggie and her family would be devastated. But then, they would never know, since apparently, this secret would die here... with her.

She must escape.

Her captor didn't react to Timmy's voice. He shoved her toward the cottage, impatient with her need to favor her injured leg. "Move it. I haven't got all day."

Can't you hear the whistle blowing?

A clap of thunder bellowed, louder than before, and the air temperature dropped noticeably.

He still did not react to Timmy's voice.

Only I can hear him.

He pushed her up the steps. She had trouble navigating the missing middle step. She wobbled backward. *Maybe I can get him off-balance.*

As she stretched to reach the top step, she pivoted to the right and pushed against him. He stumbled and windmilled his arms to keep his balance. Stepping back, he missed the bottom step and jumped to the ground.

"What the hell are you trying to do?" He bolted toward her, his arm raised. She ducked, but his fist smashed into her left eye. Lurching back, she was dazed by the searing pain that pierced her head. Blackness swirled with white starbursts for a moment, then the scene before her receded to white.

She shrank back, clasping both hands against her eye. Would she lose it? If she removed her hands, would her eyeball fall out and roll down the steps to the mud? The stinging pulsed with every breath.

Gripping her arm, he pulled her hands away and propelled her into the cottage. Her eye stayed intact, but her chance of escape decreased exponentially.

She squinted, trying to see the room, but with no lights and the stormy sky, she could only discern shadows.

He lit a lantern on a wooden table just inside the door. The glow revealed a small room with a musty sofa, a weathered kitchen table with two chairs, and an ancient pipe stove. A forlorn fireplace still held charred wood from an old fire, and a rustling sounded from behind it. A pump stood on the counter next to a sink. Moldy air irritated her nose, and she sneezed. Bile rose in her throat as she thought of the terrified boys who were held here.

As if on cue, Timmy's voice floated to her.

I don't want to play here. Where's Courtney?

"Wish I knew." She hadn't realized she'd spoken aloud.

"Wish you knew what?" He pushed her onto the sofa.

Unable to balance on her good leg, she plopped into it, raising decades of dust and the scent of mouse droppings. *Oh God, mice.*

"Wish you knew about the boys? Amazing how kids will follow you anywhere if you drive an ice cream truck." He looked off into the distance. "Almost too easy." He recovered and sneered at her. "You're too nosy. You don't need to know nothing."

The temperature shifted with a creeping chill, a chill that had nothing to do with the drop in barometric pressure. She rubbed her arms, feeling strangely comforted that Timmy was with her. Though he couldn't do anything, at least she wasn't alone.

"You just—what the hell?" As he spoke, a cloud of icy air appeared in front of his lips as if it were mid-February. He waved his hand in front of his mouth, dissipating the frosty cloud. His head swiveled as he scrutinized the room, looking for the source of the frigid blast.

"Apparently, one of your victims has returned for vengeance." Jesse chuckled.

"I don't believe in ghosts."

"Well, you'd better believe in Timmy, because he's paying you a visit."

He slapped her face, and pulled her to stand. "Shut up, bitch."

The room grew colder. He shoved her back on the couch, searching the room for the source. Lightning lit up the room, and a clap of thunder made them both jump.

When the room resumed its darkness, a soft glow glimmered by the fireplace.

"There's Timmy now." She giggled and clapped as fear dissipated into joy. She felt light, as if she could float up to the beams supporting the ceiling. *Oh no, hold on, Graham. Hold on or you're dead for sure.* She forced herself to concentrate on Ed's threatening grimace.

"What's wrong with you? Who the hell is Timmy?"

"One of your victims. He's come back to visit." A giggle bubbled up. *Steady, remember, this guy's going to kill you.* Two forces pulled at her like she was a rope in a tug of war. Ebullience that made her want to sit on the floor and play, and dread that made her all too aware that her life could end at any second. She had to let dread win.

I don't like it here. Timmy's image pulsed, soft light against the craggy brick. *The boys were crying,* he sniffled.

"I don't know any Timmy. He wasn't one of them." His nostrils flared at her as he realized his admission. "You bitch."

He's right. I've never been here before. I want to go home. Timmy hummed his favorite railroad tune, a siren song luring her in. She dug her nails into the palms of her hands.

"How are you doing that? Stop singing." His voice rose as he stared at the shimmering glow.

"I'm not doing anything. But Timmy wants to tell you something."

"I told you, I don't know any Timmy." His eyes grew so large the white encircled the iris like a spooked horse's.

Timmy's form took shape, and he pointed at Ed. *The other boys say he's a mean man. I want to go home.* His plaintive voice rang in her ears. His next words chilled her. *You need to get away. Now.*

"Make this stop or I'll kill you!"

She wanted to tell Timmy to stop, but strangely, she wanted him to stay. He was freaking Ed out, which was good. Or was it? She fought to resist Timmy's power over her.

"You were going to kill me anyway. But if you do, I can't control what Timmy does to you." She shrugged and leaned back, regretting that move since it raised more dust and odor. She ignored it, fighting back a sneeze. She had to look in control. Her life depended on it. Literally. "Just so you know, Timmy can follow you anywhere you go."

Ed shifted from foot to foot. He looked at Timmy's image, then at the door. "Let's get out of here." Grabbing her arm, he pulled her, hobbling, out into the storm.

Rain pounded them as he dragged her down the steps. As she navigated the missing step, she twisted her ankle again and fell.

"Ow!" Her cry rang out and echoed through the trees. Rain pelted her as she lay in the mud. But her clear head told her Timmy held no power over her now.

Ed kicked her in the side, and she cried out again. He searched the porch for Timmy.

"C'mon. Hurry up." He hauled her up by one arm, but she almost collapsed.

"Just let me catch my breath." She sat on the porch and leaned over. Reaching into her pocket, she slid out her keys. She clutched them, fanning them out, one each protruding from between her fingers.

"We're not staying here another minute." He towered over her, bending to hoist her up.

With all her might she thrust herself upward, head-butting him in the face. A sickening crack signaled his broken nose. Releasing her, he grabbed his face. "Shit! What the hell—?"

He grabbed for her with his right hand, a bloody claw.

Arcing her right arm back to reach maximum force, she swung her fist, the keys gouging his left eye, blood spurting out between her fingers.

His scream rang through the woods, scattering scolding birds into the sky and animals into the bush. He collapsed to the ground.

For a split second, she almost checked to see if he was okay instead of running to the car. She made it halfway to the driver's door before bolts of agonizing pain shot up her leg. She staggered forward, her breath hitching as she dragged her right leg in the wake.

She chanced a look back; he was following her, one hand covering his eye, the other reaching out to grab her—a lame parody of Frankenstein's monster.

She grabbed the car handle but lost her grip. He was closing in.

"Do it, Graham," she whispered through gritted teeth.

The door opened so quickly, she lost her balance and stepped back to catch herself. She cried out as pain seared her leg.

As his grasp caught her blouse, she plunged forward into the driver's seat to the sound of ripping cotton. Slamming the door, she hit the lock just before he grabbed the handle.

Turning the key, she started the engine, but it stalled.

No, dear God, no!

She tried again, and the engine roared. When she punched the gas, the car lurched forward, dragging him along. She hit a rut and stopped. He stumbled and fell beside the car. His fingernails scraped along the metal as he pulled himself up the driver's door until his hands and face pressed against her window. He stared at her, blood oozing out of his injured, all-white eye.

Screaming, she hit the gas again. He fell away, and she bumped down the dirt road. In the rearview mirror, he was on his knees his bloody face twisted with rage.

Chapter Thirty-Seven

❧

J esse drove blindly, her hands searching for the windshield wiper switch. At last, she located the control, and the blades swiped the teeming rain off the window. She wanted to speed far from that cabin and the madman who used it to hide his heinous crimes, but the two-track road was muddy and the Chevy slithered back and forth. She eased off the gas pedal, navigating carefully between the trees that hugged the road.

Her body shook so hard she could barely control the car. He'd intended to kill her, no doubt about that, but what made her nauseous was the image of the blood seeping from his white eyeball. With a stabbing pang, her stomach lurched. She stopped and opened the door just in time to vomit on the weeds alongside the road, the rain pelting her head as she did so. Violent spasms took hold; when she had emptied her stomach, she wiped her mouth and slammed the door.

Rain soaked her shoulders, dripping from her thick curls. Drenched ringlets stuck to her face, and she shivered.

Anxiously, she checked the rearview mirror. Could Ed have followed her? *No, you have a couple miles between you. You left him in pretty bad shape. What if he dies out here? Then I am a murderer.*

She pressed the gas pedal and drove as fast as seemed safe. The storm intensified, lightning flashing between the trees. She had to get to town. Ed needed medical help immediately.

But was she even going in the right direction? So far, there was only one choice—the two-track leading from the cabin. With the heavy rainfall, she was hard-pressed to even stay in the ruts. She came to a fork in the road where two narrow two-tracks formed a V. Which one should she take? Would one of them loop around, leading her back to the cabin? She scanned the trees, searching for a clue.

Oh, my God, please help me.

Through the raindrops cascading down the window, she spotted the Smokey the Bear sign. She took the right fork. There was no sun to help indicate east from west, but the lake had been on her left on the way in. Peeks of the lake appeared on her right intermittently. She drove. She prayed. She checked the rearview mirror.

Finally, the trees thinned out and did not crowd the road so closely. The track widened, and a cottage appeared ahead. Beachside Retreat. She laughed and cried simultaneously. Maybe she was becoming hysterical. Through the trees, the lake appeared, pummeled by the heavy downpour.

When she reached the highway, she turned toward town and punched the accelerator. The road was slick with the heavy rain, and she hydroplaned, fishtailing toward the guardrail. Still, speed lessened her anxiety, and she didn't check the mirror every five seconds.

Until the siren wailed behind her.

Thank God.

A patrol car closed in on her at breakneck speed. She pulled to the side of the road as it skidded up behind her. The cop was out of the car, revolver drawn, before she could open her door.

Pretty extreme for a speeding ticket.

"Get out of the car! Hands on your head! Now!" Rain pelted

him as he approached the Chevy then halted in the "aim and fire" stance.

She tried to open the door but forgot to unlock it.

"Hands where I can see them!" He stood, feet spread, arms straight out, pointing the gun at her head. "Now!"

The cop she thought would save her just might shoot her. One wrong move, and she was dead. This was too much.

Overwhelmed and exhausted, she trembled so violently she couldn't move. Rain coursed down the driver's side window. She couldn't see the cop's face, and he couldn't see hers.

"I'm warning you. Get out of that car or I'll shoot."

She willed herself to move. Unlocking the door, she eased it open. Holding her hands up, she tried to exit the car, but when she landed on her injured ankle, her knees buckled and she collapsed to the pavement, sobbing.

"Please don't kill me." Giving voice to what she'd been feeling for the last few hours, she knelt with her hands in the air, rain washing down her arms.

Chapter Thirty-Eight

❧❧❧

Courtney had offered her car so Maggie drove through the storm, adjusting the windshield wipers to keep up with the deluge. Perhaps she might spot something the police had missed at the cottage, something out of place, something just not right.

Sending up a silent prayer for her best friend's safety, she tried not to think of what could happen to her alone at the cottage. Surely, with the attacker elsewhere with Jesse, Maggie would be safe.

When she arrived, she parked on the grass, as close to the cottage as possible. Even though she sprinted to the door, she was soaked as she entered the kitchen. Slipping off her sandals, she turned the overhead light on against the gloom.

How ironic that this place looks so peaceful. It's like nothing terrifying happened here. Except for the piece of wood that replaced the broken windowpane.

Nothing seemed out of place. Wait. The placemat where the napkin holder and salt and pepper sat on the table was crooked. She couldn't help herself; she had to straighten it. When she did, a paper that had slipped beneath the placemat stuck out. She unfolded it.

Her heart sank. It was a note from Courtney, telling Jessie not to panic, that she was not going to get that drunk again. She would be staying at a friend's.

Courtney had been in that much despair?

Her poor sister. She'd carried so much guilt about Timmy all these years. Who could blame her for being so closed and unsociable? Courtney blamed herself for Timmy's death.

She folded the note and tucked it back under the placemat.

The only thing she'd discovered here had nothing to do with the attack on Marty and Jesse, and everything to do with understanding her sister better. Lightning flashed, accompanied by a crash of thunder, and she jumped. Maybe it was the storm, probably it was the recent events, but she wanted to get some clothes and a few toiletries and get out of here.

And back to Marty.

PIECES OF GRAVEL gouged into her knees as Jesse knelt on the road, hands raised, tears streaming down her face.

"Please don't kill me."

"Jesse!"

Joe's voice was the sweetest sound she'd ever heard. Suddenly she was in his arms, against his chest, the familiar beat of his heart rhythmic in her ears. She fell apart, shaking and crying, trying to tell them where Ed was.

But he was busy kissing the top of her head, her forehead, her cheeks, each eye. She cried out when his tender kiss pressed against her black eye.

Lifting her, he carried her to the car.

"Dave, we've got to get her to the hospital." He placed her in the back seat of the patrol car and slid in beside her.

Dave got behind the wheel.

"No! Ed is hurt. I hurt him. He needs help right away."

The two men looked at her as if she'd lost her mind.

"Don't worry, Jesse. We'll find him. First, we need to have you looked at."

"No! He'll die out there. And then I'll be a murderer."

"I'll send a patrol car..."

"They'll never find the place. It's way back in the woods. I have to take you there."

Dave looked at Joe.

"Usually, it's best not to argue with her." Joe gave her a wink.

"Okay. Will he need an ambulance?"

"Yes." She gripped Joe's hand.

Dave radioed in for an ambulance to meet them on the highway and follow them to the cabin.

While they waited, Jesse described her abduction. As she spoke, she paused at any sound and glanced toward town, hoping to see the flashing lights of the emergency vehicle. *How long will it take to get here? Put your damn siren on or Ed is going to die.*

When the EMTs finally arrived, Dave led them to the road Jesse indicated.

I don't want to go back. I don't want to see him. But please let him still be alive.

The ambulance bumped along behind them, often barely fitting between the trees. The storm had lessened to a gentle rainfall, making the trip easier to navigate than when she'd fled. She watched for the lake to appear through the trees.

"Take the left fork," she cried out when she saw Smokey. They crept along, navigating the roots and low branches that made driving the two-track dangerous. Her foot tapped a tattoo against the floor mat, matching the patter of the rain. *Please hurry.* Finally, they pulled into the small clearing.

Ed lay face down on the muddy dirt where the car had been.

Oh my God. He's dead!

Her muscles spasmed with her trembling, a jackhammer throbbing throughout her body.

Dave grabbed his revolver and got out of the patrol car. Aiming at Ed, he slowly approached, then knelt beside him. Returning his gun to its holster, he gave a nod to the ambulance driver. The paramedics jumped out and ran to him, one carrying a medical kit.

"Is he alive? Please, is he alive?" Jesse rasped. Joe pulled her to his chest.

One paramedic checked for a pulse. The other man rose to his knees and started cardiopulmonary resuscitation, pressing his hands against Ed's chest and pushing down, then breathing into his mouth. After several minutes, the other paramedic took over.

She held her fists so tightly that her fingernails dug into her palms. With every compression, with every breath the paramedics gave, she prayed, "Please. Please. Please." Clasping her hands, she continued to pray. They were not reviving him. He was dead.

She buried her face in her hands, moaning. "How could I have killed someone?"

Joe hugged her close. "They're still working on him. In any case, it was self-defense. Jesse, he was going to kill you."

Somehow that didn't assuage her guilt. She never thought she'd be capable of taking someone's life. Feeling sick, she leaned over a patch of weeds and gagged.

Joe rubbed her back. At last he nudged her. "Look."

The paramedics had stopped CPR. One was pulling out an IV line while the other was running to get the stretcher. Dave helped him, and the two paramedics lifted Ed onto the stretcher as Dave held up the IV bag. As they loaded Ed into the ambulance, Dave turned to Jesse, giving her a thumbs-up.

She collapsed against Joe. "I didn't kill him. I didn't kill him."

"No, Just Jesse. But you sure made him pay for what he did to you."

Dave climbed into the patrol car. "They think he'll make it."

A glimmer of light through the trees caught her eye. She pointed. "Dave, I think you'll find the abducted boys' remains right over there."

He peered in that direction, but Timmy was gone.

Chapter Thirty-Nine

Maggie leapt to her feet and ran to Jesse as she entered Marty's hospital room. "You're safe! Oh, Jesse, we've been so worried!" She held her at arm's length and checked her out head to toe. "You're on crutches! He hurt you!"

"Not as badly as she hurt him," Joe followed Jesse into the room.

"Look at your poor face! You have a black eye, and your lips are so swollen and cut." Maggie looked at Joe. "What could she have done to him? She looks quite beat up."

"I almost killed him." Jesse trembled, her black eye a stark contrast to her ashen face. "Ed's down in surgery. I broke his nose. And he might lose one eye. Lost a lot of blood." Jesse sank into a chair, laying her crutches on the floor beside her. "They had to resuscitate him a couple times before they could transport him."

"Right on, *bella*! We need you on the force." Marty flashed her the "okay" sign.

Maggie frowned at him. "Don't encourage her." She studied Jesse, searching for signs she knew so well—fear, anger, frustration. All she saw was exhaustion. She poured water into a paper cup and handed it to her. "Hungry?" She offered some crackers Marty had left beside his soup bowl.

Jesse waved them off. "How are you feeling, Marty?"

"Much better now that I know you're okay. Fill us in."

Jesse recounted the tale of what had happened from the time Ed accosted her outside the cottage.

Maggie leaned against the windowsill as she listened. She shifted and folded her arms, trying to tame the coils of dread seeping through her body. "You mean this Ed wasn't the man who attacked you?"

"That's right. He was confused when I accused him of it. In fact, he thought it was a gas that someone else also tried to kill me." She looked at Marty. "I remembered what you said about the attacker having soft arms. Ed is muscular. Plus, no black eye."

"That other guy is still out there." Joe sat on the arm of Jesse's chair.

She rubbed her forehead. "Something happened that I needed to remember..."

"Geez, *bella*, lots happened."

Maggie smiled as Marty's usual teasing returned. His strength was gradually increasing, and he was staying awake for longer periods of time.

"Yeah, but there was something... something I saw." Jesse rubbed her forehead again. "I just can't remember."

"If this Ed guy was the boys' kidnapper, who's this other guy? And why did he attack you? That's what I keep wondering." Joe shook his head.

"Maybe an accomplice?" Maggie offered.

"But Ed would have known about him going after Jesse." He stroked his jaw, brows knit in thought.

Courtney walked in and grinned at Jesse. "I just saw Dave downstairs. He told me what happened based on the statement you gave. Man, Jesse, I don't ever want to get on your bad side." She bent down and gave her a hug.

Maggie raised her eyebrows. Tenderness had never been a

quality her sister exhibited. At least not for the last fifteen years. To see her sister smile and hug someone melted her heart.

Jesse held Courtney's hand. "I have to ask you something."

"Okaaaay."

"Do you have Timmy's hat?"

Courtney pulled her hand away as if it burned. "No. Why?"

Before Jesse could answer, Marty, his voice weaker, said, "Thank goodness Timmy showed up."

Courtney's face morphed from happiness to her usual unemotional mask. "Timmy? Dave didn't say anything about Timmy." Now she glared at Jesse.

"I didn't tell Dave. How could he understand?" Jesse's face was drawn with pain.

Maggie pushed off the windowsill. "Jess, you look exhausted, and Marty's due for pain meds and a nap."

Joe grabbed the crutches and held them for Jesse to lean on when she stood.

"Wait a minute. You can't leave me hanging like this. Timmy showed up where? At that run-down cabin?" Courtney gripped Jesse's arm.

"Courtney, let Jesse go home and rest." Maggie kept her voice calm.

"No! I need to know." She whipped back to Jesse. "He was at the cabin? He was one of the boys...?" Her mouth turned down, her grief-filled eyes begging for an answer.

Jesse laid a hand on her arm. "Yes, Timmy appeared to us, but no, he wasn't one of the kidnapped boys. Though he did see them. He showed me where they were."

Courtney stared at her. The hard lines along her mouth softened and her eyes misted. "He wasn't one of the boys?" she whispered.

Jesse shook her head. "No."

Courtney buried her face in her hands, sobs wracking her body. *All this time, she thought he'd been abducted.* Wrapping her sister in her arms, Maggie let her cry out fifteen years of agony.

Chapter Forty

Joe turned the corner and Jesse caught site of the Cavanaugh House. Her house. Her home. The day's storm had freshened the air, and a cooling breeze blew an auburn lock across her eyes. Brushing it away, she saw pearly rose and orange clouds soften the western sky. A perfect July evening.

Jim's car was parked on the grass beside her driveway, allowing Joe to pull up as close as he could to the porch. He helped her out of the car, gently placing her crutches when she stood. As soon as he opened the door, the aroma of onion, garlic, and rosemary wafted to her. And freshly baked bread.

Jesse's stomach growled. All she'd had since breakfast at the diner was a stale cinnamon roll from the hospital cafeteria.

Susan ran to her and gently wrapped her in her arms. "Jesse. I was so frightened." She kissed her forehead then held her at arm's length. Jim stood behind her, his eyes bright with unshed tears. Susan stepped aside so he could get a hug in, too.

"I know you were my little girl many years ago, but today you are, too." He kissed her cheek.

Warmth infused every bone, every muscle, every cell in Jesse's body. This was the family she had always wished for, and now they were here. Her eyes blurred.

Finally, life can get back to normal.

"Here, come and sit." Susan swept her arm toward the living room.

Joe helped her ease down on the sofa, propped pillows behind her, then placed a pillow beneath her injured leg. Her stomach growled again, and they all laughed.

"Let me get you some chicken soup." Susan bustled out to the kitchen.

Jesse rested her head against the pillows and closed her eyes. She listened as Joe described the events as he knew them. She'd mumble an additional detail as needed.

Susan came in with a tray, and Jesse sat up. The aroma of chicken soup made her mouth water, and she spooned up a sip. The perfect temperature—hot but it didn't scald her mouth. On a plate beside the bowl, butter melted into a thick slice of home-made bread. Heaven.

"Start over when I get back," Susan said. In a moment, she returned with a tray for Joe.

"Thanks, Mom." He kissed her cheek.

When they'd caught Susan up, Jesse began to yawn. "I need to go to the cottage tomorrow."

They stared at her.

"She's on pain medication," Joe said.

"No, seriously, I need to get some stuff from the cottage." She started to sit up, but Joe gently pushed her back against the pillows.

"Do you have to go back there tomorrow?" Jim asked.

"Yes. I was working on new curriculum for the fall semester while I was there. Well, I was trying to, but between Courtney's binge and my abduction, I'm several days behind. I want to get this done before our wedding so I can enjoy our honeymoon with nothing hanging over my head. I figured since I've got to lay low for a while, this would be the perfect time to work on lesson plans, but I need those materials."

"I planned to come over tomorrow to stay with you. I could drive you out there." Susan stacked her empty dishes on the tray.

"No, Mom." Joe set his bowl and spoon on the tray. "I don't think it's a good idea to go back to the cottage. Remember, Ed was not the intruder. Someone else is stalking Jesse. And we don't know why."

Susan crossed her arms with a shiver. "You're right."

Joe nodded. "Dave Sanders offered to swing by here a few times tomorrow during his shift, too." He took Jesse's hand. "I'll take you to the cottage after dinner tomorrow."

"That sounds like a good plan." Jesse yawned again. Her swollen lip stung, and her mouth couldn't seem to form words anymore

"I'll clean up. Jesse, you need to get some sleep." Susan kissed her forehead. "See you tomorrow, sweetie." She stacked the trays and took them into the kitchen.

Joe scooped Jesse into his arms and headed up the stairs. Jim followed with her crutches.

Her eyelids drooped, and fight as she might, she couldn't keep them open. As Joe covered her with a light blanket, she drifted off into sweet, welcome sleep.

MAGGIE AWOKE to a stiff neck and a leg cramp. The soft glow of sunset peeked through the blinds, covering Marty's blanket in hazy shadows of light and dark. All his visitors had left, so he had been dozing since dinner.

Rising, she paced the room, praying for Jesse's safety. So many dangerous people had come into her best friend's life in the last year. And the ghosts.

Timmy's ghost.

She stood at the window, seeing nothing. She could barely

stand to think about Timmy not resting peacefully all these years. She didn't believe in purgatory. She doubted hell, too. *A loving God brings you right to him when you cross over. That's probably blasphemy. What kind of Catholic sister am I?*

So, where does a wandering spirit go? Was time the same when someone crossed over? Had Timmy suffered for all this time just as the whole family had? Especially Courtney. *I should have known how much she suffered.* But how could anyone? She had completely closed herself off from the family.

At least Courtney's grief was lessened with the knowledge that Timmy hadn't been abducted. But that begged the question, what did happen to him? Did he really drown?

"*Cara mia.*" Marty's voice floated to her like a dream.

She turned. He held out his hand, and she took it, sitting beside him.

His smile was soft, not his usual wide grin. He searched her face, and every place his gaze rested felt sun kissed. He drew her hand to his lips and kissed her fingers tenderly. "Thank you."

"For what?" She chuckled and squeezed his hand.

"For being here with me. You've stayed the whole time, haven't you?"

She smiled and traced her fingers along his scruffy beard.

"Maggie, I—"

She pressed her finger to his lips and shook her head. "No."

His smile dissolved into a puzzled frown. "I don't get it. I don't understand you."

"Just rest, Marty. All you need to do is rest."

His eyes closed. All the commotion of visitors and prodding medical staff had worn him out.

"You sleep. I'm going to leave for a while."

"Where are you going?"

"Hush." She pressed her fingers against his lips.

Gentle snoring signaled his sleep.

Brushing a tear away, she left for the convent.

Chapter Forty-One

Maggie immersed herself in the serene womb of the chapel. Compline wouldn't start for another half hour, and she needed some quiet time to meditate. A shower and a bite of leftover lasagna had revived her energy. She'd checked in with Jam, who wanted every detail of Marty's injuries. Then she came here, to the chapel, to soothe her soul.

She considered the symbols of her life, of what she loved so deeply. A statue of the Holy Family, St. Joseph gazing lovingly at infant Jesus in Mary's arms. The altar where Father Steve presided at Eucharist. The tabernacle housing the sacred Host. Candles flickering in the hallowed, incensed air. She inhaled, a long, slow breath.

The flames fluttering softly became little starbursts through her tears. She stared ahead, allowing the tears to flow, warming her cheeks. Retrieving a tissue she'd tucked in the sleeve of her habit, she wiped her tears. She inhaled deeply again, trying to absorb enough oxygen. The air seemed thin, unsatisfying. She tugged at the starched white linen that lined her forehead and held her veil.

"Sister John Mary told me you were back." Sister Therese stood in the aisle. She indicated the pew beside her and, at Maggie's nod, sat down, crossing herself. She stared ahead at the altar. "How is Marty?"

"Much improved, though exhausted after the scary events of last night and today."

Sister Therese glanced at her, eyebrows raised in question.

Of course. She didn't know. *Funny how when you live through something, you assume everyone else is affected equally.* She described Jesse's abduction. When she included Timmy's appearance, Sister Therese frowned and shook her head slightly. Not rejection, perhaps discomfort. But that was reality, and, as Maggie knew too well, sometimes reality was hard to accept.

When she concluded her account, Sister Therese sat in silence for a while, staring ahead.

"And how are you doing, Sister Angelina?" she finally asked.

Maggie started at her religious name. "I'm tired."

"This has been an agonizing time for you."

"Yes."

"Almost losing the man you love."

Maggie clenched her jaw. How odd to hear Sister Therese say that. She didn't answer.

"You've been struggling with what you should *do*. Perhaps you should instead consider who God is calling you to *be*. Sometimes others' enthusiasm for our vocation exceeds our own. In an effort to please, well, it might not be the right path."

That night she'd sat under the stars with her father, when that surge of excitement about a vocation tingled through her. Had that simply been a call to please Dad?

Sister Therese continued, "Vocation is living our fullest expression of who we are created to be. You might be right where you belong." She raised her hands to indicate the chapel. "Being Sister Angelina may be your best expression of God's creation in you." She took her hand. "But it might not be. I continue to hold you in prayer."

"Having to choose between two things you love is the hardest kind of choice." Maggie's voice was quiet in the gentle air.

"That's how you know the choosing is worthwhile." Sister Therese patted her hand, then rose to greet the other sisters who were arriving for evening prayer.

Maggie fingered her rosary beads. A raging headache disrupted the serenity of her surroundings.

Chapter Forty-Two

❧

J esse's apprehension increased with every mile Joe drove toward the cottage. Did she really need the curriculum materials this badly? Yes. Their wedding was just over a week away. She glanced at Joe and smiled. Nothing was going to distract her on their honeymoon.

One end of the yellow police tape had come undone, and it flapped in the wind, beckoning her. She shivered. At least she wouldn't have to struggle to get under it this time. When Joe jiggled the doorknob, the piece of wood the police had wedged into the broken window fell out, almost landing on her injured foot.

The cottage was eerily quiet. Not even the sound of waves broke the stillness. Her heart thudded as she walked to the table where her materials rested, indifferent to the danger that had threatened her here. Had it been just two nights ago?

Joe's eyes widened. "You need all this just to teach one class?"

"Sure do. I have an empty box up in my room to pack it up in."

"I'll get it. I need to find a hammer and nails to secure that wood back in the kitchen door, too."

"While you're doing all that, I'm going to run next door to thank Mr. Williamson for saving my life."

"First of all, I doubt you'll run. Second, he didn't exactly jump right in to rescue you."

A thought nagged at the back of her brain. "Nooo, but he eventually did."

"Okay. I'll meet you over there when I get this packed up and fix the door."

Navigating the uneven lawn, still wet from the rain, was tricky, and Jesse almost took a tumble twice. She finally got a rhythm down: *crutches, step, hop. Crutches, step, hop.* She hobbled toward the Williamsons' cottage, her mind puzzling over the thought that was just out of reach.

She hadn't thought through what she would say. After all, it was thanks to Mr. Williamson that the Seneca Corners police force had been out looking for the tan Chevy. Even though he hadn't told them at first.

The rubber pad of one crutch slipped across the slick surface and flew out from beneath her. Still gripping the crutches, she waved her arms trying to keep her balance.

"Shit!" She landed on her injured ankle, and the pain that seared through her blinded her with blackness interspersed with shooting lights. Planting the crutches firmly on the ground, she leaned her head forward until she could see clearly again.

Moving slower, she inched to the back door of the Williamsons' cottage. After a few knocks, she peeked through the kitchen window into the room. Dishes sat in the drainer, a folded towel lay on the counter. She knocked on the window.

When Mrs. Williamson came into view, she shifted back to stand at the door, hoping she hadn't seen her peering in like a voyeur. Her ankle throbbed while she listened to Mrs. Williamson struggle with the door.

A smile broke across her face when she saw Jesse. She pushed the screen door open. "Come in, dear. We've just finished dinner, but let me heat you a plate."

Jesse angled through the door, manipulating her crutches onto the linoleum. A tomblike silence filled the musty-smelling kitchen. "Oh, thank you, Mrs. Williamson, but I've already eaten. I just stopped by to see your husband."

Mrs. Williamson looked out the window toward the backyard, her eyes shining as if she'd just seen a lover. "Oh, he's out in the garden, dear. You know how he loves that garden of his. Tends it like a child."

"Yes." *He used to.* Jesse looked around the kitchen. The counter and appliances gleamed with care and attention.

"Where's Courtney? Is she still looking for her little brother?" Mrs. Williamson wobbled against the counter, then she looked beyond Jesse at some indefinable point.

"Courtney's... Courtney's on the beach. She fell asleep in the lawn chair."

Mrs. Williamson's face clouded over. "Oh, my."

Timmy's voice echoed in her head: *She has my hat.*

A tremor ran through Jesse as if the floor had shifted. "Mrs. Williamson, do you have Timmy's hat?"

"Why, yes, I've been saving it for him!" Her hands fluttered and a shy smile appeared. "I've put it in a special place so I wouldn't forget. I knew he'd want it back when he returned."

Jesse rubbed her arms against the icy chills slithering through her veins. "Returned from where?"

"His train ride. You know he loves trains." She pattered off to the guest room, and Jesse followed. The cottage grew stuffy, and she longed to open a window.

Pulling a stool over to the closet, Mrs. Williamson climbed up, teetering a bit. Jesse clambered over as quickly as crutches would allow; she wouldn't be much help if the woman fell. But Mrs. Williamson steadied herself and pulled down a small hatbox. She smiled and ran her hand over the top, too lovingly for the gesture to simply be to clear off the dust. She handed it down to Jesse.

Jesse's hands burned at the contact. Far off, she could hear Timmy singing *I've been workin' on the railroad...* Her hands trembled beneath the heat of the hatbox. Sweat beaded on her forehead, and she found it difficult to focus, the box swirling in front of her.

"Open it, dear." Mrs. Williamson beamed at her.

She could only stare at the box. She shuddered, and her crutches wiggled beneath her.

... *all the live-long day.* Timmy's voice was high-pitched and playful. The room spun, the dusky light growing whiter, objects fading like an overexposed photo. Perspiration rolled down the back of her neck, and she gripped the handles of the crutches to steady herself. *I've got to hold it together.*

Mrs. Williamson echoed Timmy's voice in the children's melody as she tilted the top off the box. Lying inside was a child's railroad engineer hat. Blue-and-white stripes against the yellowed tissue paper. The tissue paper quivered in Jesse's shaking hands.

"I know. I'm excited, too. He'll be so happy when he sees his hat. Take it to him right away. I can't because I have a cake just about to come out of the oven." Mrs. Williamson clapped her hands.

Jesse recalled the musty smell of the kitchen, not the fragrant aroma of an almost-baked cake.

She took the hat out of the box, the heat emanating from it almost burning her hand. To manage the crutches, she tucked the cap into the waistband of her shorts, where its warmth seeped through to her skin.

This was not what she'd planned on when she came over to the Williamsons'. There was another detail she was searching for. One that would be equally—perhaps even more—disturbing. But she wasn't prepared for this.

"Are you all right, Courtney? Don't worry, child, he's fine playing out in the garden. Go see for yourself. Then you can get back to your sunbathing." She smiled at Jesse, but her focus was on fifteen years ago.

"Yes, I'll go to the garden."

Escaping the suffocating air of the cottage, Jesse stopped

beside the kitchen stoop to get her breath. As she inhaled, her head cleared. The sun had dropped below the tree line, and shadows began to creep across the lawn. Crossing the road, she carefully picked her way along the garden path.

Mrs. Keegan had said that at one time, these gardens had been almost a tourist attraction. Mr. Williamson's knack for growing beautiful plants and spectacular landscaping was known throughout Seneca Corners.

Maggie had said that parents brought their children to climb on the child-sized train Timmy loved to pretend to ride on. He would pull the whistle and yell, "All aboard." Waving his cap, he'd make chugging sounds. The arm of the railroad crossing sign went up and down with a clanging bell, and the lantern flashed. Surrounding all of it were perennials and flowering shrubs, creating a paradise for all who visited.

But when his wife fell ill, Mr. Williamson let it go.

A small incline proved challenging because Jesse's crutches slipped on the damp ground. When she reached the top, the railroad crossing sign hung mournfully in disrepair, the paint chipped, the wood weatherworn. Rust ate away at the metal frame around the lights. She pursed her lips, weighted down by sadness. Even in its demise, she could see how magical this garden would have been for Timmy.

In among the trees, dusk was deeper, a rosy light lending an ethereal quality, as if it were a fairy garden. She would have to find Mr. Williamson soon or end up finding her way back in the dark.

"Mr. Williamson?" Her voice echoed in the twilight. "Mr. Williamson?"

"Hello, Jesse."

She jumped at the voice so close behind her. Placing one crutch down, shifting the other, and repeating, she turned to face him.

She was shocked by his hunched shoulders and downturned mouth. Mr. Williamson had been so friendly and pleasant when he'd invited them to go water skiing. He'd been so compassionate in his care for Mrs. Williamson. But now he showed no sign of playfulness or kindness. Instead his mouth drooped at the corners with sadness and resignation. His eyes that had once crinkled at the corners now were dull and lifeless.

And one was black.

Chapter Forty-Three

❦

This was the detail Jesse had forgotten. When Ed shoved her into the car and drove past the Williamsons' cottage, she and Mr. Williamson made eye contact. And his eye had been blackened.

In all her fear of Ed, she'd blocked that image from her mind. Now Mr. Williamson stood before her, shoulders slumped, studying her with a mix of sorrow and determination—and his hands grasping an ancient shovel. The heavy kind made of iron, rusty around the edges. The kind that, when swung, could cause a deadly impact.

He spied Timmy's hat tucked into her waistband. "I see." His voice was calm, a man who had accepted a distasteful task, like raking a tree-filled yard or cleaning up after driving a drunk friend home. Or killing a witness.

"It's not what you think." He took off his own engineer's cap and raked his thinning hair back, and replaced the hat. A familiar gesture—so normal in this surreal moment. "We loved Timmy. Hell, we love all the Keegan kids. We watched them grow up." He gestured helplessly as if all the Keegan kids stood before him. His eyebrows drew together as he tried to find the right words. "Timmy was special. He loved the railroad as much as I did." Shaking his head, he grinned, seeming to forget she was there. "The little guy spent hours over here with me, digging in the dirt, helping me plant flowers." He looked around at displays that sprouted weeds now. "Whenever we added a railroad fixture, he'd clap his hands and dance around it." Suddenly, he turned to her, aware of her presence once more.

Jesse stood, frozen. She certainly couldn't run from him. And despite the evidence before her, she couldn't believe this gentle man had tried to kill her. Had almost killed Marty. Had killed Timmy.

He hefted the shovel. "I don't know what else to do." He looked at her crutches. "You can't even run away from me. I don't want to hurt you. I wasn't going to hurt you the other night—just wanted to scare you. Get you away from here after what Myra said to you."

He sniffed and wiped his sleeve across his nose. "You're just so damn stubborn." He hefted the shovel again. "Well, stubborn only goes so far."

She flinched. Her mind was unable to land on a single thought. Make a single plan. Her fingers tightened around the crutches. There was no plan.

"We never meant to hurt Timmy, either." He tugged on his cap and looked back toward their cottage. "Myra, she loved to help out here, too. Prided herself on being as strong and capable as me. Sometimes we'd have contests—who could dig the most holes for planting the fastest." He chuckled. "We loved working together out here. Timmy was the icing on the cake. Like a little family, she used to say." His smile melted away.

"She could wrangle a rototiller like a champ. Loved to use the backhoe." His mouth twitched as his eyes darkened. "We figured out that she didn't see him playing in the hole." He looked at the cap hanging from her waist. "She filled in the hole and drove forward, crossing it." He stared at the ground. When he tried to speak again, he croaked out the words. "I had gone back to the shed to sharpen the trimming shears. She thought he'd gone with me."

Jesse trembled, gripping the crutches with both hands.

Can't you hear the whistle blowin'...? echoed through the still trees.

"We didn't know."

Darkness was falling, and Jesse wondered how she'd make it back in the dark. She eyed the shovel. *Fool, you won't have to worry about that.* Her legs quaked, and it took all her strength to remain standing.

... rise up so early in the morn. Timmy's voice was cheerful, a child filled with joy. Couldn't Mr. Williamson hear it? No, he was too caught up in the cumulative effect of years of guilt and sorrow. His hearing was turned inward. She steeled herself against Timmy's usual effect, but it didn't possess her. Maybe this time her fear blocked his joy.

"Later that night we were all searching for Timmy. Myra asked me what time he left me." He scrubbed his hands over his face. "That's when I wondered. But somehow the rowboat had come unmoored, and everyone thought Timmy had drowned. I clung to that theory. There was no reason to believe otherwise."

Swallowing against the tightness in her throat, she listened, tears running down her cheeks. His anguish was palpable. The horror of Timmy's death, unbearable.

"It was—what? Five years later? Maybe more. We were working in the garden near where Myra had filled in with the backhoe." He surveyed the garden, viewing memories of his torment. "We decided to transplant a maple tree. When we started digging, his hat came up in the dirt from the mound. She picked up his little cap and that's when she sort of, I don't know, lost her mind?" He looked at her as if for confirmation of his diagnosis.

Jesse wavered between heartache and fear. They were both

such kind and gentle people. This knowledge must have been devastating for them. No wonder Mrs. Williamson went delusional —her only protection for herself. And he'd protected his wife all this time. There was no way he was going to allow this discovery to be public now.

His gaze rested on Timmy's cap again. "I forgot she even still had it. 'I know they'll find him. I'll give this to him when they bring him home,' she'd said. That's when I knew Myra went sick in the head, knowing what she'd done." He held his hands out plaintively. "How could I turn her in? The Keegan family didn't need to go through all that grief again. They had come to terms with Timmy's drowning five years earlier. What good would it have done to reveal what really happened to him? Timmy was gone. Having Myra charged with manslaughter wasn't going to bring him back."

Jesse stood rigid lest she break down. Fingers of icy air tickled her face. She looked toward the mound. A soft glow appeared, and the shape of Timmy shone through.

"I've protected her all these years. I can't let her suffer. I'm so sorry." He raised the shovel, arcing it back.

Jesse pointed, "Look, Mr. Williamson."

Surprised, he swiveled around. "Good God!" Fear pierced his words, and he fell to his knees.

I've been working on the railroad... Beaming, Timmy waved at them.

Mr. Williamson crumpled, tucking his face into his raised arm to hide from the sight. "No. Please, no!"

Her fear morphed into delight. *Timmy's here. We can ride the train.* She clenched her jaw. NO. She had to hold on to reason.

Tell Courtney I'm all right. Tell her to get some sleep now. And to stop crying, because I'm happy here. His image faded into the darkness.

The air returned to a mild August night.

Delight ebbed and fear returned. Timmy was gone.

Mr. Williamson rose. "You see why I have to do this? No one

can find out. You'll tell that police friend of yours. And they'll take Myra away from me."

"Jesse!" Joe's voice cut through the night.

"Joe!" She forced his name from her constricted throat. "Joe, over here!"

A beam from a flashlight bounced through the trees, and Joe broke into the clearing just as Mr. Williamson swung the shovel.

Chapter Forty-Four

❧❧

Raising a crutch, Jesse deflected the blow aimed at her head, catching it on her shoulder. At first, she felt nothing, blessed numbness protecting her before a wrenching pain zigzagged along her arm. Without the support of both crutches, and thrown by the attack, she collapsed.

"What the hell is going on here?" Joe leapt at Mr. Williamson, but the older man swung the shovel again, landing it on Joe's left arm. A loud *crunch* echoed in the night. Joe's forward momentum reversed, and he pivoted, falling to one knee.

In a split second, he was on his feet. He grabbed the shovel from Mr. Williamson, who almost seemed to offer it as he gulped back a groan.

"I'm sorry. Oh, God. I'm so sorry." Mr. Williamson buried his face in his hands, his voice thick with remorse.

Jesse shuddered as he dissolved into a shell of grief. What this meant for the Williamsons—and the Keegans... She moaned.

Balancing one crutch, she tried to stand, but pain jolted the shoulder he'd just battered, knocking her back down. Joe looked at her helplessly, his right hand firmly gripping Mr. Williamson's arm. The irony of the situation struck her: she couldn't walk, Joe's left arm was broken, so he couldn't carry her, and for the last ten years, Mr. Williamson's whole life had been protecting his beloved wife. He was desperate enough to do anything.

Joe could leave her here for now and escort Mr. Williamson back to the cottage. But what would happen then? Even if Mr. Williamson let him return, he couldn't carry her. It was like a circle of hell. They might be stuck here looking at each other until dawn.

She turned at the sound of movement through the underbrush. *Just what we need now—a bobcat.*

"I think they're over here, Officer." Myra's sweet voice cut through the night. Carrying a railroad lantern, she emerged, leading Dave Sanders to them.

Mr. Williamson moaned. "Myra, what have you done?"

In the lantern's glow, her eyes glistened with tears and deep love. "It was time, dear. We should have called yesterday."

He wrapped her in his arms, his chin resting on her head. "Oh, Myra. What are we going to do?"

"She called the station and said a boy just died in their garden." Dave scratched his head and looked around.

"It's a long story," Jesse said, wiping her sleeve across her face.

Joe's face was pasty. "I'm going to need some help with Jesse."

Dave scooped her up, handing the crutches to Joe, who took them with his right hand. He indicated the path, and the Williamsons held hands as they led the eclectic group back to the cottage.

Over Dave's shoulder, Jesse looked back at the mound. Soft moonlight dappled the spot where Timmy finally lay in peace.

JESSE WAS SURPRISED to see the Keegan cottage glowing with lights and several cars crowding the yard, since the family wasn't due back until Labor Day weekend. As Mr. Williamson reached his cottage, he stopped and whispered something to his wife. She nodded.

"Officer, we won't give you any resistance, but it's time to let the Keegans know what happened to their son." His voice was husky.

"Okay. Maybe that will answer all my questions." Dave led them next door.

Jesse wondered what kind of reception she'd get from Mr. Keegan, but she was in so much pain, it didn't matter.

Mrs. Keegan opened the door. "Courtney told us to come out to the cottage as quickly as possible. She said Officer Sanders—" She gasped and her hand flew to her mouth. "Oh, my goodness! What happened to Jesse?" She bustled them in. Her mouth dropped open as the Williamsons followed. "Myra! How nice to see you! And you, Harold." She closed the screen door when she spotted Joe. "What in the world?"

By now, Mr. Keegan, Sean, and Courtney had joined her.

"This is quite the parade," Mr. Keegan growled.

"Hush, dear. Jesse's been injured." Mrs. Keegan was dabbing a wet dishcloth against the gash in Jesse's shoulder.

"Ma'am, it might be best if I set her down," Dave said.

As Dave carried Jesse to the sofa, Sean held the door wide for Joe, taking his good arm to steady him.

As if recalling her best manners, Mrs. Keegan gushed, "Of course. Do sit down, all of you." She led them into the living room. Dave set Jesse on the sofa, propping up her injured leg on a pillow while Mrs. Keegan covered her with an afghan, all the while taking drink orders.

If she hadn't been in so much pain, Jesse would have laughed at the Mad Hatter's Tea Party atmosphere. But she was losing the battle of staying strong, and her body throbbed from the battering of all the recent assaults.

"May I use your phone?" Dave nodded toward the kitchen.

"Sure, Dave," Courtney smiled at him as she led the way.

Joe hovered over Jesse, but his face was wan, and he swayed. He was close to passing out. "Please, let Joe sit. His arm is broken." Forcing her aching leg to bend, she made room for him.

Sean helped him ease down beside her, and Mrs. Keegan carried in a tray as if she were hosting an afternoon tea. She served each of them a cool glass of water. As Mrs. Williamson took hers, Mrs. Keegan touched her hand and repeated, "It's so good to see you, Myra."

Myra beamed at her and opened her mouth to speak, but Mr. Keegan's voice boomed out instead.

"What the hell happened? You all look battle fatigued." Mr. Keegan settled into his recliner and took a swig of his beer. Holding it up, he silently offered one to Mr. Williamson, who held up one hand and shook his head.

The Williamsons sat on the love seat. Sean placed a kitchen chair for his mother next to the recliner then dropped down to sit on the floor beside her.

In the background, Dave urgently called for an ambulance. When he finished, Courtney called someone, whispering as she spoke.

Jesse's head swam with the cacophony of sounds, voices, and movement. She noted the one voice she didn't hear and glanced at the ceiling.

Mr. Williamson took his wife's hand.

Smiling up at him, she gently nodded.

"Liam, Siobhan, we have something to tell you." He glanced at the kitchen. "Courtney, would you join us?"

She hung up the phone and took Dave's hand. Together they pulled over chairs from the kitchen table and sat down.

Mr. Williamson took a long gulp of water and began. "We know what happened to Timmy."

Mrs. Keegan gasped and clutched her throat. "Oh my God." Her voice was strangled.

Hearing the story again, and the sorrow in his voice, Jesse wanted to rail at the heavens. Why should such a tragic accident happen to such wonderful people? There was no happy ending here. Now she understood the phrase "gut wrenching."

When he got to the part about realizing the significance in

finding Timmy's hat, Mrs. Keegan jumped up, glaring, her face scarlet. She lunged toward Mr. Williamson, but Mr. Keegan caught her arm.

"No! Timmy was kidnapped. He's been living with another family. You're wrong." Her voice shook.

Mr. Keegan's voice was tender. "No, Siobhan. You always knew that wasn't true."

She stared at him, her eyes dazed. Shifting her gaze to Mr. Williamson, she growled, "How could you? Why didn't you tell us when you discovered—?"

"You believed he had drowned. Why put you through more pain?" His voice cracked. "We thought we were doing the right thing." He looked at his wife. "It was the wrong thing for everyone."

Mrs. Keegan wept. "I feel like I've lost him all over again."

Mr. Keegan took his wife's hand and patted it, swiping at his eyes in attempt to hide his own weeping. "It was an accident. In a way, Harold is right—we had buried Timmy five years earlier." He glanced at Mrs. Williamson. "I'm sorry for your loss, Harold."

Mrs. Williamson smiled, her white hair like a halo in the light from the lamp beside her.

Mr. Williamson choked back a sob and nodded.

Sean sat forward, arms resting on his knees, hands loosely folded as he stared at the floor. "So, Timmy wasn't abducted. And I was never in danger."

"In danger?" Mr. Keegan frowned at him.

"I always believed Mr. Becker next door kidnapped Timmy. He always gave me the creeps." He looked up at them. "That's why I never wanted to go near his cottage or his yard. I always thought he would kidnap me."

"I never knew that," Mrs. Keegan whispered. "So much pain." Her gaze flicked to Courtney.

Courtney did not cry; in fact, no lines creased her brow or gathered around the corners of her mouth as she sat. still as a statue. Her expression was peaceful.

Outside, crickets filled the night air, and the lake sent murmurs of comfort as waves kissed the shore. The cat clock in the kitchen swished its tail, brushing away the minutes as each dealt with their own grief.

"Thank God Timmy wasn't abducted." Mrs. Keegan broke out in a fresh round of sobbing, sorrow mixed with relief.

"I think that was always our biggest fear." Mr. Keegan swiped his hand across his eyes.

"You can thank Jesse, Dad," Courtney said. "If she hadn't connected with Timmy, we never would have known that."

Mr. Keegan scowled at Jesse. "All this damned ghost business. It's of the devil."

Courtney jumped to her feet, leaning toward him. "Then I'm of the devil, too, because I've been seeing Timmy for fifteen years. And you know what? The devil had nothing to do with it."

Mr. Keegan shot up in his seat. "What? You've never said anything about this before."

"Because you wouldn't let me. You are so damned set in your ways, if anybody does something or believes something different than you, they're automatically condemned to hell."

Mr. Keegan slumped back. His sunken eyes stared at nothing. "This is too much to bear."

Mrs. Keegan sniffled and took his hand. "I know, dear, but we'll get through it together."

Suddenly the back door flew open and Maggie rushed in, her veil askew, rosary beads clacking. "I got here as soon as I could—we'd just finished evening prayer. Thanks for calling, Courtney." She looked around the group, her brow creased. When she spotted Jesse, she ran to her, and knelt beside the sofa. "Dear Mother Mary, what's happened now?"

Sean knelt beside her. "We finally know where Timmy is."

The distant sound of sirens broke into the night.

Dave stood. "There's the ambulance. Mr. and Mrs. Williamson, you're both under arrest. Anything you say—"

"No!" Mrs. Keegan jumped to her feet. "Myra is not well. She can't endure jail. We aren't going to press charges."

Mr. Williamson bundled his wife in his arms. "Will she be put on trial?"

Dave held out his hands with uncertainty. "It's up to the prosecutor to bring charges. But you two won't have to testify against each other based on the spousal privilege statute. Anything Mrs. Williamson confided in you is privileged." Dave let that sink in.

Mr. Williamson nodded slowly.

Mrs. Williamson smiled serenely, clearly unaware of the consequence of this conversation.

"But you will face charges." Dave looked at Joe and Jesse. "Not only did you attack them, you attacked a police officer."

Mr. Williamson swiped his hand over his face. "Dear God, forgive me." He looked at his wife. "What will happen to Myra?" His eyes pleaded with Dave.

"I don't know, sir. Given her condition, she could be put in a facility rather than jail."

Mrs. Keegan took Myra's hand. "How is that going to help anything? It won't bring Timmy back to us."

Myra brightened. "Timmy is in the garden."

Chapter Forty-Five

❧❀❧

J esse scowled at Maggie, who nestled into the overstuffed chair across from her. She sprawled on the sofa, her foot propped on Joe's lap, enviously eyeing the bottle of Genesee Cream Ale Maggie grasped in one hand. In the other, she held the kitchen timer.

"Ten more minutes and we can remove the ice from your ankle."

Jesse groaned. "I'm freezing here. Can't we cut it short?" She pulled the blanket closer.

Maggie flashed her the "teacher look." "Miss Graham, do you want to have a chance to walk down the aisle next Saturday?"

"All right. If I do the entire twenty minutes, can I have a Genny, too, Sister Angelina?"

Maggie squinted an exaggerated frown. "Not with all the drugs you're on, Miss Graham."

Joe chuckled. "You are a stubborn patient. Why am I not surprised?" With his good arm, he took her hand and kissed her fingers. Then he adjusted his sling.

"Just so you know what you're getting in this wedding bargain,

Joe." She pursed her lips to the side then winced. "Ow, my mouth is still sore."

"Ed slapped you pretty hard. Twice, if you weren't speaking in hyperbole as you're wont to do." He winked at her.

"Only about mice." Her heart warmed at the memory. Had their first meeting been just over a year ago? And in just over a week, they'd be married. Life with Joe would be wonderful. Who wouldn't want to spend every day with the person they loved most in the world?

She looked at his injured arm and winced. He got hurt protecting her. She met his gaze, and he kissed her fingers again. A tickle started in her belly, and she smiled. *I was so worried about you.* She glanced at Maggie. *Just as Maggie has spent the last days worried about Marty.*

"Mags, I appreciate you being here to tend to our battered bodies, but shouldn't you be with Marty?"

"I wish I could bilocate like Saint Martin de Porres, but alas, I'm only human, not a saint." She raised her bottle to that and took a swig of beer. "Besides, Marty is doing so well he should be discharged from the hospital tomorrow or the next day. In time for the wedding, for sure."

"That's great news." Jesse moaned softly as she shifted her foot. The doorbell rang. As if expecting it, Maggie sprang up. "I'll get it. You two rest and recuperate."

"That will be Jim and Susan. I know she'll fuss over me. And I'll love every minute of it." Jesse smiled, anticipating Susan's expert nursing skills and motherly TLC.

"I don't think so," Maggie called from the hall.

Surprised, she sat up when the Keegans instead entered the living room, Mrs. Keegan holding a bouquet of flowers. She thrust them into Mr. Keegan's hands and smiled angelically at Jesse.

"How are you feeling, dear?"

"I... uh, I'm fine, thanks, Mrs. Keegan. Hi, everybody."

Mr. Keegan shifted from foot to foot, his face red. Anger? Embarrassment? Certainly discomfort.

Jesse recovered her manners. "Please, have a seat." She tried to stand, but Mrs. Keegan touched her shoulder to ease her back down.

Sean helped Joe bring in extra chairs from the kitchen. As they sat, the doorbell rang again. Based on the aroma that floated to her, Susan and Jim had come bearing enough food to compete with the loaves and fishes. They headed straight to the kitchen to unload the feast, then returned to check on Jesse.

After introductions were made and everyone was seated, Mrs. Keegan nudged her husband, who still gripped the flowers like a freshman on his first date.

Mr. Keegan cleared his throat. "Red, I mean Jesse, I owe you an apology." He extended the flowers to her.

Jesse took them, not sure what to do with the offering.

Susan took them. "Let me put these in a vase."

Courtney took her father's hand.

He frowned at them. "I still don't like the idea of ghosts or speaking with the dead, but Courtney explained, that is, she described how... well, how Timmy appeared to you. How he helped you learn what really happened to him." He glanced at Courtney. "And how he saved your life there at that cabin with the Good Humor man."

Soft chuckling interrupted him, and he shot each one a confused look.

"Dad, it just sounded funny, you saying Timmy's ghost saved her from the Good Humor man," Sean explained.

Jesse held in another chuckle. *Story of my life, Mr. Keegan.*

Mr. Keegan nodded, still befuddled. "Anyway. She said Sister Angelina here," he nodded at Maggie, "I mean Margaret—Maggie —said it wasn't satanic." He shrugged one shoulder. "If Sist—that is, if Maggie believes that, so do I. And I want to apologize for kicking you out. You're welcome to stay at our cottage any time."

Grinning, Courtney chimed in, "After all, with your red hair, you could be his third daughter."

Maybe it was the drugs, maybe it was exhaustion, maybe it was from God. Wherever it came from, Jesse welcomed the incredible joy that started at her heart and surged through her body like the blood coursing through her veins.

"Thank you, Mr. Keegan. I'd be honored to be your honorary third daughter." She took Joe's hand. "And now I have an even larger family." She smiled at Susan and Jim.

Maggie's voice was soft. "God bless us every one."

Mrs. Keegan dabbed at her eyes. "Yes." She whimpered into her handkerchief.

Only one thing dampened Jesse's joy. "What will happen to the Williamsons? Joe and I did not press charges for his attack on us, but what other charges will they face?"

Courtney leaned forward. "Mrs. Williamson has been taken to Geneva Hospital for a thorough examination. She will probably be cared for in their mental health ward until a court date is set. It's still unclear if the prosecutor will even bring charges since Timmy's remains have not actually been uncovered."

Sean nodded. "Mr. Williamson may be charged with accessory after the fact, but because he's her spouse, he may not be charged depending on spousal protection laws. In any event, he has to wait for her court date—if there even is a trial."

"It's all so tragic." Mrs. K blew into her handkerchief.

Sean patted her shoulder. "But now we all know that Timmy wasn't abducted."

"Amen." Courtney made the sign of the cross.

Jesse wasn't sure how to ask her question. "About Timmy..."

Mrs. Keegan started to speak but managed only a garbled gulp.

"We've found enough evidence of Timmy's remains." Sean came to her rescue.

Mrs. Keegan wept.

Sean continued, "Because Timmy was so happy in that garden, we plan to leave him interred there. Mr. Williamson is deeding us that section of his property. We're planning a memorial Mass for him in September."

Jesse nodded. Timmy was at peace now; he was no longer visiting her. But what about Courtney?

As if reading her mind, Courtney said, "Any more visits from Timmy, Jesse?"

"No, how about you?"

"No. For the first time in fifteen years, I think Timmy is resting peacefully."

"Amen!" Maggie said.

Susan smiled at Maggie. "How is Marty doing?"

Maggie glanced at her father. He sat back and crossed his arms.

"Thanks for asking, Susan. He'll be released tomorrow or the next day. His recovery will keep him off his feet for a while, but he's tough." Her face was radiant.

Mr. Keegan grunted.

Jesse recalled that saying about old dogs and new tricks. Who knew what would happen between Maggie and Marty, but the process was shaking up Mr. Keegan's old-time religion. "Who needs a beer? Sean, I know you want one."

He laughed. "And I can 'cause I'm legal now."

"Like that ever stopped you before," she whispered in an aside nobody could miss.

Boisterous teasing broke out.

Jim stood and took drink orders, and though Jesse tried to slip in a request for a Genny, Maggie gave strict orders for a ginger ale.

As exhausted as Jesse was, this gathering of her family exhilarated her. Joe squeezed her hand. Looking up at him, her heart soared. He understood. And he loved her no matter what.

She felt like crossing herself and saying a prayer of gratitude. Maggie would faint if she knew.

Chapter Forty-Six

❧❦❧

After leaving Jesse in Susan's care in the bride's room, Maggie excused herself and went to the restroom. She stared at her reflection in the ladies' room mirror. Her gaze traced the outline of her veil and the stiff white linen against her face that secured it, then traveled to her habit, buttoned up to her neck.

Gently, she unsnapped the fastener at the nape of her neck and slid the veil back off her head. The vanity light above her gleamed off her short, dark hair. She fluffed the pixie cut, finger-combing the hair along her face and forehead.

With trembling fingers, she unfastened the top button of her habit. Her hands dropped to her sides.

Can I do this? Turn away from a commitment I'd intended for my lifetime?

Out in the hall, she heard Marty's infectious laugh.

How can I not? My life is on the other side of that door.

She unbuttoned the remainder of her habit, letting it slip to the floor. Stepping out of it, she unzipped the garment bag that hung on a hook, then ran her hand along the rosy pink shantung dress she'd tried on at Shelby's. Laughter bubbled up as she pulled it out and held it up against her body.

Never in her life had she felt so sure, so lighthearted, as if she were soaring above mountains, looking down at the earth with clarity, with certainty, and with a heart bursting with love.

Slipping into the dress, she turned to look over her shoulder at her reflection. Eyes bright with joy smiled back. She stepped into beige heels and paced the room a few times. She hadn't worn heels this high since her senior prom, but Jam had coached her with a pair she had hidden in her closet.

The height only increased her sense of floating, drifting off into the heavens. Picking up her habit, she draped it on the hanger the dress had occupied and zipped it into the garment bag. On the counter next to her veil was a small, beige purse, which she unsnapped. She pulled out a rose-blush lipstick and savored the silky feel of it gliding across her lips.

Someone knocked on the door, almost causing her to smear her lipstick.

"Maggie? Are you ready? Father Steve is waiting to start." Marty's attempt at a whisper echoed through the wooden door.

"I'm ready."

Maggie opened the door to Marty sitting in his wheelchair. His gaze, at her waist level, slid up to hers, his eyes growing wide with wonder.

Their eyes met. All her indecision, all her doubts, all her tears were worth the look on his face. His brown eyes, widened in shock, softened with love and tenderness. She could melt into his arms right on the spot.

"*Cara mia.*" His whisper carried a depth of passion beyond her dreaming. He pulled himself up to standing.

She propped her shoulder beneath his to steady him, and he wrapped her in his arms.

"I'm a little wobbly here."

"Like having one foot on the dock and the other in the boat?" She smiled at him.

He laughed. "You never did tell me where I landed in that metaphor."

"I no longer have one foot on the dock, Marty. I want to be in the boat with you. Let's sail away together."

She was used to his bluster, his loud Italian voice, his boisterous laughter, even his sometimes-crude jokes. But she wasn't used to this look in his eyes, this untethered passion that cocooned the two of them in a time and space all their own. All sound but their breathing faded away: the organ, the people talking, the birds outside the window. In this moment, only they existed.

His finger traced her cheek, his gaze followed until reaching her lips. Then he locked his eyes on her, mesmerizing her until their lips met. Did she hear angels singing? Did she hear violins playing? Damned if she didn't.

Marty swayed, and she caught his weight against her shoulder.

"Be careful, Marty. The doctor allowed you to be in the wedding if you stayed in the wheelchair. You need that support."

He buried his face in her hair. "You are all I need."

She raised her face to his, searching his eyes. "I love you, Marty."

"I have loved you for so long, *cara mia*." His lips touched hers as the organ began playing "Jesu, Joy of Man's Desiring."

SITTING BEFORE THE MIRROR, Jesse studied her reflection. With her auburn hair piled up in Grecian curls, her eyes were more brilliant green than ever. Maybe it was the excitement that made them sparkle like emeralds; certainly it was her love for Joe. She ran her finger along the bateau neckline of her sleeveless, satin dress, and adjusted the wide band of ebony satin that circled her slim waist.

Susan placed the lace-trimmed mantilla over her hair, securing it with the attached comb. "If we nudge your veil forward just a bit, it might hide your black eye. It's almost long enough to hide the wound on your shoulder."

Jesse smiled at her in the mirror. "Hey, I'm proud of my battle scars. Besides, if you want to fit in with this wedding party, you've got to limp, bleed, or show bruising."

Susan laughed. "Well, I'm honored to fill in back here for Maggie while she wheels Marty up the aisle to the altar."

Jesse grimaced. "Maggie's scars are all internal. And still, she thinks about me. She worried so much about wearing her habit today, but I told her, hey, I'm black and blue, and we'll both be in black and white. It's perfect." She checked the clock on the wall. Father Steve was running late, that wasn't like him. "Do you know what the hold-up is?"

Susan shook her head. "No. Joe was here an hour ago, pacing like a tiger. Not sure if it's nerves or just wanting to see for himself that you're all right." She smiled. "I suspect it's the latter."

"He'll see me in a few minutes." She laughed. "We planned a simple, unconventional wedding so we could walk down the aisle together. But who could predict that the side I'd be on would be determined by his broken arm?"

A knock sounded on the door. "Jesse? Mom? Are you ready?"

"Time for Joe to escort *me* down the aisle." Susan kissed her cheek. "I'm so happy that you'll be my daughter."

A lump rose in Jesse's throat. Finally, someone was happy to have her as a daughter. But Helen would have felt the same way. A soft breeze brushed her cheek. *Thank you, Helen.*

Susan dabbed at Jesse's eyes with a tissue, careful not to smear her mascara. "Oh, dear. I didn't mean to make you cry."

She laughed. "I'm fine."

"Mom? You ready?" Joe called through the door.

As Susan left, she closed the door quickly so he couldn't see Jesse.

Jesse chuckled. *Good Lord, these ancient customs make me crazy.*

In a few moments, Joe returned and opened the door. He halted, gazing at her, and then a slow grin broke across his face. He drawled in his best John Wayne imitation, "Why, ma'am, you clean up real good." His winked at her, then said softly, "You look beautiful."

She pressed her hands against her belly where desire tickled and spread south. "We could run out the back door and start the honeymoon immediately."

He kissed her. "And disappoint all those people? No way."

She stood and caressed the cast that encased his left arm. "Thank you for coming to my rescue."

"Anytime and every time." He kissed her again.

She grabbed the cane resting against the dressing table. The doctor had agreed to let her forgo the crutches on her way down the aisle provided Joe and the cane could support her weight. Lacing her hand through the crook of his right arm, she smiled up at him and together they walked to the entrance of the chapel.

She halted at the view of the altar, stunned. There sat Marty in a wheelchair, grinning like the Cheshire Cat. Across from him stood Maggie. In the rosy-pink shantung dress.

Jesse's vision blurred. How could her body hold so much joy? Today she would marry the man she loved with all her heart. Today she would become a member of a loving family. Today her best friend had found peace. It was too much.

"Oh, my God," she whispered.

Joe tightened his grip on her arm. "Does your leg hurt? Do you need your crutches?"

Smiling, she stared into his hazel eyes, so filled with love. "No, Joe. I have all the support I need." She had to ask. "Life with me will be complicated. Are you sure you don't want to get out while the gettin' is good?"

"I promise." After crossing his heart, he pressed two fingers to his lips, then to hers. "Not a ghost of a chance, Just Jesse."

The organ resounded, and they started down the aisle.

Note to Readers

Dear Readers,

Thanks for sharing my characters' journey. Want to know more? Click and be the first to know about new books, freebies, and giveaways available only on my blog. Be privy to deleted scenes and upcoming ideas from my books so you can step into the world of my characters and know them better than any other readers. You may even help me name characters or decide on a plot direction—see your ideas in print!

Want to leave a review? That would be great! Click here or visit my Amazon Author page. Thank you.

Elizabeth

Visit Elizabeth at:

Amazon Author Page

Website: www.elizabethmeyette.com.

Facebook: https://www.facebook.com/elizabethfmeyette/

Twitter: @efmeyette

Acknowledgments

For writers, family support is crucial, and I am abundantly blessed. As always, my beloved husband, Rich, has been my main supporter, cheering me on when I despair, listening to my ideas during our "staff meetings" which often included adult beverages. I am eternally grateful to you, my beloved.

My daughter, Kate Bode, gets as excited about my books as I do, urging me with, "write faster, Mom, I want to read your book." Thank you for your infectious enthusiasm. Often it spurs me on when I'm in a slump. Thanks to my daughter-in-law, Rachel, for providing resources for legal aspects in the story. Thanks to Lou and Karen Meyette for sharing their sanctuary on the lake that inspired so many scenes in this book. Your hospitality provides an environment where creativity floods my mind.

I am fortunate to be surrounded both locally and online by amazing authors who share the blood, sweat, and tears of our crazy profession. To my CR Sisters and my MMRWA chapter mates, I thank you. A special shout-out to my Monday write-in group, Kate Bode, Patricia Kiyono, Annie O'Rourke, and Diana Lloyd, who traveled the journey of this book with me. Thanks to my Plotting

Peeps, Annie O'Rourke, Linda Fletcher, and Deb Moser, whose wisdom and wine sharing offered new ideas—in *vino veritas* indeed.

When I hand over my "baby" to readers for the first time, I feel a mix of excitement and trepidation, but my trusted beta readers take special care of her. A special thanks to H.J. Smith, Luana Russell, and Sara Yoder, who traveled with me during our journey as teachers and continue to support and encourage me as my beta readers, but more importantly, as dear friends.

My thanks to my editor, Julie Sturgeon, who patiently answered all my pre-edit questions, affirmed my unconventional ideas, and talked me off the ledge when edits arrived. With every stroke of the pen (or stroke of a character in Track Changes), she helps me to become a better writer through her insight and expertise.

As always, special thanks to my muse, Boris. Readers ask where I get my ideas from or how I come up with a plot. I am not kidding when I say this: Boris tells me. There are times when I read what I had written the previous day and scratch my head asking, "Did I write that?"

Finally, to all you readers who trust me enough to enter the story that my characters and my muse, Boris, have whispered to me, I thank you.

About the Author

Author, blogger, poet, and believer in dreams-come-true, Elizabeth Meyette enjoyed a career in education before turning to writing full-time. To quote her friend, "She's not retired, she's 'refired'!" and loves her second career path.

Her Finger Lakes Mysteries, *The Cavanaugh House*, *Buried Secrets*, and *The Last Crossing*, are set in 1968 in the Finger Lakes region of upstate New York. Her Brentwood Saga historical romances, *Love's Destiny*, *Love's Spirit*, and *Love's Courage* are set during the American Revolution.

Elizabeth and her husband, Rich, enjoy living in west Michigan surrounded by the beauty of the Great Lakes. They made an agreement that she cannot cook on writing days after he endured burnt broccoli and overcooked chicken. Fortunately, Richard is an excellent cook.

She credits her muse, Boris, for keeping the stories coming. When Elizabeth is not working on a novel or poetry, she is busy keeping up with her blog, *Meyette's Musings*.

The Cavanaugh House

Book One in The Finger Lakes Mysteries

This house held secrets. Secrets that wafted through rotting window sashes on the winter wind. Secrets that spiders wove into webs anchored between the ceiling and walls. Secrets that scuttled on the feet of cockroaches across stained kitchen linoleum and scurried into its cracks. Secrets that peered from holes in the baseboard from glinting mouse eyes. This house held the secrets close to its bosom where they had slept for decades. No one had disturbed these secrets in all the years the house sat decaying from neglect. There was no reason to, and there was no desire.

June 1968

This might be the biggest mistake I've made yet, thought Jesse Graham.

She climbed out of her three-year-old yellow 1965 Volkswagen Beetle and waded through tall grass and weeds that scratched at her sandal-clad feet. Looming before her, the two-story house—her house—hovered, insinuating more height than it could actually claim. Wrapped in chipped and peeling greenish-yellow paint, the house looked weary, and the once-red front door had faded to a dull russet. The roof sagged, and the tiny porch appeared to be giving up the fight to support the small roof above it. She stared at the house, and the windows stared back, blank. Above the front door, two windows mirrored her dismay as the wood trim above them bowed down. In her twenty-eight years, she had never seen a sadder looking house.

"Oh my God, what have I done?" she breathed.

She closed her green eyes, as startlingly brilliant as her mother's. She suspected they were all she had inherited from the aloof, career-focused woman, for she could see no other similarity. Once again the fear that she had been the cause of her parents' divorce in her early childhood crept into her mind: did her father leave because of her? Jesse always supposed that her father had wanted a boy, and when she arrived, his disappointment caused him to flee. She shook her head.

"That's nonsense. People don't run away because of the gender of their baby," she said aloud.

She combed her fingers through her thick auburn hair, a gesture she made when concentrating or trying to work through a difficulty. So much sorrow had entered her life recently both on a personal level and a national level with the assassination of Robert Kennedy two weeks earlier and Martin Luther King just months before that. Too much sorrow, and now she faced the consequences of her recent break-up with her fiancé, Robert.

She scanned the yard, which deepened her apprehension. Overgrown bushes hugged the house as if begging it to remain and the lawn had conceded the fight with weeds years before. Now crabgrass, nutsedge and dandelions grew knee-high, hiding even a path to the door. Age-old maple and oak trees dotted the property, providing shade from the June sun, their leaves motionless in the early summer air. The few houses on this road weren't adjacent as they would be in the town, but they were close enough to view this forlorn yard that perched at the dead end of the street. Anything she did would be an improvement.

Jesse's shoulders shook as she began to laugh, silently at first, then shaking with mirth. At first she feared she might be descending into hysteria, but she didn't feel out of control. In fact, she felt very much in control knowing that if she didn't laugh, she would cry. What had she expected? Valet service and a mint on her pillow? The house had been abandoned for over twenty-five years —weeds were going to grow, paint was going to chip. But they were *her* weeds and *her* chipped paint; no one was going to tell her what to do about them. And no one was going to take them away.

Circling the house, she was pleased to see that the windows, with the exception of one that was cracked, were intact, albeit the originals from when the house was built circa 1920. They would not keep summer heat and winter cold at bay.

"No, they're not 'bay' windows," she laughed, then groaned. "Geez, I even make lame jokes when I'm alone."

The house was wider than it was deep, although an addition at the back accommodated a kitchen. Two outbuildings stood farther back on the property, one an outhouse, the other a small carriage house.

"Oh, Lord, I hope there's indoor plumbing."

Plumbing! Not yet; she hadn't contacted the local utility companies to have water or gas and electricity turned on in the house. She checked her watch, relieved to see that it was just 1:30 p.m. She still had time to make it into town and take care of that.

Returning to her car, she rustled through her purse in search of the keys her mother had given her. Her fingers found the horse-shoe-shaped key ring, smooth brass worn down by years of use holding three keys: a standard Yale lock key, a smaller brass key and a skeleton key. She headed for the front door and tested the first of three steps leading up to the porch. Feeling confident that they would hold her, she climbed them and faced the door. Her body tingled as if ants crawled beneath her skin; what would she find in there? This was the first step to her new-found independence. No one was coming to her aid if her plans failed. The house was a tumbled-down mess, but wasn't she as well? She had burned many bridges in Rochester, and the bridge with her mother was smoldering. Her father had been out of the picture for years, and she was an only child. Her dear friend Maggie was her sole support system. Whatever existed on the other side of the door was now a part of her existence, too. This abandoned and rejected house was all she had. And she was all this house had. *We're in this together.* Straightening her shoulders, she took a deep breath and selected the key. She was surprised that the Yale key worked so easily in the old lock. Her heart pounded as she turned the doorknob and entered the house.

It took a moment for Jesse's eyes to adjust to the dim interior, for the windows were thick with grime, and the trees filtered out most of the sunlight. The centrally located door opened into a small foyer, a room on either side. Straight ahead was a staircase, and beside it, a hall led to the kitchen. Musty air invaded her nostrils, dust turned everything a dull pale gray, and she felt ancient, powdery motes settle upon her like a second skin. Lacy cobwebs stretched from the high corners to the brass light fixtures hanging in the middle of the ceilings. She heard scurrying at the far end of the hall and resisted the urge to run outside.

To her right was the dining room with a door on the far wall that led back to the kitchen. Turning left, she entered the living room, sparsely furnished with drop cloths draped over the pieces. A chair sat perpendicular to a sofa with a round coffee table in front. A floor lamp hung its head in the space between the sofa and chair, and nestled in a far corner was an oak secretary with a drop-down desk. Drooping at the windows were barkcloth drapes that once had boasted white gardenias on a rose background, but now hung in faded tatters, eaten away by dry rot.

Jesse turned slowly, surveying the room.

"Wow," she said. "Wow, wow, wow."

Her thoughts traveled to Robert's apartment with its white leather furniture, glass and chrome accent tables, and carpeting so thick it was like walking on moss. It was as though she was on a "Rat Pack" set when she was there; everything was sleek and modern, tasteful and expensive. She had lived in that world for the past two years. And like its furnishings, that world had turned out to be less ideal than it appeared. A world more than just miles away from this dilapidated house.

Mustering her courage, she pulled the fabric off the sofa. She shrieked as a flurry of grey shapes scattered in all directions—one straight toward her. She panicked as paws scurried across her sandaled foot. Mice! Goosebumps prickled her skin and adrenalin shot though her body. Heart pounding, she ran out the front door, off the porch and bolted to her car. Her knees gave out and she collapsed, trembling.

"Are you okay?"

Grabbing the door handle, she pulled herself up and looked around for the voice's owner.

"I'm over here," he said.

She looked toward the road and saw a blue pickup truck at the end of the driveway. Leaning out the driver's-side window was a man about her age, with tousled red hair. Humor lit up his mouth and softened his strong jawline and rugged face.

"Are you okay?" he repeated as he climbed out of his truck and started toward her.

Jesse brushed herself off and ran her fingers through her hair.

"Oh, yes, I'm fine," she said.

She saw his hazel eyes twinkle with amusement.

"I can see that. In a hurry to get somewhere? I noticed your quick exit."

She looked at her watch and gasped. It was after 2 p.m. If she were going to get any utilities started, she needed to get to town.

"I need to get my utilities started."

Oh, that sounded intelligent. She was a little off balance, and not just because of the mice encounter; this man's gaze was warm and unsettling. He chuckled.

"Well, I would never want to keep a woman from that."

"What I mean is..."

He held out his hand.

"Joe Riley."

She shook his hand and smiled.

"Jesse Graham."

"Nice to meet you, Jessica," he said.

"Not Jessica, just Jesse. The nickname for Jessica is J-E-S-S-I-E. I'm J-E-S-S-E. Pronounced the same, spelled differently."

"Oh, like Jesse James," he said.

"Yeah, I've never heard that one before," she tossed back.

"Sorry. Wow—I'm making a great first impression," Joe said as he scanned the property, avoiding her eyes. "So you bought the old Cavanaugh House, 'Just Jesse.'" It was a statement more than a question. His eyes studied the place, traveling over the roofline, down to the foundation and back to the outbuildings. "Mighty brave."

"I didn't buy it; I inherited it from my Aunt Helen."

He raised his eyebrows and nodded but didn't say anything.

"I just met the current residents—all one million of them, I think—when I pulled the drop cloth off the sofa. The mice took me by surprise. I panicked and ran."

He laughed and looked back at the house.

"If there were a million, I'd probably do the same."

"Okay, maybe a thousand. At least a couple hundred." Jesse laughed, feeling at ease with him. "I think a call to an exterminator is also in order. I'd better head into town and get things started."

"Can I help?" His face was earnest, his smile genuine.

"No, thank you. I can handle things myself," she said.

"Well, you can't stay here tonight with a million mice living in there. You'd be welcome to stay at my place."

She lifted her chin and looked at him sideways. "Right. Your place."

"No, no, no. You don't understand. I live with my mother less than a mile from here." His face was the color of summer toma-toes. "It's all legit. Mom would be a proper chaperone, and we have a spare room. I'm sorry. I didn't mean to imply..."

Jesse was touched by his sincerity. He was falling all over his words.

"No offense taken. And that is a sweet offer. It's just that… well…I need to take care of things myself. It's important to me."

"Oh, got it." He took a step back and looked around the yard. "Well, then, I'd best be leaving."

She saw his discomfort and rethought her words.

"No, Joe, it was very kind of you to offer, and truly, I take no offense. I'm just at a place where I need to depend on myself right now." She smiled at him, and he nodded and turned to leave.

"Wait, there is something you could help with."

He turned back to her.

"I do need a place to stay, but I have a friend in town who may have room for me. May I use your phone to call her?"

"Sure, follow me." He hopped into his truck as she locked the house and then backed her Beetle out to follow him. Looking back at the house, she was filled with ambivalence. On the one hand the house scared her, on the other, she already felt like she belonged there.

As she drove, Jesse remembered the day she found out about her house. On her twenty-first birthday her mother had presented her with a large manila envelope.

"You will probably want to sell this as soon as possible. Oh, and happy birthday," Eileen Graham said as she tossed the envelope to her daughter.

Opening the envelope, she sensed her mother's green eyes on her. She pulled out a sheaf of papers and leafed through them. Her Aunt Helen's will, the deed for the house, and the mortgage forms created a thick stack that intimidated her. Something else was in the envelope; she tilted it and a set of keys slid into her hand. She looked at her mother who shrugged, lit a cigarette and then examined her manicured nails. Breathing smoke as she talked, she gestured at the papers.

"For some reason, my sister wanted you to have the house. There was nothing I could do about it."

Jesse wondered at her last statement, but dismissed it as she looked through the documents.

"I own it free and clear. Aunt Helen has a trust that will pay the taxes," she said.

Her mother stubbed out her cigarette and left the room.

Jesse had never sold the house and, according to her mother, it had stood vacant for all twenty-eight years of her life. She'd had no idea what she would find when she arrived, but it would be hers and the house would be away...far away.

Want to read more of *The Cavanaugh House*? Click here or visit my Amazon Author Page.